SEAL'S PROMISE

REBECCA DEEL

Copyright © 2020 Rebecca Deel

All rights reserved.

ISBN-13: 9798615024269

DEDICATION

To my amazing husband, the love of my life.

ACKNOWLEDGMENTS

Cover by Melody Simmons.

CHAPTER ONE

An explosion obliterated the hushed silence of night in Antigua, Mexico. The building shuddered, throwing Rachelle Carter to her hands and knees. Popping sounds rose from the street below the five-star hotel, and a strange orange glow lit the darkness.

Amy Morales, daughter of the US ambassador to Mexico, staggered to the window and peered outside. She gasped. "An army of men is firing guns. Is this a coup?"

Heart slamming against her ribcage, Rachelle stood and said, "Get away from the window. You're making yourself a target."

A hard rap on the door. "Amy, open up."

She flung open the door to admit a member of her security detail. "What's happening, Tim?"

"Terrorist attack. We have to evacuate you and Rachelle."

Amy shook her head. "We'll be safe here if we barricade the suite door until help comes."

"Help isn't coming. The city government and law enforcement will have their hands full rescuing hotel guests and fighting armed thugs shooting everyone in sight, including first responders."

"We can wait until the men are gone."

"You're a high-value target. Terrorists would love to post your picture as the latest prize in the war against the US."

Rachelle tugged Amy toward the bedroom. "How long do we have, Tim?"

"Two minutes. Faster is better."

"What are we doing?" Amy asked as Rachelle nudged her friend inside her bedroom.

"Change into clothes you can run in. Hurry. Every second of delay endangers us and your security detail." She hurried to her own room.

Rachelle yanked on a pair of black jeans and a long-sleeved black t-shirt. She slid her feet into running shoes, snagged her visa and money along with a black waterproof hooded jacket, and shoved them into her lightweight backpack. A suitcase would slow her down and speed was critical. The possibility of being in the middle of a terrorist attack had been the furthest thing from her mind when she'd agreed to spend the week with her best friend from college.

She raced back to the living room. Tim scanned her from head to foot and nodded in approval.

Not sure what might lie ahead, Rachelle added protein bars and three bottles of water to her pack as well as sunscreen. She slid her satellite phone into her pocket, grateful her boss at Fortress Security had insisted she take the phone in case of emergency. A terrorist attack definitely qualified as an emergency. If she and the others failed to escape the hotel, she'd call Fortress.

Gunfire continued to echo in the night. Shouts and screams added to the cacophony of sound rising in an ever-growing tidal wave of terror. To her left, the balcony door shattered.

Tim swore viciously. In a crouch, he sprinted toward Amy's room and threw open the door. "Time to go."

"I'm not ready," she protested. "I haven't packed my bags yet."

"No time." He tugged Amy into the living room. "We can't wait. The shots aren't just in the street. The terrorists are inside the hotel. If we don't leave now, we'll be shipped home in body bags."

Rachelle shrugged on her pack and handed Amy her purse. "Come on. Your belongings are replaceable. You aren't."

Tim motioned for them to stay in place and opened the door to the suite.

Eric, his partner, glanced over his shoulder. "They're two, maybe three floors away."

Amy darted into the hallway and headed for the elevator. "Let's get out of here."

Eric caught her arm and tugged her back to his side. "No elevators."

She scowled. "Why not?"

"They're metal coffins."

Rachelle swallowed hard. No exit. Fortress operatives hated to ride elevators. Terrorists could wait until the elevator doors slid open, then spray bullets into the interior. The occupants would have no place to hide from the deadly projectiles. "Stairs?"

"If we can." Tim motioned for his partner to lead the way, guiding the women toward the right stairwell.

Eric jogged to the door and eased it open. He checked the interior, glanced at his partner, and shook his head. He held up three fingers.

What did that mean? Screams came from the stairwell followed by rapid gunfire. Rachelle clamped a hand over her mouth. Terrorists were shooting people in the stairwell. Worse, she heard more gunfire in the left stairwell.

Tim's scowl confirmed her suspicions. Her heart sank. She would love to have one of the Fortress operatives by her side, especially a certain former Metro Nashville homicide detective.

Tim and Eric were good at their jobs. Cal Taylor had been a Navy SEAL before he joined the police department. His training put him into a different category altogether, one that was miles beyond Amy's protection detail.

Rachelle forced herself to think past the fear. Her life depended on the decisions made in the next few minutes. There must be another way off the fifth floor besides the elevators and two main stairwells.

"The service elevator is at the back of the hotel with service stairs around the corner from the elevator. The door is tucked away in an alcove out of sight." She discovered them while looking for the vending machine earlier in the day.

Eric wrapped his hand around Amy's and headed that direction. Tim and Rachelle hurried after them.

How long did they have before the terrorists breached this floor? She guessed a few minutes at most. So far, no sounds of gunfire or screams came from the service stairs. Either the terrorists weren't sweeping up that stairwell yet or they stationed some of their people at the bottom with weapons.

Would her suggestion lead them into a death trap? Her hand fisted. What choice did they have? This was the only option unless they rappelled down the outside of the hotel, and none of them had the equipment.

At the service stairs, Eric nudged Amy to the side of the door. With weapon in hand, he peered inside the stairwell and signaled for them to wait. Eric slipped into the darkened interior. A moment later, he returned. "It's clear for the moment," he whispered.

Once again, he led the way with his hand wrapped around Amy's. Tim followed, gesturing for Rachelle to stay close.

They descended three floors without incident. When they started to descend to the first floor, the door at the foot of the stairwell burst open. Two men charged inside. Spotting Eric, they raised their weapons.

Tim yanked Amy toward the exit to the second floor. Rachelle scrambled after them as gunshots echoed in the stairwell.

Amy screamed. Rachelle gasped as bullets smacked the concrete wall and shards of concrete nicked her cheek. She ducked and rushed onto the second-floor hallway behind Tim and Amy.

"This way." He ran toward the corner, towing Amy behind him. At the corner, he peered into the next corridor, then continued on.

Rachelle heard stumbling steps behind her. She spun, expecting to see one of the terrorists barreling toward her with his gun raised. Instead, Eric staggered toward her, hand pressed to his stomach, blood oozing between his fingers.

"Eric!" She hurried toward him. When he stumbled and almost went down, she wedged her shoulder under his.

"Leave me," he rasped. "More are coming."

"Save your breath." Rachelle wrapped her arm around his waist and urged him to move. When she thought she'd go down under his weight, Tim ran toward her.

"I've got him. Go. Linen supply room on the left. Hurry."

She sprinted around the corner and saw Amy gesturing to her from a doorway.

"Where's Eric?"

"Tim is helping him."

Amy's face paled. "He's hurt?"

"He's been shot. I don't know how bad." She didn't want to upset Amy more than she already was, but unless Eric received medical help soon, she feared he wouldn't live.

"We have to help him."

Amy headed for the hallway, but Rachelle caught her arm and tugged her back inside. "If you go out there, Tim will divide his attention between protecting you and helping Eric."

"You don't understand. I love him."

"Newsflash, Amy. I knew that the first day I saw him with you. He wouldn't want you to put yourself in danger."

Seconds later, Tim hauled Eric across the threshold.

Rachelle closed and locked the door. The lock wouldn't keep out a determined intruder for long. She glanced around, grabbed the chair sitting off to the side, and wedged it under the knob. "What now, Tim?" No second exit from this supply room."

"We're taking the express elevator to the garage." His lips curved.

Express elevator? Her gaze shifted to the small metal door on the right side of the room. "The laundry chute?"

Amy's eyes widened. "Can you and Eric fit into the chute?"

"We'll make it." Tim gestured for Amy to climb inside the chute. "A laundry bin is down there with linens inside. It's straight down two floors. If you scream, you'll bring the terrorists down on us. Go."

Amy perched on the chute ledge and let go. Tim motioned for Rachelle to go next.

After securing her pack in front, she climbed over the metal lip and dropped, clamping her lips shut against the scream rising in her throat.

Seconds later, she landed on a mound of sheets and towels, and scrambled out of the bin into a darkened room lit by a dim exit sign.

Another person dropped into the bin. A low, soft moan came from Eric as he struggled to move out of Tim's way. Seconds later, the other man landed in the bin and hoisted his wounded comrade over the edge.

Once Rachelle and Amy steadied Eric, Tim hauled himself over the lip of the bin and hurried to the door. He opened it a crack, then motioned for the others to stay put and slipped from the room.

"Where is he going?" Amy whispered.

"To retrieve your SUV. Eric can't run." What an understatement. The wounded man swayed where he stood.

"Eric needs to go to the hospital." Her friend's voice shook. "He's losing a lot of blood."

"Need you safe," the man mumbled.

"I need you alive," she retorted.

Tires squealed outside the door. Seconds later, Tim threw open the door. "Go. Amy, into the backseat with Eric."

Rachelle grabbed a handful of towels and dashed after Amy and the others. Once Eric and Amy were inside the vehicle, she scrambled into the shotgun seat and handed the towels to her friend. "Put pressure on his wound. We have to slow the bleeding."

Tim shoved the vehicle into gear and burned rubber racing for the nearest exit. "Can you fire a weapon, Rachelle?"

"No, but I'll try."

"Let's hope it doesn't come to that."

If it did, they were in serious trouble.

"Amy, hand Eric's weapon to Rachelle. Keep your finger outside the trigger guard."

A moment later, Amy handed over the weapon.

"There's no safety on that weapon, Rachelle. Just point and pull the trigger."

"If I have to fire, do you have any advice?"

"Don't close your eyes, and hold the grip tight. The Sig will buck in your hand."

Fantastic. Hopefully, she wouldn't shoot out the tires of their own SUV. "Right."

When Tim rounded a corner and barreled up a ramp to the exit, a man with a gun in his hand stepped out and fired at their vehicle. Instead of slowing down or taking evasive action, Tim pressed down on the accelerator and clipped the guy as he leapt out of the way.

After a quick right turn out of the garage, they raced down a side street away from the hotel, and hung a fast left onto a six-lane street swiftly filling with vehicles fleeing the area around the hotel. Tim wove in and out of traffic, his gaze scanning the mirrors and peering through spiderwebs of compromised glass.

"Do you know the location of the closest hospital?" Amy asked Tim.

"We always know where to obtain medical help in case you're injured."

"Hurry." Her voice was choked with tears. "Eric's unconscious."

The drive to the hospital couldn't have been more than a few miles. However, with the number of vehicles on the roads, the race for medical help seemed to last hours.

Finally, Tim swerved into the hospital parking lot and sped toward the ER entrance. When Rachelle would have opened the door, he said, "Wait."

He glanced around the area, exited the vehicle in a rush, and came around to the passenger side to open the door and haul Eric out. "Get in front of me," he ordered Amy and Rachelle. "Go."

In less than a minute, they were inside the safety of the hospital. One look at Eric, and the nurse motioned for Tim to take Eric to an examination room.

Amy hustled after them, leaving Rachelle in the corridor outside the room. A medical team rushed inside. Soon, Tim joined Rachelle. "How is he?" she asked.

"They're prepping him for surgery."

"What are his chances?"

"Not good."

Oh, no. "Does Amy know?"

He nodded. Tim glanced at her, zeroing in on her cheek. "With everything happening so fast, I didn't have the chance to ask if you were all right."

"I'm fine, thanks to you and Eric."

"You did great back there."

Shouts and screams came from the reception area, followed by the distinctive sound of gunfire.

Amy opened the door. "What's going on?"

"Trouble." Tim yanked her from the doorway and shoved her and Rachelle away from the pandemonium. "Go. Hide."

"We can't leave Eric alone. He's vulnerable."

"The terrorists want you. Once I neutralize the threat, you can return." He palmed his weapon. "Move, Amy."

Rachelle gripped her friend's arm and tugged her down the corridor at a run. Once they rounded a corner and were out of Tim's direct line of sight, she headed for the stairs leading down to the bottom level of the hospital.

"Where are we going?" Amy whispered. "We can't go far or Tim won't be able to find us."

"Someplace safe where I can call for help."

"We're in a hospital. How much safer can we get?"

Rachelle could think of several places. Out of this city topped her list.

"Are you calling the police?"

More gunshots, closer this time.

She pressed her finger to her lips to warn Amy to be silent. Rachelle didn't know what was going on or why, but they were being hunted. If they didn't escape soon, she and Amy wouldn't live to see the sun rise.

CHAPTER TWO

Cal Taylor poured coffee into his mug and headed for his boss's office. He nodded at Brent Maddox's administrative assistant who waved him into the office without interrupting her phone conversation.

He gave a perfunctory knock on the door and twisted the knob. Five men looked up when he walked into the office, their conversation petering out.

"About time you showed up," Eli Wolfe drawled. "I thought we'd have to send out the National Guard to track you down."

"I haven't been to bed yet, Sleeping Beauty, so don't push your luck."

"Shouldn't have been out partying so late." Rafe Torres' eyes twinkled.

Cal snorted. "I'm not the one with a hangover this morning. That would be my principal, a hard-drinking, skirt-chasing Chase Hancock."

Medic Jackson Conner's eyebrows rose. "The country music star?"

"That's the one."

"Did he cooperate with your orders?" Brent asked.

"Of course not. He balked at every security precaution, not wanting to disappoint his adoring fans. To top it all off, when his date for the evening got fed up with Hancock ogling every woman at the event and dumped him, the star struck out when he tried to pick up another woman. To his annoyance, she was with another man and refused to ditch him for Chase."

Jon Smith folded his arms. "Sounds like a bad soap opera. What's the rest of the story?"

"He decided I should reserve a suite for him at Opryland Hotel and arrange for a prostitute to visit his room. When I pointed out that soliciting sex was illegal, he fired me on the spot and became angry when I insisted on escorting him to his home before I went off the clock." He slid a look Brent's way. "I should demand extra pay for putting up with him."

"We took him on as a client as a favor to his father." Anger burned in the CEO's eyes. "That's the last time we provide protection for Hancock unless he agrees to our terms." A slow smile curved his mouth. "Since he'll hate the new terms, Fortress won't have to provide protection for him again. As soon as this meeting is over, go home and get some rest."

He planned to sleep eight straight hours. If Rachelle had been at work today, he would have delayed his agenda to have coffee with her. However, she was visiting a friend in Mexico.

The thought of her in that dangerous country without her own security team made him twitchy. Amy Morales had a security detail, but their priority was the ambassador's daughter, not her college friend. Only two more days. Rachelle would be at work on Monday. Maybe he'd finally work up the courage to ask her to dinner.

Jon glanced at his watch. "Dana is taking our daughter to the pediatrician for a checkup. I'm supposed to meet them at the doctor's office in 90 minutes."

Cal dropped into the empty chair beside him. "Everything okay?"

"One-year visit. Dana's worried because Chloe is small."

"Are you?"

"She's perfect, but Dana needs to hear that from the doc." His expression darkened. "Chloe's regular doctor is on vacation. This visit is being covered by the partner, a man Dana isn't familiar with. She's still skittish around men she doesn't know."

Understandable given her stepfather's abusive behavior toward Dana.

"This won't take long," Brent said. "I brought all of you in to discuss creating a new team with the five of you."

Cal straightened. Finally. Brent had been hinting at this for months. Cal had missed being on the Teams. Since Jon and Eli were his former SEAL teammates, partnering with them on a new team would be a real treat.

"We don't have enough teams to cover assignments now," Brent continued. "It's time to expand the number of units in the field. As of now, you'll be known as Wolf Pack."

Jon turned his head to stare at Eli who grinned at his best friend. "You put him up to that, didn't you?"

"Maybe."

Rafe, another SEAL, rolled his eyes. "Lame name."

"Perfect name," Eli countered. He shifted his gaze to Brent. "What about Curt Jackson? I requested him for this team as well."

"I have other plans for Curt. I wasn't kidding when I said we need more units."

"He's heading up another team?"

A slight nod. "I'm activating your unit as of now. I want to give you more time to train as a unit before you deploy. No guarantees, though. Several places around the globe are heating up. Eli, you are the unit leader, although any member of your team could take the lead." His lips curved. "We all know, however, that you and Jon take charge automatically whenever you're on a mission."

In the midst of Eli's protests of their innocence, Brent's office door flew open and Micah Winter, the Fortress logistics coordinator, hurried inside, satellite phone in his hand. "We have a problem." He tapped the screen and said, "You're on speaker with Brent and one of the Fortress teams. Tell them what you just told me."

"The hotel in Antigua where I was staying with Amy Morales was attacked by terrorists."

Blood drained from Cal's face. "Rachelle, are you safe?"

Her breath caught. "Cal, you have no idea how glad I am to hear your voice. The answer to that question is no, we're not safe. Terrorists shot one member of Amy's security detail. We brought Eric to the hospital for treatment, but within minutes, the terrorists showed up here."

Here? His stomach tightened into a knot. "You're still in the hospital?"

"Tim told us to find a place to hide."

Adrenaline poured into his bloodstream. "Leave the hospital. The terrorists are hunting for you and Amy. Find a place to hole up until we arrive."

"Are you close?"

Regret had him closing his eyes, wishing he wasn't hundreds of miles to the north of her position. "We're six hours away. You have to protect yourselves until we reach you."

His boss leaned closer to the phone. "Rachelle, it's Brent. Are you or Amy injured?"

"No, sir."

"What happened to the other members of Amy's security detail? Are they with you?"

"There are only two."

Cal gritted his teeth, glancing at his teammates. Their expressions were grim. The women should have had at least four, if not six, security people with them. Certain areas of Mexico were volatile. Antigua happened to be one of the least stable areas. "Where are you in the hospital?"

"The morgue. I figured it was the last place they'd look for us."

"Smart." Instead of running for the nearest exit which would have landed the women in the hands of the terrorists, Rachelle had chosen a place they wouldn't search first. "Morgue's have outside exits for the delivery of bodies. Get out of the hot zone and find a safe place to wait for us."

"Cal?"

"Yeah, sweetheart?"

"Hurry," she whispered.

His hands clenched. "We'll be wheels up within the hour. Is my number programmed into your phone?"

She hesitated a moment, then said, "I have Micah's number and yours."

The other men in the room looked surprised at that. Tough. He wished she'd called or texted. He'd missed her. "You and Amy need to go. When you leave the building, don't run unless the terrorists are on your heels. Otherwise, running will draw attention to you."

"Okay."

"Call me as soon as you're safe. Rachelle?"

"Yes?"

"Be careful."

"I'll do my best." She ended the call.

Brent picked up his handset and called one of the pilots on standby. "Prepare the jet for a flight to Antigua, Mexico. Wheels up in one hour." He ended the call and looked at Cal. "Something you need to tell me?"

"No."

His friend's eyebrow rose. "Care to reconsider that?"

Cheeks burning, he scowled. "Coffee dates. I want more. That's all you're getting from me."

Brent rounded on Micah. "Did you know about this?"

A snort. "Hard to miss."

Great. He thought he'd been subtle about his slow pursuit of Micah's administrative assistant. Her comment about saving his phone number in her sat phone contact list made him wonder if Rachelle was interested in him as more than a friend, too.

Cal stood. "Are we done here?"

The rest of his team rose.

"The Texas unit will join you in Antigua. They're on the way home from a mission. We'll reroute them to meet you at the airstrip."

"Wouldn't it be better to slip into Antigua with one team instead of two?" Jackson asked.

"We don't know how large this terrorist cell is or even if the attack was carried out by terrorists. If the group is large enough, you'll be lucky to escape with the two women. Two teams might not be enough."

Eli flashed a grin. "If we bring the cool toys, we'll be fine."

"Pack heavy," Micah said. "Better to have more equipment than you need. We'll update your intel as we get it."

Wolf Pack left the office and headed to the vaults to load up with supplies. While he replenished his gear, Cal noted that Jackson stuffed his mike bag with medical supplies. He prayed the medic didn't need to use any of the supplies on Rachelle, Amy, or the operatives.

Within ten minutes, he and his teammates grabbed their Go bags and headed for the elevator.

Cal drove from the underground garage and toward John C. Tune Airport, pushing the speed limit as much as he dared. The sooner they were wheels up, the better. Wolf Pack had intel to gather and an op to plan.

Hopefully, Rachelle would call soon to tell him she and Amy were safe. In the meantime, he'd consult every map he could find of Antigua and the surrounding area. Jon had a photographic memory, but if the teams had to split up into smaller groups, Cal needed to know the layout of the city. The knowledge would aid in making a quick exit when their routes were blocked.

By the time he parked at the airport in the private area designated for Fortress, Cal had to hold himself back from running to the jet. His SEAL teammates wouldn't believe it if he told them. He'd been known for having nerves of steel. Knowing Rachelle was on the run with armed men hunting her and her friend made his blood run cold.

When he brought Rachelle back to US soil, he wasn't waiting any longer to ask her on a date. Life was too short. He didn't want to waste more time, refusing to consider that he and his teammates might be transporting her body home.

Cal grabbed his Go bag from the cargo area of his SUV and headed for the jet. He stored his gear as the rest of his team boarded the plane. Choosing a seat, he prayed the jet caught a tailwind and shaved time off the journey.

Within minutes, the jet powered up and taxied down the runway. Once the jet reached cruising altitude, Eli walked to the conference table. "Time to get to work, boys. We have damsels in distress to rescue."

Jackson frowned as he joined them. "We don't know where they are. How can we plan an extraction?"

"We'll have more information soon." Jon dropped onto a seat next to Eli. "With an operation like this, Brent will tap Zane to gather intel."

After Cal settled next to Eli, he sent Zane a text, requesting the link to track Rachelle's sat phone location. He received a response less than a minute later. Tapping the link, he watched as the flashing red dot continued to move.

Rafe sat beside Cal. "Information already?"

"Tracking Rachelle's phone." Was she with the phone? That was the question plaguing him. If one of the terrorists caught the women, he could have killed them and taken the phone.

Jon grabbed a laptop and brought up a map of Antigua. "Let's get started. We have a lot of work to do and little time."

CHAPTER THREE

When Rachelle glanced at Amy, her eyes widened. "Lower your head," she reminded her friend. "Security cameras are everywhere. If the gunmen want you bad enough, they'll hack into the cameras and track you."

"It's the middle of the night. No one's going to see me."

"Streetlights and dim lighting from the stores make it easy to recognize you."

Amy sighed as she lowered her head. "Sorry. I forgot about that. How did you think of it?"

"I work for a security company, remember? I hear coworkers talk about such things all the time." How ironic that working for a security company made her more aware of how unsafe she was most of the time.

They walked in silence for a few more blocks with Rachelle using an erratic zig-zag pattern instead of walking a straight line. The further from the hospital they walked, the better she felt about their chances of escape. Although they weren't out of danger yet, no one stopped them or showed any interest. Hopefully, their luck would hold.

Fifteen minutes later, the traffic was sparse enough that she and Amy no longer had to turn into darkened alleys or doorways when a vehicle drove by. They'd walked for hours. Time to find a place to hide.

Rachelle studied the area as they continued on. Warehouses. Perfect. Some of the warehouses should be unlocked or abandoned. Abandoned was better. If Cal and his teammates didn't arrive in Antigua before dawn, she and Amy might have to stay hidden until the sun went down again and it was safe for the operatives to come for them. Good thing she'd brought water and protein bars.

"This way." She headed into the maze of warehouses, sticking to the shadows in case security cameras were mounted and operational.

In case they were being pursued, Rachelle continued to choose a random path toward the back of the warehouse district. The further they walked, the seedier the warehouses became with less lighting.

If she could locate an abandoned warehouse with an unlocked door or windows, they might have a chance to escape notice if the terrorists tracked them this far.

"We have to stop soon," Amy murmured. "I'm almost too tired to walk."

"Me, too. Just a little farther."

"This is spooky."

"In this case, spooky is good."

"If you say so. Personally, I'm not a fan. This is the kind of place where criminals hang out."

"Let's hope the criminals are too busy plying their trade to be around at the moment. Once we're in place, they won't know we're here." She hoped.

When they reached the last row of warehouses, Rachelle glanced to either side and turned left. The warehouse in the corner appeared abandoned as were others nearby.

In case a camera was operating this far back, she tugged Amy into the alley between two warehouses and walked to the back of the buildings. A wooded area stood about twenty feet away. If necessary, she and Amy could hide there.

Hiding out in the woods, however, wasn't on her list of things to do while on vacation in Mexico. Rachelle didn't like bugs or spiders. From what she'd observed so far, Mexico hosted many varieties of each.

When they reached the back of the target warehouse, Rachelle checked the first window. Locked. As she and Amy continued to the next, she scanned their surroundings. So far, no one was around.

At the next window, Rachelle held her breath and lifted. To her relief, the window rose albeit with a few loud creaks and groans. Once the window was raised, she waited to see if someone came to investigate the noise.

When no one shouted or came to investigate, she motioned for Amy to climb into the building. Hopefully, their luck would hold when Rachelle lowered the window again. She would have left the window up if not for the fact that every other window that she'd seen was down.

As soon as Amy was inside, Rachelle hauled herself up and over the sill. She dropped onto the other side, then quickly lowered the window, wincing at the noise.

"It's pitch black in here," her friend whispered. "I can't see a thing."

Hoping she wasn't about to make a serious tactical error, she turned on her phone's flashlight app. A narrow, dim light appeared.

Rachelle relaxed. Thank goodness. She should have realized that Micah would let her borrow one of the phones designated for the operatives. Their apps were designed for use during missions. A bright flashlight app would bring the enemy straight to an operative's location. Still, she aimed the narrow beam toward the floor in case someone was nearby.

Their footsteps echoed in the empty building as she led the way across the cavernous interior in search of an office.

If someone came into the open warehouse, she and Amy would be sitting ducks unless they found a place to hide.

Rachelle turned right and began to walk along the wall. If they didn't find shelter on this side of the warehouse, they'd have to try the left. That option, however, would leave her and Amy too far from the tree line. The back of the warehouse on that side was at least ten feet farther from the woods. A huge expanse of land when you were running for your life.

The wall abruptly ended. Swinging her flashlight that direction, relief weakened Rachelle's knees. She reached back for Amy's hand and tugged her into the hallway.

"What are we doing?"

"Looking for an office or a closet with a window so we can escape into the trees if we have to make a quick getaway."

Amy chuckled. "Sounds like we're a couple of criminals on the lam."

"You and Eric will have a wild story to tell your kids one day."

"May I borrow your phone to call the hospital and check on him?"

"I thought about that earlier, but I'm afraid to call attention to him. What if one of the terrorists overhears the conversation and goes after him?"

"There must be some way to find out how he is, Rachelle. I'll go crazy if I don't know."

"We'll figure out something." She understood Amy's deep desire to check on Eric. If anything happened to her favorite coffee date, Rachelle would be frantic to learn about his condition.

Hearing Cal's voice on the phone earlier had calmed the panic threatening to overwhelm her at the hospital. What she wouldn't give to be in his arms.

She sighed. Nice thought. Wouldn't happen, though. Despite frequent coffee dates, Cal Taylor hadn't asked her for a real date. She probably wasn't vivacious enough for an operative. Where many of the women the operatives dated or married were outgoing and the life of every party they attended, Rachelle's personality was at the opposite end of the spectrum. She preferred meals at home and found parties stressful unless the people in attendance were good friends.

Since the handsome Navy SEAL hadn't asked for a date after all these months, he likely wasn't interested in her beyond friendship. A depressing thought. Cal had fascinated her from the first time she'd seen him outside Micah's office.

On both sides of the hallway were several open doors. Rachelle and Amy checked each one, closing each door afterward, until they reached the last office, the one closest to the woods. Like the others, this office had a heavy wood desk pushed near the back wall.

Rachelle walked closer and studied the gap between the wall and desk. Although a tight fit, she and Amy should be able to hide from sight underneath the desk if all else failed.

Next, she unlocked the window and tried to lift it. The window slid up without resistance or, even more important, noise. "This is perfect. We'll wait here for Fortress."

"Fantastic." Amy sank to the floor and leaned her back against the wall. "I might have cried if we had to walk further. My feet and legs are killing me. How long before your friends arrive?"

Rachelle checked the phone's screen for the time. "Three hours at least. Once they land, they'll have to figure out where we are and avoid terrorists on the way here."

"Would your friend Cal be able to learn Eric's condition?"

"If he can't do it, he'll know someone who can." She brought up her contact list and touched Cal's number.

He answered on the first ring. "Are you safe?"

Her eyes burned at his question and obvious concern. "For the moment."

"Where are you?"

"I'm not sure exactly. We took a meandering path instead of a straight line away from the area."

"Good. That's exactly what you should have done. Were you followed?"

"I don't think so. We used roads off the main drag, and no one seemed to pay attention to us." She swallowed hard. "I'm sorry, Cal. I couldn't keep track of the roads we walked."

"It's not a problem, Rachelle. We have a tracker on the sat phone. As long as you have the phone with you, we know exactly where you are. I was asking about your hiding place. What did you choose?"

She relaxed again. Thank goodness. If she'd had to give him an address or something, she and Amy would be in serious trouble. "An abandoned warehouse in the warehouse district. There must be 50 warehouses in this area, and the one we chose isn't the only abandoned one in this section."

"Perfect. Good job. Sit tight. We're three hours out. All you have to do is stay hidden and quiet."

"That's the plan. Can you do me a favor?"

"Name it."

"Can someone check on Eric's condition? Amy's worried."

"Hold." Cal's voice became muffled as he spoke to someone, then he returned. "Jon will see what information he can dig up without alerting the wrong people."

She frowned. "Jon Smith?"

"That's right."

"But he's a sniper."

Cal chuckled. "He's also the best hacker out there, on a par with Zane."

Wow. Who knew the quiet, intense SEAL had those kinds of skills? "Tell him thanks."

"Sure. How much battery life do you have on the phone?"

She checked. "Almost a full charge. Why?"

"Excellent. Leave the call live. If you see or hear anything that concerns you, let me know."

"Okay. Cal?"

"Yeah?"

"Thank you for coming to get me."

"I would have insisted on coming with any team deployed to come for you. It's my good luck that Wolf Pack was in Brent's office when you called."

She grinned. "Wolf Pack?"

"Eli is to blame for the name."

"I like it."

"That makes two of you, then." He paused, then said, "Rachelle, I'm handing my phone to Jon for a minute."

A moment later, Jon Smith's distinctive deep voice sounded in her ear. "Eric Hoss is in recovery at St. Cecelia Hospital."

"What's his prognosis?"

"According to the doctor's notes, he'll make a full recovery. However, he'll be out of commission for a while. Amy will have a different security team guarding her for several months."

"What about Tim?"

"I'm sorry. He didn't make it. I'm handing the sat phone back to Cal. We have plans to adjust."

"Rachelle?" Amy's hand clamped on her arm. "You're crying. What happened? Is Eric all right?"

"He's in recovery and expected to be as good as new in a few months." Her voice broke.

"Those aren't tears of joy. Why are you crying?"

"It's Tim. I'm sorry, Amy."

Her friend stared. "He's dead?"

Rachelle nodded as Cal's voice came through the phone.

"You okay?" he asked, voice low.

"Tim was a good man. He sacrificed himself to protect us and Eric."

"For that, I will be forever grateful. I'm sorry, Rachelle."

"Me, too."

"I'm especially sorry I'm not there to hold you."

Stunned, Rachelle's eyes widened. "Are you serious?" she whispered.

"Very."

Butterflies exploded into flight in her stomach. Oh, wow. Maybe she'd been dead wrong about Cal's interest. If she was very lucky, she'd have a chance to spend more time with him. "In that case, I'll expect delivery of said hug upon your arrival."

"As soon as it's safe."

"I'll hold you to that promise. I need that hug in the worst way."

"Soon. Rest for a while. I'll be here if you need me."

She gave a watery laugh. "I already do," she said softly.

Cal groaned. "You're killing me."

"Since I want that hug, I'll behave." Rachelle glanced at Amy. "You thirsty, Amy?"

She straightened. "I hope you're not kidding. I'd kill for a drink of water right now."

Rachelle set the phone on the floor beside her and shrugged off her pack for the first time in hours. She dug into the depths, grabbed a bottle of water, and handed it to Amy. "I don't know how long we'll be here. Might be best to drink half and save the rest." If Cal and his teammates were delayed in reaching them, they would be in for a hot, stressful day of waiting. If their luck didn't hold, she and

Amy would be on the run with a little water and protein bars to sustain them until help arrived.

"You packed water?"

"And protein bars. Want one?" Amy held out her hand. "I don't like them much, but I'm hungry."

She laid a wrapped bar on her friend's hand. "Gourmet cuisine at its finest."

"Not even close, girl."

"Think of it as an appetizer."

Amy grinned and bit into the bar, making a face at the taste.

They each ate a protein bar and drank some water. When they finished, Rachelle said, "Sleep, Amy. We'll be out of here soon."

"I want to return to Eric. He's alone in the hospital. Who's going to protect him?"

Rachelle stared at Amy. "You can't do it. You don't have training or weapons. More important, you're a target. You're the one the terrorists would love to capture. You'll put his life in danger if you stay. He wouldn't want you to be in danger to protect him."

"I love him. I can't leave him here alone."

She wrapped her hand around Amy's. "We'll talk to the operatives when they arrive. Maybe they'll have a solution to help Eric."

Amy lifted her chin. "If they don't, I'll refuse to leave."

CHAPTER FOUR

Cal pressed his phone to his ear, scanning the darkened airstrip with two large SUVs waiting for them. The second Fortress team had gathered near the lead vehicle, weapons within easy reach. "Rachelle?"

A thumping noise, then, "Yes, Cal?"

"We're outside of town. I need both hands free so I'm ending our call for now. If you need me, text. I'll contact you as soon as I can."

"Be safe."

"Always." Especially now that he knew his interest in her might be reciprocated. "I don't know how much resistance we'll encounter, so don't let down your guard. If you have to run, find another place to hide and wait for us. No matter what, remember that I'm coming for you. Nothing and no one will stop me from finding you."

Rachelle drew in a shaky breath. "All right."

"See you soon." Cal ended the call, switched his phone to vibrate, and slid it into his pocket. He glanced at Eli and gave a short nod.

"Load up," Eli said. "We have two damsels and a wounded warrior to rescue."

Eli and Jon consulted with the Texas team leader, Brody Weaver. Seconds later, Eli clapped the other man on the shoulder, then Weaver and his team climbed into the first SUV, heading for the hospital and Eric Hoss.

Jon climbed behind the wheel of the remaining SUV. As he left the airstrip, the Texas team's jet taxied down the tarmac. Both teams would travel to the US on Wolf Pack's jet. Considering the strong feelings between Eric and Amy, the team leaders had agreed that flying everyone home together would be best.

The medics would handle Eric's care until they reached Bayside, Texas where Ted Sorenson, one of the Fortress trauma doctors, would take over. If Eric needed more time in a hospital, Fortress would provide security.

Once word leaked about his feelings for Amy, Eric might find himself reassigned. The Diplomatic Service frowned upon agents falling for their principals.

In the shotgun seat, Eli placed a call to Zane Murphy, the Fortress communications and tech guru. With two teams involved in this operation, Zane was providing technical support for Wolf Pack while another tech assisted Texas.

"Yeah, Murphy."

"It's Eli. You're on speaker with Wolf Pack. What do you have for us?"

"Antigua is still in chaos. Even though the affected area is only five square miles, the whole city is on edge."

"Any red flags on the Internet?"

"Oh, yeah. Rumors are circulating about the terrorists hunting for two women. Their descriptions match Amy and Rachelle."

Cal's gut tightened. "Do they have a lock on them?"

"Not yet. The search is moving closer to their hiding place, though."

"Estimation?"

"An hour or less."

The SUV leapt forward as Jon floored the accelerator.

"Copy," Eli said. "Notify Sorenson that we'll be flying into Bayside."

"Roger that. I'll monitor Web chatter and contact you if a problem arises." He ended the call.

"I hope we don't hear from him," Jackson muttered.

Rafe snorted. "Unlikely. No mission goes according to plan."

Eli glanced at Cal. "Keep an eye on Rachelle's tracker."

He gave a tight nod and checked the tracking app again. Rachelle hadn't moved. Hopefully, the terrorists would keep searching in the wrong direction. His hand tightened around the phone, silently willing Jon to drive faster.

His teammate took side roads when they were within the five-mile chaos zone. From one block outside the zone to just inside the boundary, the atmospheric difference was stark. Outside the zone, traffic moved at a brisk pace as citizens hurried to their destinations. Inside, traffic was sparse, as though the zone held its breath, waiting for another terrorist strike.

Eli's phone signaled an incoming text. He glanced at the screen and made a call, placing it on speaker. "Talk to me."

"One of our satellites is in position to scan the area where the women are hiding. The terrorists are searching the warehouse district."

Adrenaline poured into Cal's bloodstream. "How long?"

"Fifteen minutes, probably less."

Not long enough if they met resistance.

"We can't leave the SUV outside the red zone," Eli said. "We'll need a fast getaway."

"The target warehouse is close to a half-mile area of woods. You can park the SUV park under tree cover and reach the women on foot."

Eli grunted. "Doable although not ideal if they're injured. We'll make it work. Once we're in position with the comm system activated, we'll bring you into the loop."

"Copy that."

Eli looked at Cal. "Text Rachelle. If she and Amy hide in the woods, it will make our jobs easier."

After firing off a text, he received a response seconds later that sent a river of ice water into his veins. "Three armed men are walking the back perimeter of the warehouse district. If they leave the warehouse, they'll be spotted."

He sent another text. "Hide. We're ten minutes out. Where are you in the building?"

"Corner office closest to the woods."

"Hold tight. I owe you a hug." He slid his phone away. "They're in the corner office at the back of the warehouse."

"Good." Eli glanced over his shoulder. "We'll move as soon as our boots hit the ground."

The last few minutes of the drive, Wolf Pack geared up in the close confines of the SUV and went through a comm check. When all was ready, Eli contacted Zane and looped him into the network. "Any change?"

"Yeah, none of it good. The terrorists are searching the last row of warehouses. They're three warehouses away from Amy and Rachelle."

"How many?" Jon asked.

"Ten."

"Piece of cake." Eli grinned.

Another time, Cal would have agreed. He didn't like the odds with Rachelle's life on the line. The terrorists wanted Amy. Rachelle would be collateral damage.

Two minutes later, Jon hid the SUV in the deep shadows of woods.

Wolf Pack exited the vehicle and spread out. "On the move," Eli whispered to Zane.

"Roger that. Three bogeys moving your direction, ten feet apart. Two hundred yards out."

"Copy." Eli motioned for Jon to take the man on the left and Rafe the one on the right. They melted into the shadows. After signaling that he wanted the man in the middle, Eli sent Jackson and Cal for the women.

Suited him fine. Resolve hardened inside him. Didn't matter how many men stood between him and Rachelle. They wouldn't stop him.

One hundred yards into the woods, Cal held up his fist. Jackson dropped to a crouch behind a tree, weapon up and ready.

A twig snapped to their right. Mission clock running in his head, Cal grabbed his Ka-Bar. A gun battle would draw more terrorists to their location.

"Fourth bogey in the woods, twenty yards to your right, Cal," Z murmured.

Cal acknowledged the information with a click of his comm device. Time to end this before the women were found and spirited to another location or killed.

He signaled Jackson to hold position and moved toward his target. Another twig snapped, followed by a low-voiced curse in Spanish. Cal adjusted his course to circle behind the terrorist.

Zane's voice came over the comm system a minute later. "Fifth bogey following behind the fourth, same heading."

He glanced over his shoulder at his teammate and motioned for him to take the fifth terrorist, then acknowledged Zane's information with another comm click.

Jackson moved toward the new threat.

Cal tracked his target a few more feet. Motion to his right caught his attention. He scanned the darkness, waiting. There. An armed man dressed in black crept through the woods, doing his best to be silent but failing miserably as he continued to step on twigs and stumble over rocks and tree roots.

He slipped up behind the man, clamped a hand over his mouth, and drew the sharp blade across his throat. Easing the body to the ground, Cal wiped his blade on the man's pants and sheathed his knife. He activated his comm system. "Bogey four is down," he said in a toneless whisper.

One by one, the rest of his teammates reported that their targets were down.

"Five more bogeys joined the party in the warehouse district," Zane reported. "Three are still roaming the perimeter near the women. The rest split up and are searching the remaining three warehouses."

Cal moved toward the warehouse where Rachelle hid with her friend. "How many inside with the women?"

"Three."

"Stay on task," Eli whispered to Cal. "We're two minutes out."

Right. He scowled. At least six men stood between him and Rachelle with more ready to aid their comrades at the first sign of trouble.

At the edge of the woods, Cal crouched beside Eli and watched the men patrolling the perimeter. When Jackson, Jon, and Rafe joined them, Eli leaned close to Jackson. "Dart the guy on the corner. Jon and I will take care of the other two. Rafe, Cal, go after the women while we bag the trash."

When Jackson was ready, Eli waited until the other guards turned away from the corner man. "Go."

Jackson pulled the trigger. The dart lodged in the man's throat. Eyes widening, the thug removed the dart. Seconds later, he was on the ground, unconscious.

Eli and Jon came up behind their targets and took them down with no fuss.

While they moved the bodies out of sight, Cal and Rafe ran to the back door of the warehouse.

Rafe tried the knob, looked at Cal, and shook his head. Great. Another delay. His teammate grabbed his lock picks. Seconds later, the tumblers clicked.

Stepping to the side, he twisted the knob and eased the door open. When no one fired a shot or shouted, Rafe slipped inside the warehouse with Cal on his heels.

Noises came from the area of the warehouse where Rachelle and Amy hid. Praying he wasn't too late, Cal headed toward the offices.

Flashlights glowed in two offices, one on each side of the corridor. Peering into first office with movement, Cal spotted one man searching the interior of the room.

He signaled Rafe that he had one man in the office. Rafe indicated the same. Cal grabbed his Ka-Bar and slid into place behind his target. Seconds later, he eased the body to the floor.

Moving to the next office, he checked the interior. Empty aside from a desk, chair, and a few boxes. He continued to the next office, the one beside the corner office. A muffled curse came from inside the room.

Cal palmed his Ka-Bar. When the terrorist stalked from the office and turned toward the corner room, Cal slipped up behind him, clamped his hand over his mouth, and plunged the blade into the man's kidney. He dragged the man out of sight and lay the body on the ground.

Rafe joined him in the hall and they walked to the corner office. Cal looked inside. No terrorist. No sign of the women.

He frowned. Were they hiding in a different place? "Rachelle, it's Cal."

A soft gasp sounded from the direction of the desk. A moment later, Rachelle crawled out from under the desk and ran to him.

Although protective gear prevented him from feeling more than her slight weight, he wrapped his arms around her and held her close. "You okay?" he whispered.

"I am now. Is it safe?"

"We neutralized several terrorists. More are close."

Rafe helped Amy from beneath the desk as Cal activated his comm system. "Packages secured."

"Copy," Eli murmured.

"Incoming," Zane said. "Eight bogeys heading to your location."

"Move, Cal," Jon said.

"Copy." Cal released Rachelle and wrapped his hand around hers. "Got company. We have to leave."

"The window opens without noise. I checked."

He flashed her a grin. "Good job." He activated his mic. "Coming out the corner office window."

"Wait," Jon murmured.

While Cal raised the window, Rachelle slipped her pack over her shoulders and stood beside Cal with her back to the wall.

"Amy doesn't have her ID or visa," she whispered.

"Zane will take care of the clearance."

"Go," Jon said. "Thirty seconds before the warehouse is breached."

On the other side of the warehouse wall, Eli and Jackson waited to assist the women through the window. Cal turned to Rachelle. "You first." He lifted her to the ledge. His teammates helped her to the ground.

Rafe helped Amy over the ledge, then followed her through the window opening. Cal brought up the rear.

"Fifteen seconds," Jon murmured.

Holding Rachelle's hand, Cal tugged her toward the woods. They'd have to move fast. While operatives were trained to move in silence through any terrain, the women weren't. Cal didn't want Rachelle and Amy in the middle of a firefight between Fortress and the terrorists.

"Rafe, Cal, go," Eli snapped. "Jackson, you're with me and Jon."

Weapon in his right hand, Cal ran, urging Rachelle to keep pace. She did her best to follow in his steps.

Rafe ran with Amy's hand clasped in his about ten feet to their left.

Over the comm system, Eli snapped, "Jon."

A shot rang out. "One down," came the sniper's response. Another shot. "Two down. More incoming."

"Go."

Another shot. "Three down," Jackson said.

"Go. We have room."

A small buffer. Cal poured on a burst of speed, forcing Rachelle to run faster. Although he hated to push her, an unknown number of gunmen were pursing them. The journey to the jet would be a race against terrorists determined to stop them from lifting off.

Eli said, "Texas has their package and is en route to the jet."

"Copy that," he murmured. Now, all Wolf Pack had to do was reach the jet before terrorists caught up with them. Piece of cake.

Rachelle stumbled. Cal righted her, slid his arm around her waist and forced her to keep going.

More gunfire sounded behind them. Shouts from the terrorists, a scream of pain.

"How much farther?" Rachelle gasped.

"A few hundred feet. Can you make it?"

"Watch me."

He smiled, looking forward to spending time with this spunky woman in the coming days.

Eli's voice said, "Rafe, take the wheel. We'll need Jon with a weapon in his hand. Z?"

"Right here."

"Tell the pilots and Texas we're coming in hot."

"Copy that."

Cal swung Rachelle into his arms and sprinted the last two hundred yards to the vehicle. He yanked open the back door and stuffed her inside. "Move to the other side and drop to the floor." He followed behind her as Rafe burst from the trees with Amy in his arms.

He shoved the ambassador's daughter inside the vehicle. "On the floor." He slid behind the wheel as the rest of Wolf Pack ran into view.

Rafe cranked the engine and raised the hatchback for Jon who dove into the back compartment. Once the hatchback returned to its original position, the sniper kicked out the back window.

Eli and Jackson scrambled into the vehicle, and Rafe took off.

"Any injuries?" Jackson asked.

Rachelle shook her head. Amy did the same.

The ball of ice in Cal's stomach began to melt. Excellent. If they got the women onto the jet and into the air without injury, he'd call this mission a rousing success.

"Fantastic. I love not using my supplies on a mission."

Eli rolled down the passenger-side window. "Let's hope we keep it that way. Floor it, Rafe. We have a slim lead. The firefight pinpointed our location for interested parties."

The SUV surged ahead.

Rachelle didn't say a word, but her hand cupped Cal's calf.

He brushed his fingers across her cheek. "A few more minutes, and we'll be in the air." But how many obstacles would Wolf Pack go through to make that happen?

CHAPTER FIVE

Rachelle lay flat on the floor, heart pounding in a mad rhythm. "What's happening?" she asked Cal.

"We're widening the distance between ourselves and the terrorists."

"Will we lose them?"

He hesitated, then glanced at her. "Unlikely." Cal didn't elaborate.

Cal didn't have to elaborate. Rachelle realized the operatives would have to fight their way to the jet. If they lost the fight, she and Amy along with the operatives would pay a heavy price.

"We can't leave Eric in Antigua," Amy said. "The terrorists will kill him if they find out who he is."

"Eric's with our second team and on his way to the jet," Eli said.

Her breath caught. "You're serious?"

"We never leave one of our own behind. If we could have brought Tim's body without endangering the other team, we would have. The State Department will handle the arrangements for Tim through official channels."

"What about my parents?"

"On a plane to Washington, D.C. No one wants you targeted in a bid to force your father's cooperation with a terrorist agenda." Eli paused, staring out the back window. "Jon."

"I see them," came the grim response.

"What is it?" She knew the floor was the safest place for her and Amy, but Rachelle hated that she couldn't see anything.

"Three vehicles are pursuing us," Cal murmured.

Amy gasped. "How will we escape?"

"Have a little faith. Fortress always completes a mission."

"But you're outnumbered."

Cal shrugged. "Probably."

Rachelle's lips curved. He acted like the odds being against them was normal, and maybe it was.

Brent Maddox hired the best people for Fortress. Wolf Pack was more than capable of pulling off a miracle against the odds.

She looked at Amy. "We'll be fine. These guys are the best."

Her friend frowned. "My team is the best, too, and look what happened to them."

Rachelle shook her head. "They're good. Fortress is better."

Amy didn't look convinced, but she lapsed into silence.

"Cal, target the vehicle on your side," Eli said. "Jon, take out the others. Two more incoming from the front."

Rachelle's hand tightened around Cal's calf. Five vehicles filled with terrorists. Holy cow!

"We've got this," Cal said to her, then levered himself out the window, sitting on the frame.

"Ladies, it's going to get loud in here," Jackson said. "Cover your ears."

The operatives opened fire.

"One down," Cal announced. A massive rending of metal ripped through the night.

"Two down," Jon said. Two shots later, he announced, "Three down."

"Four down," Eli said. "Cal, inside. Rafe, evasive maneuvers. We can't let the last group disable the vehicle."

"Copy that. Hold on." After several quick turns, the SUV accelerated.

"Go, Jon," Eli ordered.

Two shots later, the sniper sat up. "Five down. Get us out of here, Rafe."

"Is it safe for us to sit up now?" Amy asked.

"For the moment. If we run into more trouble, you'll be back on the floor."

Cal helped Rachelle to the bench seat beside him.

She shivered, cold to her bones. Stupid in this tropical climate.

Cal wrapped his arm around her shoulders and tucked her against his side to share his body heat. "Adrenaline dump," he said, voice soft. "It'll pass soon."

"You're not hurt?"

He shook his head and leaned down until his mouth was beside her ear. "I still owe you a real hug." His lips brushed the shell of her ear as he spoke, sending another shiver cascading through her, this time for a much better reason.

For a man sporting hard muscle all over, his lips were soft and warm. What would they feel like on hers? Rachelle stilled. Good grief. What was wrong with her? They were running from the enemy, not out on a date.

She looked at him. "I'm holding you to that." She craved the feel of his arms around her.

A slow smile curved his mouth. "I'll deliver that and more."

Rachelle's eyes widened. What did that mean? When he winked at her, butterflies took flight in her stomach again. Wow. Did the interest go both ways?

A phone signaled an incoming call. Eli tapped the screen of his phone. "You're on speaker, Brody. Go."

"We're five minutes from the jet." The sound of gunfire came through the speaker. "We have two bogey vehicles in pursuit." The Texas team's leader reported their position.

"We're one minute behind you. Take them out if you can, but your main mission is transporting the package to the jet. Maintain communication so we can coordinate."

"Copy that."

Eli snagged his bag from the floorboard and pulled a big gun from the depths. "Amy, Rachelle, on the floor. Sorry. I know it's not comfortable."

"Bogeys ahead," Rafe said.

Eli said, "Brody, ease your vehicle to the right. We'll target the left vehicle first."

"Copy."

"Hold it steady, Rafe." Eli's voice was muffled. A moment later, an explosion lit the night. "One down. Brody, floor it. We'll slide between you and the remaining bogey, and cut them off. Jon, you ready?"

"Yep."

"Go, Rafe."

The SUV's engine roared as the driver demanded more speed from the vehicle. Cal slid from the seat and covered Rachelle with his body. Jackson did the same with Amy.

"More protection for you since we'll be close to the pursuit vehicle," Cal said.

"I understand." He was heavy, but she wouldn't complain.

"Here we go," Eli said. "Let's get this done, and go home."

Cal wrapped his arms around Rachelle's head, his body curved over hers.

She hated that Cal was in danger to protect her. A bullet coming her way would have to go through him first. Rachelle shifted one of her hands to thread her fingers through his.

He tightened his hold on her. "I've got you."

Gunfire sounded nearby. Glass shattered. Cal grunted.

Rachelle felt a trickle of warm liquid on her cheek. "Cal!"

"I'm okay. Stay still."

"You hit?" Jackson asked.

"Bullet kissed my arm. You can slap a Band-Aid on it when we're in the air."

Rachelle's eyes stung. Even though Cal acted as though the injury was nothing for concern, she wouldn't believe that until she saw the evidence for herself.

Gunfire sounded in the cabin. Two shots, then Jon said, "Two down. We're clear."

"Pack your gear," Eli said. "We're one minute from the jet. Ladies, stay down until we're on the tarmac."

The operatives readied their bags.

"Thirty seconds," Rafe said.

Cal looked at Rachelle. "When we come to a stop, stay in place until we're sure it's safe. You up for one more run?"

She nodded. She'd do anything necessary so Cal received medical attention.

He smiled. "Almost to safety."

"I can't wait to see Eric," Amy said, her voice shaking. "I want to see for myself that he's all right."

Rafe skidded to a stop. The operatives scrambled from the SUV.

A moment later, Cal plucked Rachelle from the floorboard and set her on her feet. "Run!" He clasped her hand in his strong grip, and they sprinted for the jet with

Amy and Rafe a few steps in front of them. Jon, Eli, and Jackson hung back, weapons up and ready.

"Incoming," Eli shouted over the jet powering up.

Cal swept Rachelle into his arms without missing a step and ran faster. She wrapped her arms around his neck and glanced over his shoulder. Three vehicles raced up the road toward the airstrip.

Rafe took the stairs to the jet two at a time with Amy in his arms. Cal surged up to the cabin in his wake. "Clear," he called to his teammates.

Cal set her in a seat, shrugged off his pack and stowed it in the overhead compartment. He dropped into the empty seat beside hers. "Strap in."

Eli, Jon, and Jackson bounded into the cabin.

"Go, go, go," Eli called to the pilot as he and Jon secured the door.

The jet began to move as three vehicles careened onto the tarmac.

The operatives stowed their gear and strapped into seats.

Picking up speed, the jet lifted from the ground. Rachelle gripped Cal's hand, hardly daring to breathe as the jet gained altitude.

"Oh, yeah, baby," one of the Texas team called out. "That's what I call an adventure."

A dark-haired man slid a glance to his more enthusiastic teammate. "Give it a rest, Max. I don't think the ladies are a fan of this kind of adventure."

An understatement. Rachelle's idea of an adventure was a day at the zoo. Running from terrorists wasn't an item on her bucket list.

"It's more energy than a four-shot espresso," Max said.

"Where's Eric?" Amy twisted in her seat, worry in her eyes. "I want to see him."

"In the bedroom at the back of the jet," Rafe said. "I'll take you to him as soon as the jet levels off."

"Is he all right?"

"He's fine for now," the dark-haired man said. "Our medic is with him. When you see Eric, keep in mind that he should still be in the hospital."

"What does that mean?"

"He's in a lot of pain and worried about you. Reassure him that you're fine and encourage him to take the pain meds so he can sleep through the flight. Aside from seeing you, that's the best thing for him."

Five minutes later, the jet leveled off, and Rafe escorted Amy to see Eric.

Jackson grabbed his bag from an overhead bin and approached Cal. "Let me look at your arm. After you're patched up, I'll help Jesse with Eric."

The medic crouched beside Cal and used a big knife to rip the sleeve to see the injury better. He gave a soft whistle. "That needs more than a Band-Aid, buddy."

Dismayed, Rachelle twisted to see for herself. The ragged furrow across Cal's upper arm looked red and swollen. "Oh, Cal," she whispered. His arm must hurt, yet he didn't act as though the pain fazed him.

"I've had worse."

"But you were hurt protecting me."

His gaze locked with hers. "Better me than you."

Jackson reached into his bag. "I'll numb your arm and give you antibiotics. Once the lidocaine is working, I'll clean and stitch that arm." The medic glanced at Rachelle. "Cal's not a fan of needles. Distracting him while I work will make my job easier."

Cal's eyebrow rose as he stared at his friend.

Hmm. Guess Jackson was stretching the truth. Rachelle didn't have the right to ask for the one thing she wanted. A long, soul-stealing kiss.

Cal shifted his attention back to her. "Talk to me."

Not as good as a kiss, but she could do that. "About what?"

"Tell me about the terrorist attack from the beginning."

Jackson swabbed Cal's arm and readied a hypodermic needle.

Rachelle told him about the explosion that rocked the hotel, the gunfire, and screams inside and outside the building, the escape from the hotel, and the hospital. When she finished her tale, Cal asked her to go through it again. This time, he interrupted at several places to ask for details.

When she completed the telling a second time, he raised their clasped hands to his mouth and kissed her knuckles. "You're incredible, Rachelle."

"All I did was run and hide with my knees knocking the entire time."

He shook his head. "You used your brain and thought through the options. You could have let fear paralyze you. Instead, you came up with a smart plan and went with it. When possible, you called for help."

"Tim's dead," she whispered, her heart aching all over again at the loss of a good man.

"Because of your actions, you, Amy, and Eric are alive. You put yourself at risk to help them. Without you, Amy would have been captured by the terrorists. You used what you learned at Fortress."

"I did what anyone else would do."

"Most people look after themselves. You didn't."

Jackson returned to Cal's side with a stool and sat. He pinched Cal's arm. "Feel that?"

"Pressure only."

"Perfect. Rachelle, snuggle up to Superman so he's more relaxed."

Not a hardship assignment as far as she was concerned. She glanced at Cal. "You don't seem nervous about stitches."

"I'm cringing on the inside." Lips curving, he wrapped his uninjured arm around Rachelle's shoulders and settled her against his chest. "Close your eyes and tell me something I don't know about you."

She frowned. "Are you trying to distract me?"

"Is it working?"

"No."

He chuckled. "Close your eyes and pretend it is."

Rachelle rested her head against Cal's shoulder. "In the interest of preserving your superhero status, what do you want to know?"

"What's your favorite type of food?"

"It's a tossup between Italian and Mexican. What's yours?"

"Steak and baked potato. Favorite type of movies?"

"Action adventure with a romance thread."

His hold around her tightened. "Chick flicks?"

"Hate them. What about you?"

"I'm not a fan of chick flicks, either."

Jackson snorted.

Rachelle smiled. "What kind of movies do you like?"

"Action adventure, romance thread optional. Do you have siblings?"

"One of each, both older. You?"

"Two younger sisters who were the bane of my existence growing up. They still stick their noses into my business at every opportunity."

"Nieces or nephews?"

"Both. You?"

"Same. Is it safe to look, Jackson?"

"Not yet. Two more minutes."

A moment later, soft material settled against her back.

"Thanks, Jackson," Cal murmured.

"Yep. Did you sleep at all overnight, Rachelle?"

"No time. After the hotel and hospital were attacked, Amy and I were on the run. Once we hid in the warehouse office, I encouraged Amy to rest while I kept watch."

Cal tightened his grip. "Protecting your friend again."

"She didn't volunteer to take a watch shift?" Jackson asked.

"Amy was exhausted."

"So were you." A pause, then the medic said, "You're all set, Cal. I'll give you a mild pain reliever when the lidocaine wears off."

"Thanks for the patch job."

"You say that now. Wait until you receive my bill. Rachelle, do you have injuries?"

"My left arm hurts."

The medic checked her arm. "Looks like thorns or brambles tore your sleeve and cut you. The cuts aren't bad, but I need to treat them to prevent infection."

Once he finished, Jackson gathered his medical detritus. "If you develop a fever, I need to know about it. How long ago did you drank water?"

She frowned, thinking back through the nerve-wracking hours. "I don't know."

Jackson walked up the aisle and returned a moment later with bottles of water for her and Cal. "Drink this, then take a nap. We have food on board if you're hungry."

Rachelle's stomach lurched at the thought of eating. Maybe later.

The medic looked at Cal. "I'll check on you in an hour." He checked the other Fortress operatives for injuries.

Cal tapped her bottle of water. "Better drink part of that. Jackson won't be happy if he comes back to find the bottle unopened."

She wrinkled her nose. "I'm not sure I can keep the water down."

After she drank a few ounces, Cal set the water aside and showed her how to recline the seat, then lowered his own and urged Rachelle to lay her head on his chest again. He tugged the blanket over them both. "I feel like I drank a vat full of caffeine."

"You'll crash soon."

Although skeptical, she resolved to hold still so Cal would rest. Surprisingly, the warmth and safety of being held in his arms seeped into her body and a heavy lethargy stole over her muscles.

"Relax," Cal murmured. "I've got you."

With his words echoing in her mind, sleep overtook her.

CHAPTER SIX

Cal knew the moment Rachelle dropped into sleep. Her entire body went boneless, much like his nieces and nephews did when they gave in to the need to rest.

He relaxed deeper into the seat, easing Rachelle more fully against his chest. The tension that racked his body from the moment he learned Rachelle was in trouble finally dissipated. Despite the fast-paced effort to rescue her and Amy with two Fortress teams, the women had been lucky to escape Antigua unscathed.

They'd have repercussions in the aftermath of the violence they witnessed. His gaze dropped to the woman in his arms. Would she look at him differently when her shock wore off? Knowing he was an operative and accepting what he did for a living after seeing his handiwork were two different things.

Cal had killed men in the course of his missions. He wouldn't apologize for doing his job and protecting his team, but he wanted Rachelle to accept the necessity for violence on missions and see the real Cal Taylor.

An hour later, she stirred in his arms, her breath catching. She moaned. "Cal."

He tightened his hold. "I'm here. Sleep." When Cal kissed her temple, Rachelle snuggled close and made a purring sound of pleasure.

The corners of his mouth tugged upward. He hoped to hear that when he kissed her while she was awake. Closing his eyes, Cal drifted into a light sleep until Jackson returned to check his arm.

"Looks good," the medic whispered. He glanced at Rachelle. "How is she?"

"Restless."

"In another hour, I'll give you meds to help with the pain."

"Nothing to knock me out. How's Eric?"

"Holding his own."

"And Amy?"

"Hasn't left his side for an instant. I think wedding bells will ring soon."

"Might be the only way he can stay with her."

Jackson returned an hour later to give Cal two capsules to swallow, then pressed a small packet of the medicine into his hand. "Two every six hours," he murmured. "If you need more, let me know."

He slid the envelope into his pocket and dosed for two hours, rousing when Rachelle stirred again. This time, she opened her eyes and gave him a deer-caught-in-the-headlights look. Amused at her reaction, he whispered, "You okay?"

She nodded. "I'm sorry. You can't be comfortable." She shifted as though planning to move.

Cal stilled her movement by tightening his hold. "Are you uncomfortable?"

Her cheeks turned pink. "No."

Satisfaction zinged through him. "Good."

"Aren't you?"

"This is the best rest I've had in months." Although she looked skeptical, he wasn't exaggerating. "Let me hold you."

"Tell me if holding me hurts your arm."

"It won't." He wouldn't give up this privilege because of a little pain. The pleasure of holding Rachelle was too great. "Sleep if you can."

She watched him a moment, then rested her head against his chest again. Within minutes, her breathing was deep and steady. She didn't stir when the jet landed to refuel or when the aircraft resumed its journey toward Bayside, Texas.

Three hours later, the jet began the final approach to the airport. Time to wake Rachelle. He hated to release her. Holding Rachelle was fast becoming an addiction.

"Rachelle," he murmured.

She sighed, her breath warming his neck.

"Time to wake up. We'll land soon."

She tilted her head back to look at him. "How do you feel? Don't sugar-coat your answer."

Cal blinked. He couldn't remember the last time someone other than a medic asked him that question. "My arm hurts, but I've had worse injuries."

"Let Dr. Sorenson check it."

"Jackson is a great medic," he said, voice soft.

"I know. Do it for my peace of mind."

"After he examines Eric." And Rachelle. He wanted assurance that she was all right after her ordeal. The doc's bedside manner was abrasive with operatives, but he was a softy with the women and children Fortress rescued. Besides, Sorenson liked Rachelle. The doc mentioned her when Cal had the unfortunate necessity to be a guest at the clinic.

He retrieved her bottle of water. "Here. Drink more before Jackson has my hide for not taking care of you."

She smiled and drained the remaining water.

Excellent. When they arrived at the clinic, he'd encourage her to eat a light meal. Whether she realized it or not, Rachelle burned many calories fleeing from the terrorists and running to the SUV. He'd be surprised if her body wasn't sore after the long hours of stress and tension.

Once the jet stopped on the tarmac, Cal helped Rachelle to her feet. She swayed and gasped as her knees buckled.

He caught her with an arm around her waist as operatives unbuckled their seatbelts and retrieved their bags. "Easy."

"I feel like I just finished a marathon. My muscles are sore."

He drew her against his side. "I'll ask for over-the-counter pain relievers at the clinic."

"How's Eric?"

"Stable. Jesse and Jackson kept him sedated." He eased her away. "Better?"

She nodded. "Thanks."

Hoisting his Go bag over one shoulder, Cal held out his free hand to Rachelle. She shrugged into her pack and slid her hand into his.

He squeezed gently and led her toward the door. Two of Sorenson's crew boarded the jet and headed for the bedroom.

"Who are they?" Rachelle asked.

"The doc's assistants. They'll help the medics transport Eric to the clinic."

Three SUVs were parked nearby, a driver at the wheel of the first vehicle. After Eric and Amy were ensconced in the back of the second SUV with Jesse, Eli motioned for Cal to escort Rachelle to the first vehicle. Eli and Rafe joined them while Jackson headed for the second SUV, and Jon the third. The rest of the Texas unit split up between the SUVs. Sorenson's men climbed behind the steering wheels.

The three vehicles headed for the veterinary clinic. Within fifteen minutes, the teams provided a hedge of protection around Eric, Amy, and Rachelle as they exited the SUVs and entered the building. Another one of Sorenson's assistants motioned for his coworkers to take Eric to the exam room.

Ted Sorenson joined them in the hall. "Maddox wants an update." He frowned at Eli. "Call the man so he'll leave me alone."

He acknowledged the doctor's surly order with a snappy salute. "Your wish is my command."

A snort. "In my dreams." He stalked to the exam room and paused in the doorway to glance at Cal. "You're next."

"After you check the women. I'll keep."

With a nod, Sorenson walked into the exam room.

"I don't need a doctor," Rachelle protested. "I have a few scratches."

"You want the doc to check me?"

She narrowed her eyes. "You're blackmailing me?"

"Absolutely."

"A scratch isn't the same as a bullet wound."

He shrugged. "That's the deal. Take it or leave it."

"You're hardheaded."

"When your health and wellbeing are at stake, you bet."

Rachelle sighed. "Fine. I'll let Dr. Sorenson look at my scratches."

"Once Eli talks to Maddox, we'll have a better idea of the timeline for flying home."

"What about Amy and Eric?"

"That's up to Sorenson." Based on what he'd learned from Jackson during the flight, Eric wouldn't be traveling with them unless his or Amy's safety was at risk.

Eli passed them on his way to Sorenson's office. "I'll report in. We'll meet in the kitchen as soon as I'm finished."

Cal nudged Rachelle toward the kitchen. "Come on. We'll deliver the message and see what food Sorenson stocked for us."

"Whatever he brought in won't be enough to feed this army."

He grinned. Probably not. "We should hurry, then. Otherwise, you and I will have to order takeout." As he suspected, the operatives were devouring the spread of sub sandwiches Sorenson had provided.

Rachelle winced at the sight of the food.

Hmm. Guess she wasn't ready to eat a heavy meal. "Eli's reporting to Maddox," he announced to the others. "Meeting here when he's finished."

Cal drew Rachelle aside. "You need to eat."

"I know." She swallowed hard. "I can't handle a sub."

"I'll find something for you." Sorenson kept a variety of food on hand for his staff, including the vet techs on the other side of his business.

He checked the refrigerator. "Blueberry bagel and cut fruit sound better?"

Rachelle brightened. "Perfect."

After preparing a plate for her and seating her at the table, Cal rummaged in the cabinets until he found a stash of herbal tea. He held up a packet. "Hot tea, soft drink, or water?"

"Tea."

He nuked the water and tea bag, then set the mug in front of her. That done, he slapped together a sub for himself and dropped into a seat beside her.

When Rachelle finished her last bite, Jackson walked into the kitchen. "Rachelle, you're the next customer in Sorenson's exam room."

Cal rose to accompany her, but Rachelle laid her hand on his arm. "Finish your meal."

He grabbed his plate and bottle of water. "I'm next anyway. I'll eat in the hall."

A small smile curved her mouth. "Still protecting me?"

"Always." Something about the terrorists' determination to capture the two women bothered him. While he couldn't pin down what it was, he didn't like it. Cal followed her to the exam room.

Sorenson pointed at the table. "Sit there, Rachelle. Taylor, scram but don't go far."

"Yes, sir."

He closed the door behind him and dragged a chair from the office into the hallway. After polishing off his meal, Cal looked in on Eric and Amy. Jesse came to stand beside him in the hallway.

"How are they?"

"Amy's fine. Eric will be laid up for weeks. Although the surgeon did a good job, Eric has an infection. Sorenson put him on strong antibiotics."

"Prognosis?"

"Full recovery, but it will take a while." He inclined his head toward Cal's arm. "What about you?"

"A few stitches. Rachelle wants the doc to check my arm anyway."

The medic's eyebrows rose. "Didn't know you two were an item."

"She doesn't, either."

Jesse flashed a grin. "Like that, is it? Well, this will be fun to watch."

"Want me to bring you a sandwich?"

"I'll fix my own when Jackson returns."

The door to the exam room opened, and Sorenson pointed at Cal. "Next."

"Wish me luck," he said under his breath.

Jesse clapped him on his uninjured shoulder with a chuckle. He took Cal's empty plate and bottle. "I'll take care of these for you," he said, then returned to his patient.

Rachelle was still seated on the table. He made a beeline for her, searching her face for an indication of a problem. Seeing none, he breathed easier. "Verdict?"

"I'm fine." She flicked a glance at the doctor. "Dr. Sorenson recommends that I talk to one of the Fortress counselors."

"A precaution," the doctor assured him. "I suggested the same for Amy."

"It's a good idea," Cal said.

"Have you talked to one of the counselors before?"

"Many times. Talking to a counselor helps you process what you saw and experienced." And perhaps aid her acceptance of what he did for a living.

"Let's see your arm, Taylor. I have furry patients waiting." The doc removed the bandage. After a moment, he said, "Jackson does good work." Sorenson removed his rubber gloves. "Looks fine. If you have a problem, see one of the doctors in Nashville."

"Thanks, Doc."

"Out. I have real patients who need me."

With a grin, Cal lifted Rachelle from the exam table and ushered her to the kitchen to wait for Eli.

Soon, Wolf Pack's leader walked in, his expression grim. Cal went on alert as did the other operatives in the room.

"We have a problem."

CHAPTER SEVEN

Cal stiffened. He didn't like the sound of that. "What kind of problem?"

"The Dark Net is buzzing about a target slipping through the net in Mexico."

Rafe scowled. "Nothing more specific?"

"There's a contract on the target."

"How much?" Jon asked.

"Two million dollars."

"We still need more than that to go on." Brody Weaver folded his arms. "While two mil isn't chump change, I can think of half a dozen potential targets off hand aside from Amy Morales and her family who are as valuable to the right person in Mexico at the moment. We have to know if Amy's the target because we can't be constantly on the move with Eric's injuries. I doubt Amy and Eric are willing to separate."

"Maddox is preparing two safe houses while Zane is scrounging for more intel."

"Texas will provide security for Eric and Amy?"

"That's the plan. Phantom will be assigned to assist you."

A slow nod. "Understandable with an HVT and a critically-injured principal. When will Maddox give more details?"

"As soon as he has all the pieces in place."

Max inclined his head toward Rachelle. "What about her?"

Cal's eyes narrowed. He wouldn't leave Rachelle while her safety was in question. If necessary, he'd request a leave of absence. Maddox wouldn't be happy. Tough. Rachelle was his priority. "She stays with me. End of discussion."

Eyebrows rose at his declaration.

"Lucky for you, we've been assigned to Rachelle until we're positive she's not a target," Eli said.

Rachelle frowned. "Why would terrorists be after me?"

"Protection is a precaution."

"An unnecessary one," she insisted.

"We'll discuss that later." Eli smiled. "You can hash that out with Maddox and your boss. Both of them believe you need a shadow."

Rachelle rolled her eyes. "I'll talk to Micah and persuade him to see reason."

Good luck with that. The Fortress logistics coordinator had been in this business for a long time and had a nose for trouble. While Cal didn't always agree with Micah's assessments, in this case he did. Too many unanswered questions lingered about the terrorist attack and the frenzied search for the women.

"Orders?" Rafe asked.

"Wolf Pack has the watch. Texas will stand down for the next few hours." When the other team dispersed to replenish their supplies and rest, Eli eyed the remaining operatives. "Jon, you and I will take the perimeter. Rafe, tap your FBI and CIA contacts. Find out what they've heard. Cal, you're with Rachelle. Jackson will watch Eric and Amy."

"How would the terrorists find us?" Rachelle turned to Cal. "They can't know who rescued us from Mexico."

"Enough money changes hands, and people will talk. We didn't have time to avoid security cameras or interrupt the feed. Anyone who studies the images will know we're well trained. Fortress has a reputation in Mexico, and the fact that you work for Fortress leads to the conclusion that we extracted you and Amy. If someone wants you and Amy bad enough, they'll find you. Amy knows who you work for. What are the chances that she mentioned your employer to someone?"

"A hundred percent. But would that information lead them to the clinic and to Wolf Pack and Texas?"

"I won't risk your safety or Amy and Eric's by trusting that the terrorists haven't tapped every resource to find you."

Rachelle was silent a moment. "While we wait for the next order, is there anything I can do to help?"

Might not be wise to let her too deep into research in this situation. She hadn't had a chance to process her narrow escape.

Cal glanced at Eli. His team leader shook his head slightly. He shifted his attention to Rachelle. "I have an idea. Wait here a minute."

He sought out Sorenson. "Do you have a dog who needs TLC?"

The vet's eyebrows rose. "You're volunteering for petting duty?"

"Hey, I'm a dog fan. I'm not asking for me, though. I thought Rachelle would enjoy some pet therapy."

"She having trouble?"

Wouldn't surprise him, but that wasn't the reason behind his request. "We're at loose ends until Maddox lines up safe houses, and I don't want her wandering around the neighborhood. I'm not convinced she's safe here."

"We have Molly, a black lab whose owner dropped her off for a checkup. Molly loves being brushed and playing with a tennis ball. I have a fenced-in area where we take the dogs for exercise. Rachelle will be safe there. The door to the play yard is in the holding room."

"Thanks, Doc." He returned to the kitchen where Rachelle waited alone for him. Cal held out his hand. "Come with me. I have a treat for you."

She followed him into the hallway. "Where are we going?"

"You'll see." He located the holding room and opened the door. Immediately, a cacophony of barks rang out in the room.

Cal located a leash and tennis ball on one of the shelves, and freed the black Lab from the holding pen. He attached the leash and led Molly and Rachelle outside.

Crouching, he rubbed the Lab's big head. "This is Molly. She's here for a checkup. Want to play with her for a while? I'm sure she'd love some time outside the crate."

She smiled. "I'd love to." Her smile faded as she glanced around the yard. "Is it safe to be outside with her? I don't want to put her in danger."

Cal wasn't surprised that she'd thought of the dog's safety before her own. "The privacy fence prevents anyone from seeing you. Enjoy the sun and a sweet dog who loves to play."

For the next hour, Rachelle took turns with Cal petting Molly and throwing the tennis ball. By the time the dog flopped down in the sunshine for a nap, the ball was wet, and Molly had been brushed until her coat gleamed. Molly's owner would be pleasantly surprised at how tired the Lab was when she went home tonight.

"Thank you, Cal. This was fun." Rachelle beamed at him.

Glad he could do something to distract her from the situation she was in, he squeezed her hand. "I enjoyed being out here myself. It's been a while since I had a chance to play with a dog."

"Did you have a pet growing up?"

"My family owns a farm. We always had dogs running around, usually four or five."

"Sounds like fun. Are you close to your family?"

He smiled. "I am. I don't spend as much time with them as they'd like, but I talk to them every week." Cal winked at her. "Even my bratty sisters."

They spent a few more minutes enjoying the sunshine, then he escorted Rachelle and Molly inside. After giving the dog water, they returned her to the crate to rest and walked to the kitchen for water for themselves.

They'd just tossed their empty bottles into the recycle bin when Eli strode in. "Get your gear. We're leaving in fifteen minutes."

Cal's blood ran cold. Not good. Orders to move that fast signaled trouble.

Rachelle stared. "Why?"

"Internet's burning up with references to an HVT in this area of Texas."

"That's still not a specific target or city."

"Close enough. If trouble comes, we don't want Sorenson or his family caught in the crosshairs."

"What about Eric and Amy?" Cal asked.

"They're coming with us. We'll split up and take Rachelle to the second safe house once Phantom is in place. Right now, it's too risky to leave the Texas team without backup."

While the other operatives gathered their gear, the medics consulted with Sorenson on Eric's best course of treatment.

Amy stood in the doorway to the treatment room, concern in her eyes. "Why are we leaving? Eric isn't ready to travel."

"Someone is hunting for you and Rachelle," Eli said. "A sizable reward has been offered, and rumors are circulating that the hunters are looking in this area. We need you, Eric, and Rachelle in a defensible location."

"Isn't there something else we can do? I'm worried about Eric."

"The medics are consulting with Sorenson."

"They're not doctors."

Jesse walked up in time to hear Amy's words. "If Sorenson didn't think we could handle Eric's medical care, we'd make other arrangements."

"The doc wouldn't pull his punches to spare the feelings of our medics," Eli said. "His priority is always the patient."

"What if Eric needs more help than the medics can handle?"

Rachelle squeezed Amy's hand. "The Fortress teams will make sure he gets it."

Amy looked at Eli for confirmation.

"If the medics say Eric needs to be in the hospital, we'll admit him under a false name."

"I don't want to cause you trouble, but my first concern is Eric's health."

"I understand. Tell Eric we're leaving in five minutes." When she hurried off, Eli moved closer to Rachelle. "How are you?"

"A few sore muscles."

"When we're airborne, Micah wants to talk to you."

"I intended to call him anyway."

When it was time to leave, Sorenson's assistants helped the medics transport Eric to the SUVs. A fifteen-minute drive later, the caravan came to a halt on the tarmac near the Fortress jet. Once Eli and Jon determined that they were secure for the moment, Eli signaled Cal and Rafe to escort the women to the jet. Within minutes, the jet powered up.

"Do you know where we're going?" Rachelle asked Cal.

"Maple Valley, Tennessee."

She blinked. "Why there?"

"It's near Nashville and advanced medical care for Eric." He looked at her. "Maple Valley is also close enough for Fortress to send reinforcements if we need them."

"Is that likely?"

"I hope not."

"That's not comforting."

"Would you rather I lie to you?"

"Never. I'd rather face a problem head-on than be caught unprepared."

Once the jet lifted off and leveled out, Eli called the operatives together to make security plans for the safe house. Only the medics were exempted from the planning session.

Cal squeezed Rachelle's hand briefly. "While we're working on the security details, call Micah and get his take on your situation."

"Good idea."

Yeah, she said that now. The lady might not be so enthusiastic when Micah didn't back down from his recommendation that she go into hiding. Cal kissed her cheek, then joined his teammates at the conference table.

Every step of the way, he felt her gaze on his back. If she knew how much he longed to share a real kiss with her, would she be shocked?

As Jon brought up the schematics of the safe house and satellite images of the area surrounding the house, Cal was aware of Rachelle's low-voiced conversation with her boss. Although not close enough to hear the words, he recognized the tone easily. She was irritated. A few minutes later, she got up and walked to the bedroom at the back.

Rafe gave a low whistle. "Your lady isn't happy."

"I'm glad she's ticked off at Micah instead of me."

The operatives chuckled, then the teams debated the best places to set the perimeter and the guard rotation.

Jon tapped the screen. "This bedroom will offer the best defensive position for Eric's safety. It has the advantage of being a suite. Amy won't want to be separated from her boyfriend. She'll also be close to the panic room if the terrorists track us down and slip past our perimeter defenses."

"Where do you want Rachelle?" Cal asked.

"Second floor. There are multiple ways off that floor. Cal, you'll take the room next to hers. The rest of Wolf Pack will be in rooms close by to offer another layer of protection. Texas will be on the first floor. Phantom is already on site and setting up perimeter alarms."

He frowned. "Shouldn't we take Rachelle to the second safe house?"

"That was the original plan." Eli rubbed the back of his neck. "Maddox might have to reassign Phantom to another hotspot."

"What about the Shadow unit?"

"Deployed this morning. We can handle this ourselves."

No question about that. His main concern was protecting Eric since the agent wasn't mobile. Good thing the safe house had a panic room. With the way things were heating up, they'd need it.

CHAPTER EIGHT

Rachelle tapped lightly on the jet's bedroom door. Her gaze shifted to the man on the bed. "How's Eric?" she asked Amy.

"In pain." Her eyes glistened with unshed tears. "We should have remained in Bayside until a clear threat emerged."

Waiting until trouble arrived with guns blazing, then moving an injured man in a hurry wasn't the best plan. While Rachelle understood Amy's concern, she saw the wisdom of using a safe house off the grid since the terrorists were in southern Texas, searching for Amy. "You're too valuable to risk, Amy."

"My father's valuable, not me. I was on the goodwill tour because Dad was in meetings. Fortress could have doubled the guards at the clinic instead of moving Eric again." Her gaze shifted to her boyfriend. "What if I lose him, Rachelle?"

Jesse laid his hand on Amy's shoulder. "You won't. We're keeping a close watch on him. If we think Eric is in trouble, we'll transport him to a hospital."

"But he's in horrible pain."

"We'll keep him as comfortable as possible," Jackson said.

"Amy." The rough whisper drew their attention.

She rushed to Eric's side. "How do you feel?"

"Like a truck ran over me. Glad to be in the US." Eric turned his gaze to Jesse. "Where are we headed?"

"A safe house in Tennessee. We need you and the women off the grid."

A frown. "Why?"

"The terrorists are hunting for Amy and Rachelle," Jesse said. "Two million dollar contract for capturing them."

Eric wrapped his hand around Amy's. "A WITSEC safe house?"

"It's one of ours. Less chance of a leak."

The wounded agent grimaced. "Wise." He shifted position. "I don't know how I'll pay you for this. Fortress protection comes with a high price tag."

Jesse grinned. "Don't worry. Maddox will stick the government with the bill."

"You're worth every penny. I didn't think I'd leave that hospital alive."

"What happened when the terrorists arrived?"

Shadows filled Eric's eyes. "The medical personnel rushed me to the surgical suite before the terrorists saw me. Tim fought the terrorists near the exam room where I'd been. He sacrificed his life to protect me. After the surgery, a terrorist confronted the doctor. Dr. Gomez claimed my wife shot me for cheating on her."

"Gomez must be a stellar liar because the terrorists bought the story long enough for us to evac you."

"The terrorists would have returned to confront me and question my nonexistent wife." Eric shifted his gaze to Rachelle. "Thank you."

"For what?"

"Helping me at the hotel. I wouldn't have made it without you." Another grimace.

"I kept you moving for a short time, but Tim did the hard work."

"Tim was a good man." Eric looked at the medics. "What are the arrangements to bring him home? His family deserves closure."

"The State Department is working on it, but the chaos in Antigua is complicating things." Jackson laid his hand on the wounded man's shoulder. "We don't leave one of our own behind. If the government can't get the job done, Fortress will bring Tim home. We owe him for saving Rachelle."

"Thanks." His eyes began to close.

"Sleep, Eric," Jesse murmured. "You and Amy are safe. If anything happens, we'll tell you."

A slight nod, then his breathing deepened as he succumbed to his body's demand for rest.

"Did you mean what you said about Tim?" Amy asked, voice soft.

"Yes, ma'am."

"Are my parents safe?"

"They landed in Washington, D.C. two hours ago with their security detail. They're worried about you."

"May I talk to them?"

"When we're at the safe house. They know you're out of danger and with Eric."

Jackson eyed Rachelle. "How are you?"

"Sore." Who knew running from terrorists caused sore muscles?

He rummaged in his bag and dropped two capsules onto her palm. "Over-the-counter pain meds to take the edge off."

"Thanks." She swallowed the medicine with water. "What about you, Amy?"

"Same, but Jesse took care of me." She sighed. "I didn't know I was so out of shape. As soon as I'm safe, I'll sign up for a gym membership."

She'd had the same thought while they ran through the woods. "I'll check on that for myself."

"You won't need a gym membership," Jesse said.

"Why not?"

"Fortress has a gym on site for employees."

She stared at the medic. Was he nuts? She couldn't go in there. "The operatives use that gym."

"So?"

"I'm not an athlete. I refuse to embarrass myself on a treadmill beside men and women who run 5 miles without breaking a sweat." The thought of Cal watching her stagger through a mile or two made her flinch. She hated to run, and it showed.

Jackson smiled. "Operatives won't notice. When Eli runs us through PT, we're focused on survival."

Amy tilted her head. "He seems like a southern charmer, not a drill sergeant."

"Eli is a southern gentleman except in training when he's tough as nails and a hundred times meaner than a drill sergeant."

Surprised, Rachelle looked at Jesse for confirmation. From her observations of Eli and Jon, Eli was the gentler of the two men. Ice seemed to run through Jon's veins instead of blood. Even his face didn't show much emotion, unlike Eli. Wolf Pack's leader possessed a great sense of humor.

Jesse grunted. "He's right. Don't let Wolfe fool you. He's just as dangerous as Jon, maybe more so, because you don't expect him to pull the trigger."

Wow. Good to know. She turned to Amy. "Do you need anything? Water, soft drink, snack?"

"I'm fine." Her friend smiled, mischief temporarily displacing the worry for Eric in her eyes. "I'm sure your handsome friend misses you."

Rachelle's cheeks burned. "He and the others are working on safety plans. I doubt Cal noticed I'm not in the main cabin."

Jackson snorted. "He knows."

Although she didn't argue the point, Rachelle didn't believe him. Cal appeared engrossed in the security planning.

Jesse inclined his head toward the door. "If you don't return soon, he'll look for you."

She wrinkled her nose. "I don't think so."

The medic's lips curved. "Haven't you noticed the protective streak of Fortress operatives? Cal Taylor is a protector at heart. He notices everything about you."

"We're friends." Although her heart said otherwise. "We get coffee together when he's in town." Not as often as she wanted. Once Cal signed on full-time with Fortress and trained at PSI for a few weeks, Brent had frequently assigned him to missions.

"Open your eyes, lady. Based on what I've seen on this mission, the connection goes deeper than infrequent coffee dates." He opened the door to the main cabin and nudged Rachelle into the aisle.

Her gaze sought out Cal. Were Jackson and Jesse right? She'd been crazy about the Navy SEAL since she met him.

The operative rose in the middle of the discussion and walked to her. "Everything okay?" he murmured as he reached for her hand and threaded his fingers through hers.

"Eric is sleeping."

He studied her expression a moment. "Are the medics worried?"

She shook her head.

"If Eric's not worrying you, what is?"

She grimaced. "I'm that transparent?"

"We're friends."

Her heart sank. Friends? She didn't want a friends-only relationship with Cal. After squeezing his fingers, Rachelle released him. "Go back to your meeting. I hear Eli is a hard taskmaster."

Cal frowned. "He can be." The operative edged closer, turning his back to his teammates and blocking their view of her. "I hurt you."

She added observant to his list of admirable qualities. "Of course not. You wouldn't do that." At least, not intentionally.

"Rachelle."

She closed her eyes for a few seconds, cheeks burning. "Don't ask. Please."

"Baby, I can't fix what I did wrong if I don't know how I hurt you."

Her breath caught. Baby? Did he mean that?

"Tell me," he whispered.

She had to know if he viewed her only as a friend or not. If he did, she'd shore up the walls around her heart and get on with her life. "You said we're friends."

Cal stilled. "Aren't we?"

For a moment, she thought hurt flickered in his eyes. In the next instant, he'd masked his expression and his eyes showed nothing except intense focus on her. "Is that all we are?"

He cupped her cheek. "I want more. Do you?"

"Yes."

The operative relaxed, his thumb brushing across her bottom lip in a touch so light her nerve endings sparked to life. "Thank God. I was afraid you'd reject me and break my heart."

"Why would I do that?"

"You're beautiful, smart, and funny. You could have any guy you wanted and deserve better than me."

"I disagree. Besides, you don't have competition. None of the Fortress men have shown interest in me."

He snorted. "You haven't noticed the looks and hints thrown your way."

"You're the only man I'm interested in."

His gaze dropped to her mouth. "You have no idea how much I want to kiss you."

"I wouldn't object," she whispered.

Cal groaned. "Don't tempt me. When I kiss you the first time, I don't want an audience."

"Rain check?"

"Definitely." He bent his head until his mouth brushed the corner of hers. "I can wait. Maybe."

A tiny turn of her head and her mouth would be against his. So tempting. Rachelle returned the favor by kissing the corner of his mouth. "It's later. Kiss me now?"

His lips curved. "Still have that audience."

"Bummer. Think they'll notice a short kiss?"

"Our first kiss won't be short. So, yeah, they'll notice." With a soft groan, Cal eased away from her. "I have to go or Eli will grab me by the scruff of the neck and drag me back on task."

"Is there anything I can do to help?"

He shook his head. "I have my laptop with Zane's iron-clad encryption. Would you like to use it?"

"I'll check my work email."

"I'm sure Micah would appreciate that. He brags about you all the time."

"Really?"

"Yes, ma'am. All the division heads would love to poach his assistant. He's threatened to fire anyone who steals you."

That made her laugh. Nice to know she was appreciated.

Cal retrieved his laptop. Once he logged her into the system and the hotspot, he returned to the conference table.

Although she didn't know how long she'd be out, she refused to leave her boss short-handed. Rachelle settled back in her seat and got to work.

CHAPTER NINE

"Nice of you to join us," Eli drawled when Cal sat.

"Bite me," he muttered.

The other man flashed him a grin. "Pass. I prefer to nibble on my wife." He sobered as his gaze shifted to Rachelle. "Is she all right?"

He thought she was flat out amazing and way too good for the likes of him, but he had no intention of telling his fellow teammates that. They already had enough to tease him about as it was. "She's good for the moment. Once we're in Maple Valley, I'll set up a session with a counselor. Memories of her time in Antigua will plague her when she lets down."

Max nudged him. "Didn't look like your conversation centered around terrorists. What gives, frog boy?"

He lifted one shoulder in a shrug. "I told Rachelle I'm interested in her."

Brody's eyebrow rose. "Yeah? And?"

"Lucky for me, the interest goes both ways."

A slow smile curved the Texas leader's mouth. "Nice."

Better than nice. A miracle. "Thanks."

Jon rolled his eyes. "Are we finished with the gossip session, ladies? If so, we still have work to do."

Logan Fletcher, Texas team's EOD man, groaned. "Come on, Jon. We've already talked through five different scenarios and made contingency plans for each. Enough already."

Wolf Pack's sniper turned his cool gaze to the other man. "We need at least five more scenarios with contingency plans."

Sawyer Chapman lightly punched his teammate on the shoulder. "Give it up, buddy. Even though I hope this planning is overkill, I won't risk the lives of our principals because I think Wolf Pack is filled with overachievers."

Rafe snorted. "Not overachievers. More like the voice of experience. No mission goes according to plan. In fact, missions tend to go off the rails early and often."

Brody frowned. "A result of poor intel?"

"Nope. This is our first team mission. The rest of our missions have been as individuals or part of other teams." He shrugged. "Maddox knows our capabilities and pushes us to our limits."

Logan scowled. "He's not holding back on Texas, either."

"Maddox only hires the best," Eli said. "You wouldn't be part of Fortress if you couldn't handle the job."

"What makes your team different from ours?" Sawyer asked.

"Five SEALs."

The members of Texas exchanged glances. Brody rubbed his jaw, his beard rasping against his fingers. "You win," he muttered.

"It's not a contest of skill," Jon said. "Because of our background, our training is more extensive than yours."

"On a mission, getting the job done is priority," Cal said. "Texas is ranked at the same level as the rest of the elite teams at Fortress. You're doing everything right."

Brody glanced at Eli. "Let's finish this planning session. We land in Nashville in three hours."

"Let's get to it, then."

For the next hour, Cal divided his attention between the planning session and keeping an eye on Rachelle.

Finally, Eli stood. "That's it for now. When we land in Nashville, Texas will transport Amy and Eric. Maddox has two SUVs waiting for your use. The rest of us will drive our own SUVs and form a loose circle around your vehicles. Zane will send the safe house address to your phones. I'll talk to the medics about Eric. If they say he can't handle the drive, we'll make alternate arrangements." He headed toward the bedroom.

Cal returned to his seat beside Rachelle. She closed the laptop lid.

"Thanks for letting me use the computer."

"Get a lot done?"

She nodded. "Is it possible to stop by my apartment for clothes?"

He hated to disappoint her. Though she probably wasn't the primary target, he didn't want to take the risk. "Wouldn't be wise. It's the first place someone will look for you."

Rachelle sighed. "I understand, but I'll need clothes and toiletries."

His lips curved. "Maple Valley and the surrounding towns have stores."

"I don't have cash with me. I used my credit card in Mexico, but that leaves a trail."

He threaded his fingers through hers. "I'll take care of it."

"If someone discovers I'm with you, you'll be a target. I don't want you hurt because of me."

"I have alternate ID complete with a credit card courtesy of Zane's mad computer skills."

She stared. "As a former law enforcement officer, does using a fake ID and credit card bother you?"

He kissed the bridge of her nose. "I'm not defrauding anyone. I'll pay the bill. Using a fake ID is a way to protect you."

"Does Zane create alternate IDs for all operatives?"

He nodded. "We have several at our disposal, complete with histories." He studied her a moment, wondering how she would react to his next words. "Most of us also have IDs not created by Zane."

"Why?"

"In case of a data breach. It's another layer of protection in case things go south and our lives are at risk along with our principals."

"Is a data breach possible? I thought Zane was the ultimate computer geek."

"He is, but no protection is airtight. That's why Zane changes our security protocols on a regular basis and experiments with new programs. Staying ahead of super hackers is a never-ending battle."

She sighed. "Remind me not to complain the next time he introduces new security measures."

"Deal." His gaze dropped to her mouth. Man, he'd give anything to have the privacy to kiss her. Not the time, he reminded himself. Soon, though. Waiting much longer to feel her mouth under his might kill him.

Rachelle drew in a shaky breath. "Not fair," she whispered.

"What isn't?"

"I want that kiss you promised me, but we're still not alone."

"Tell me about it." Cal reclined his seat and extended his arm to her. "Come here. Even though I can't do what I want, I can hold you."

She settled against his side and rested her head against his chest. "I don't think I can sleep. Too much on my mind."

"Let your body rest, then. In the military, I learned to sleep in short spurts."

"You should sleep if you can. I'll keep watch for you."

Delighted with her, Cal kissed Rachelle's temple. "If you need me, wake me." More content than he'd been in years, Cal closed his eyes.

Minutes later, Eli returned from the bedroom. "New plan," he announced. "The medics consulted with Sorenson. They don't think Eric can handle the drive from Nashville to Maple Valley. Maddox will have a helo at the airport to transport Eric, Amy, Jesse, and one other member of Texas. The rest will drive the SUVs. Brody, you and your teammates decide who's going with Jesse and the helo."

While the members of Texas discussed the situation, Cal tightened his hold on Rachelle who had fallen asleep in his arms. Good to know she trusted him enough to sleep this close to him. If she knew what he was capable of, she might not be so comfortable with him.

When the pilot announced they were on final approach, Cal rubbed Rachelle's back to ease her to wakefulness. "Rachelle, wake up."

"Mmm."

His lips curved. She sounded like a content kitten. "We'll be landing soon."

She sighed and tilted her head back to smile at him. "Guess I fell asleep. Sorry. Some watch assistant I turned out to be. I didn't intend to fall asleep on you."

"I'm not complaining."

Her gaze drifted to his mouth. "How soon will we arrive in Maple Valley?"

He chuckled. "Not soon enough."

When the jet stopped on the tarmac, a Fortress physician boarded and hurried to the back bedroom.

"What's going on?" Concern clouded Rachelle's eyes as she looked toward the back of the jet.

"The medics don't think Eric can tolerate the ride to Maple Valley. He, Amy, and two members of Texas will fly up by helicopter. The rest of us will drive."

"Is Eric worse?"

"He's holding his own, but Jesse and Jackson feel he's pushed himself as far as he can without a setback in his recovery."

Fifteen minutes later, the doctor exited the bedroom. He clapped Eli on the shoulder. "How's it going, Eli?"

"Not bad." He inclined his head toward the bedroom. "How's Eric?"

"On track. He's exhausted, though. The helo is the best plan to get him out of Nashville and to the safe house."

"Any instructions for us?"

"Once Eric is at the safe house, don't move him unless it's a dire emergency. I've given instructions to the medics and the medicines they need for his care. If there's any change, have the medics call me or Sorenson. You need a game plan for an emergency medical evac."

"Already done, Doc."

"Jesse and Jackson are to update me every four hours on Eric's condition. Let him sleep as much as possible. He needs to stay in bed for a few days. The medics will know when he's ready to get up. Don't let Eric decide for himself. He's as bad as Fortress operatives, already wanting to know how soon he can get moving."

"Yes, sir."

"I have a stretcher and two medics with me. We'll get him ready to transport while you and the others secure the area."

Eli glanced at his team and said, "Wolf Pack, recon."

Cal rose along with his teammates. He bent and kissed Rachelle's cheek. "Stay here until I come back for you." He turned and looked at Brody, who nodded, acknowledging the silent order to protect Rachelle until Cal returned.

He and his teammates spread out across the tarmac, weapons in hand, as the doctor motioned for the medics to bring the stretcher from the specially-equipped van used for patient transport.

Cal scanned his assigned area but saw nothing to raise his suspicions. A short distance away, the helo's rotors slowly turned as the pilots awaited the patient and other passengers.

Soon, the medics and doctor exited the jet with Eric and Amy. Wolf Pack closed ranks around the pair, alert for signs of trouble as they crossed the tarmac to the waiting helo.

Within minutes, Eric, Amy, Jesse, and Max were on board the helicopter. As soon as Wolf Pack, medics, and doctor were clear, the bird lifted from the tarmac, rotors whipping dust and grit into a whirlwind.

After the doctor and medics left, Eli signaled his team to return to the jet. When Cal stepped into the cabin, his gaze sought out Rachelle. The knots in his stomach untied themselves when he saw for himself that she was safe. He turned to Brody. "Thanks."

"No problem."

Rachelle's brows knitted. "Did I miss something?"

"Eric and Amy are on their way to Maple Valley."

"That's not what I meant."

"We'll talk about it later. I want you off this jet and in my SUV." Despite not seeing signs of a threat, Cal's skin crawled. Had he missed a threat to Amy and Rachelle?

"Grab your gear," Eli told the remaining operatives. "Time to go. Cal, escort Rachelle. The rest of us will provide protection for the two of you until you're inside the SUV. The plans we made to escort Eric and Amy will shift to providing a secure perimeter around Rachelle and Cal."

Cal grabbed his Go bag as well as Rachelle's pack. He held out his hand to her. "Let's go."

He escorted her to the door where Rafe took Cal's Go bag. With a nod of thanks, Cal wrapped his arm around Rachelle's shoulders and tucked her against his side.

Gaze scouring the area as they left the safety of the jet, he hurried her to his SUV. Rafe deposited the Go bag in the middle of the back seat and strode to his own vehicle.

Cal drove from the parking area designated for Fortress and headed for Maple Valley surrounded by his teammates. With luck, they would arrive at the safe house without incident.

His jaw tightened. No matter the cost to himself, no one would hurt Rachelle on his watch.

CHAPTER TEN

Rachelle enjoyed the beautiful sunset as Cal maneuvered through Nashville traffic. "You're good at combat driving. Would you like to apply for a job as my permanent chauffeur?"

The operative chuckled. "I could be tempted by the right persuasive technique."

"That sounds promising. What persuasive tactics would I have to use?"

"Two things. First, I would require kisses. A lot of them."

Did he think that would discourage her? Fat chance. She couldn't wait to share kisses with the handsome operative. "What's the second thing?"

"I want an exclusive dating relationship with you."

Rachelle blinked. Was he serious? "We've only been on coffee dates."

"Those don't count, and I'll remedy that as soon as possible."

While she didn't have a problem committing to a relationship with him, Cal might regret the impulse when he realized how uneventful her life was. He lived life on the edge. She lived a life of routine.

He glanced at her, his expression neutral. "Too soon to ask for that privilege?" he asked, voice soft.

"No. I'm afraid you'll find me boring." Her cheeks burned, embarrassed to lay her greatest fear at the feet of the most interesting man she'd ever met.

"I haven't yet."

"You live an exciting life, and I'm all about routine. I prefer staying home to going out. I'd rather read a book than go on a week's long vacation in some exotic location."

"I have more excitement than I want. Being in a crowd means I'm constantly on alert. When we're together, I want to concentrate on you, not on protecting you from potential threats." He glanced at her before returning his attention to the road. "If you prefer reading a book to exotic vacations, why did you go to Mexico for a week?"

"Amy didn't want to go on the tour for her father by herself. She's not a fan of public speaking and thought having me along would make the week more fun."

"Was it?"

"Yes, until terrorists attacked."

"You're a good friend."

Rachelle grimaced. "In this case, I wish I had refused to go." Running from terrorists would stay fresh in her memory for a long time.

Another glance at her. "Back to my question. Are you interested in exclusive dating or do you need more time to decide?"

"I'll agree on one condition."

"Name it."

"Tell me if our relationship isn't working for you. Don't delay the inevitable because you don't want to hurt my feelings." She tilted up her chin. "Holding back the truth will hurt worse."

Cal was silent for a few beats. Finally, he wrapped his hand around hers. "Who hurt you?"

Stunned, Rachelle's head whipped his direction. How did he know? "It doesn't matter."

"Yeah, it does. I want his name so I'll know who to be on the lookout for in case he decides he wants to return to your life."

"That won't happen. He's married to my former best friend now. They're expecting their third child soon."

He squeezed her hand. "You keep up with him?"

"My mother does, and she's not shy about sharing the latest gossip. I don't ask about him or stalk his social media pages. I'm not carrying a torch for him."

"I still want a name."

"Stubborn, much?"

He grinned. "You have no idea."

Yeah, she was getting the picture. "Brad Delke."

"Did you mean what you said?"

"That I'll date only you? You bet. My mother didn't raise a fool. I've wanted to date you for months."

He relaxed in his seat, still holding her hand. "Fantastic. Now I have the right to spoil you."

That made her smile. "As long as I have the right to do the same."

"Deal." Cal raised her hand to his mouth and kissed her knuckles. He glanced in the mirrors and frowned.

Rachelle's stomach tightened. "What's wrong?" No one could have followed them from Mexico or Bayside. Could they?

"Not sure if there is anything to be concerned about."

"But you think there is."

Without acknowledging her comment, he released her hand and activated his Bluetooth system.

A moment later, Eli's voice sounded in the SUV's cabin. "I see him," was his greeting. "Jon and Brody are moving into position to cut him off if he becomes a problem."

"If this guy is a threat, we can't deal with it on the interstate. Too dangerous for other drivers."

"Suggestions?"

"Backroads." He named the exit he wanted to take. "The road will give us room to maneuver without endangering others."

"I'll pass the word to the others. Follow Rafe and Sawyer. The rest of us will slide between you and the unknown driver."

"Copy that." He ended the call.

"How did the terrorists find us?" Rachelle's fingers tightened around Cal's. How had the danger followed her home? They couldn't know she would be in Nashville at this time.

"We don't know if this driver is a threat. My job is to protect you from anything that might develop into a problem." He glanced at her. "We'll handle it. All you have to do is trust me."

"I can't be safer than with a Navy SEAL and a homicide detective."

Satisfaction bloomed on his face. "I won't let you down."

"I'm not worried about that, Cal."

He squeezed her hand. "Good." Glancing in mirrors again, he returned his hand to the steering wheel.

Ahead of them, two Fortress SUVs took the Ellendale exit. Cal followed suit. A glance behind them told Rachelle that the rest of their entourage had fallen into line behind them. "Will you set a trap for the tail?" she asked.

"Your safety is my priority. I won't put you at risk."

The Fortress vehicles followed the winding road through the shadowed countryside. A short time later, Cal's phone signaled an incoming call.

He tapped the display screen on the dashboard. "Taylor."

"It's Logan. The bogey is still on our tail. What do you want us to do?"

Cal's expression hardened. "Cut him off. I don't want him near Rachelle. If you can, detain and question the driver. I want answers."

"Copy that. I'll pass the word to Brody and Sawyer."

"I'll contact the rest of my team." He ended the call, then contacted Eli.

"I'll stay on your tail and send Jon to help Texas. If this guy has answers, Jon will get them. Stay alert, Cal. There's usually a backup plan when an HVT is involved."

"Yes, sir." He ended the call. "The next few minutes could be rough."

"Why are the terrorists so persistent? I'm not an HVT like Amy or her parents. This doesn't make sense."

He trailed his fingers down her cheek without taking his gaze from the road. "We'll find the answers. I won't rest until I do. Nothing and no one will touch you on my watch."

Rachelle nuzzled against his palm, reveling in the feel of his calloused skin pressed. When she left for Mexico, she never dreamed she would have this privilege. "Can Eric and Amy be followed to the safe house?"

"Only if someone learned we were using the chopper and placed a tracker on it. I'll alert Jesse to have the pilot check the helo before they unload Eric and Amy. If they've been compromised, the pilot will lift off again and Maddox will come up with another plan while they're in the air."

Jesse answered Cal's call and promised to have the helicopter checked for a tracker.

"How is Eric?" Rachelle asked.

"Sleeping like a baby. With all this traveling, he'll be sore and grumpy for days. Everything okay on your end, Cal?"

"Don't know. Looks like we picked up a tail. Your teammates and Jon will corner this guy and find out what he knows."

A soft whistle came over the sound system. "I'd hate to be on the receiving end of Jon's interrogation."

"No kidding. Later." He ended the call.

"What did Jesse mean by that?"

"Jon is one of the best interrogators employed by Fortress. If our pursuer knows anything, he'll be begging to talk before Jon is finished with him."

Good grief. She stared at Cal. "Will he kill the man?"

A brief glance her way. "What do you think?"

She considered what she knew about Jon Smith and the kind of men Maddox hired. "He won't unless the man attacks and they can't contain him."

"That's right. Jon's a world-class sniper. He's killed many terrorists over the years and won't hesitate to do so again to protect innocents. But he doesn't kill unless it's necessary. If he kills the man, you can be sure he didn't have another option."

Rachelle twisted to look at Cal. A question burned in her mind, but she hesitated to ask. It felt intrusive.

He glanced at her, his expression resigned. "Ask."

"Would you kill the man following us?"

"If he threatened you and put your life at risk, I wouldn't hesitate." After a beat of silence, Cal wrapped his hand around hers. "Want to take back your agreement to date me?"

"Not a chance, buddy. You're not sliding out of your promise, and I'm not welshing on mine. You owe me kisses, and I intend to collect."

He flashed her an intense look. "Believe me, I'm happy to deliver."

His phone rang. Cal tapped the dashboard screen again. "Yeah, Taylor."

"It's Brody. We have the man in custody. Jon's working with him now."

"Copy that."

"Stay alert. He's claiming he and his crew never fail."

Crew. Rachelle's hand tightened around Cal's. Eli was right. This man wasn't working alone. What did that mean for them?

"We need to know the target's name and why they want her."

"Copy." Brody ended the call.

Cal updated Eli.

"Not what I wanted to hear," he growled.

"Might be best to backtrack and return to the interstate."

"Or we could run into the rest of the crew." After a moment, Eli said, "Keep moving forward, but anticipate trouble."

"Yes, sir." Cal glanced at her. "You okay?"

"Peachy. Who needs coffee to stay awake."

He chuckled. "Adrenaline buzz does wonders for you, but you crash hard after the crisis is over."

They continued through the dimly-lit countryside. Where before she'd enjoyed the sunset, now Rachelle wished for daylight to see potential danger. Their headlights pinpointed their location for anyone interested. On this sparsely traveled road, four vehicles traveling together would capture attention. Traveling without headlights wasn't an option.

Up ahead, two vehicles raced toward them. Cal's hands tightened around the steering wheel. "If I tell you to get down, do it without hesitation."

"All right."

As they neared an intersection, the two vehicles swerved and skidded to a stop, blocking both sides of the road. A third vehicle raced from the crossroad and slammed into the passenger side of Cal's SUV.

CHAPTER ELEVEN

The impact of the blow shoved Cal's SUV across the intersection, over the grass-covered shoulder, and down into the ditch.

He glanced at Rachelle as he drew his Sig. His heart sank. Her head lolled toward him, blood covering the side of her face. "Rachelle!"

No response.

Praying she was still alive, he touched his fingers to the side of her neck. Cal breathed a sigh of relief when he found a strong pulse. Gunfire echoed in the still night air and bullets smacked into the side of his SUV.

Hoping he wouldn't cause further injury, Cal lowered the back of her seat until Rachelle laid flat. The SUV's armor-plated exterior would offer better protection. While the glass was bullet resistant, if enough rounds impacted the windows, they'd shatter.

Cal opened the driver's door and slid out. Using his vehicle for protection, he fired two shots at one of the men sent to grab Rachelle and dropped him.

Another attacker fired multiple rounds at Cal, forcing him to crouch near the wheel well for protection. The sound of booted feet running across the asphalt alerted him to another possible attacker coming for Rachelle. Cal scrambled around the front of his vehicle, using the incline for concealment.

When the man raised his weapon to fire at the SUV, Cal fired two shots, one bullet to the chest and one to the head.

The night grew eerily quiet as gunfire ceased.

"Cal," Eli called. "I'm coming in soft. We're clear."

Cal kept his weapon up and ready until Eli appeared alone.

"Rachelle okay?" his teammate asked.

"No. Jackson!"

A moment later, the medic hurried down the embankment and around the hood. Jackson crawled into the damaged vehicle with his mike bag as Cal scrambled into the backseat.

Rachelle groaned and batted at Jackson's hands as the medic checked her for broken bones and internal injuries.

Thank God she had come around. Cal captured her hand in his. "Jackson is checking you for injuries."

"Head hurts."

He glanced at the side of her forehead and hissed in fury. "I'll bet. You have a gash on the side of your head. As soon as Jackson says it's safe to move you, we'll get you out of here." The sooner, the better. He didn't know how many more members of this crew were in the area. He didn't want Rachelle caught in the middle of another firefight.

"Does anything hurt besides your head, Rachelle?" Jackson asked.

"Ribs."

"Right side?"

"Yes."

The medic ran his hands over her ribcage, eliciting more moans from her. He glanced at Cal. "Cracked.

Doesn't feel like they're broken. When we're in a safe place, I'll tape them. She's going to be uncomfortable for a while."

Jackson continued his examination, asking questions to determine if she had more injuries. Finally, he sat back. "We should be able to move her."

"Internal injuries?" Cal asked.

"Not that I can find."

"Let's get her out of here, then. My skin is crawling."

The medic's expression was grim. "Same here." He laid his hand on Rachelle's shoulder. "Let us do the work."

"Is Amy okay?" she whispered to Cal.

"I'll find out when we're on the move again." He glanced at Jackson. "What's the best way to do this?"

"Raise the hatchback and slide her out the back."

Cal lowered the seat and raised the hatchback.

"How can I help?" Eli asked after he slid down the embankment.

"We need to move Rachelle to Jackson's SUV. Grab my gear."

"I'm all right," she insisted. "I can climb out on my own."

Not a chance. He laid a hand on her shoulder and squeezed gently. "Indulge me. The accident shook me up."

Her lips curved. "Right."

She might think he was exaggerating, but he wasn't. Cal had never been so afraid in his life as when the other vehicle slammed into Rachelle's side of the SUV.

Cal and Jackson slid Rachelle across the seats and into the cargo area. While Jackson held her steady, Cal gripped her upper arms.

"I'm going to move you toward Cal and help you sit up, nice and slow," Jackson said. "If you become dizzy or nauseated, I need to know."

When she nodded, the medic climbed from the vehicle and worked with Cal to ease Rachelle into a sitting position.

Although he watched her face, Cal didn't detect signs of nausea or pain. "How do you feel?"

She was silent as she assessed her body's response to the change in position. "A little lightheaded. I'm also starting to stiffen up."

With the speed of impact, he wasn't surprised. She'd be hurting for several days.

Eli grabbed Cal's gear from the SUV. "Let's roll. Zane has a cleanup crew on the way." He slid a glance to Cal. "The skin on my nape is prickling."

Not a good sign. Cal needed to get Rachelle situated in the other SUV and get her out of here. Eli's instincts were never wrong, and in this case, they agreed with his own.

"What's that mean?" Rachelle asked.

"Trouble's headed our way." Cal could have lied. He wouldn't if he could avoid it. He didn't want their relationship to be based on untruths. He wanted the same kind of rock-solid relationship with her that Jon and Eli had with their wives.

"Wonderful. I'm ready to go."

"I'm carrying you. Don't argue. I need to hold you in my arms." When he gently lifted her into his arms, she wrapped her arms around his neck. Trusting his teammates to have their backs, he moved quickly to Jackson's vehicle and set her on the backseat. Jackson tossed him the vehicle remote and climbed into the backseat beside Rachelle with his mike bag at the ready.

Although Cal hated to be separated from her even by a few feet, he wanted Rachelle to have her cut examined as soon as possible. He'd seen enough injuries during his career to recognize when someone needed stitches, and she did.

He cranked the engine. Cal fell in behind Rafe with Eli bringing up the rear.

"I'm going to clean your cut so I have a better idea of what we're dealing with," Jackson said to Rachelle.

Minutes later, he said, "Congratulations, pretty lady. You need stitches."

"I'm not a fan," she muttered. "You sure I can't get a second opinion?"

Cal smiled. He didn't blame her. He'd received more stitches than he wanted during his years in the military, law enforcement, and black ops work. "Sorry, sweetheart. He's right."

"Traitor," she groused.

Jackson patted her shoulder. "I understand your reluctance. However, the cut on your forehead won't close on its own without leaving a significant scar. I can stitch the cut or we can have a doctor brought in to do the honors. Your choice. The cut is near your hairline. With your hairstyle, the stitches won't show, and you shouldn't have much of a scar."

A sigh. "Cal, what do you recommend?"

"Jackson's an excellent medic."

"That's a good enough recommendation for me. You're hired, Jackson. At this point, I don't trust anyone I don't know."

Wise choice. Whoever headed this terrorist group was well connected. He'd prefer Jackson or Jesse work on Rachelle unless she was critically injured. That possibility made his stomach twist into a knot. He wouldn't let anyone that close to the woman coming to mean so much to him.

"Excellent." Jackson told her he was going to use lidocaine to numb the area.

The medic continued to talk her through his treatment steps as Cal drove a winding road through the countryside, alert for more trouble. As he drove, he listened to the question-and-answer session with Rachelle and Jackson.

Minutes later, Cal's cell phone rang. He placed the call on speaker. "You're on speaker."

"How is Rachelle?" Eli asked.

"She needs stitches. Jackson has already used lidocaine. We're waiting for the medicine to kick in. Do you have an update?"

"Nobody on our six. Amy and Eric have landed. The pilot and Max are checking the helo for a tracker. Jackson, can Rachelle tolerate detours to the safe house?"

Rachelle answered for herself. "I'll be fine while you and the others make sure we don't lead the terrorists to Amy and Eric."

"I hear you. Tell Cal if you reach the point where you can't handle any more."

"Yes, sir."

But Cal heard the stubbornness in her voice. She'd rather suffer than endanger Eric and Amy. He glanced in the rearview mirror and caught Jackson's eye. The medic gave a slight nod. His teammate would monitor Rachelle.

Ten minutes later, Jackson said, "Do you feel this, Rachelle?"

"Pressure."

"Perfect. Cal, we need a smooth ride for a few minutes."

"You got it."

"Turn on the overhead light. Why don't you talk to the lady unless you need me to plead your case for you."

He snorted. "No thanks, buddy. If she listens to you, I won't stand a chance with her."

"Cal is a good guy, you know," Jackson said. "Even though he is a rough around the edges. With coaching from me, he'll make a passable boyfriend."

His eyes narrowed. Great. Some help he was. "Thanks for the ringing endorsement, Jackson. I'll be lucky if she doesn't dump me before we arrive in Maple Valley."

The medic was silent a moment, then said, "Wait. You mean you two are an official couple?"

"If you haven't convinced Rachelle that I'm not worth the risk, yeah, we are."

"Fat chance of that," she murmured.

"All right!" Jackson said. "About time you manned up, Taylor."

"Shut up, Conner."

His teammate laughed. "Been waiting for you to grow a backbone. I was ready to ask Rachelle out myself since I didn't believe you'd follow through."

He growled. "You're pushing your luck." His aggravating teammate laughed at Cal's embarrassment. "Pay attention to your job."

"I'm half finished. If you talk to her, I won't share interesting bits of information."

"Lighten up, Jackson," Rachelle said. "Cal's been talking to me."

"Is he saying anything worth listening to?"

"Jackson," Cal snapped.

More laughter from the medic. "Problem, my friend?"

"Not for much longer. Dead men can't talk."

"Tell me about yourself, Jackson." Amusement filled Rachelle's voice. "Is there a special woman in your life?"

"Not at the moment. I'd been holding back for a chance with you. Now, my hopes are dashed, and my heart is shattered into a million pieces."

Cal glared at his soon-to-be former friend in the mirror.

"Ha. I don't believe that for a minute." She continued to pepper the medic with questions.

When Cal followed Rafe onto the interstate, Jackson said, "You're all set, Rachelle. I placed a waterproof bandage on the cut so you'll be able to shower. Don't linger in there, though."

"Thanks for patching me up, Jackson."

"No problem. When was your last tetanus shot?"

"Last year."

"Good. Take these pain capsules. By the time we arrive at our destination, the lidocaine will have worn off.

Wrap up in this blanket and take a nap. You're going to crash soon."

"I can help you keep watch. I'll be fine until we reach Maple Valley."

The invisible band around Cal's heart squeezed. Even injured, she was thinking of them instead of herself. "We've got this, Rachelle."

"All right. Wake me if you need my help."

"Absolutely." He wouldn't. The offer, though, made his heart turnover in his chest.

Jackson climbed into the front passenger seat and remained silent for a few miles. He glanced over his shoulder. "She's out," he murmured.

"How is she?"

"She'll be fine in a few days. I'll keep her on light pain meds. I also gave her an antibiotic because of the cut." The medic clapped Cal's shoulder. "You're a lucky man. Rachelle is one tough lady."

She had to be tough to thrive in a relationship with a man who deployed without notice. Worse, he could never tell her where he was going, what his job entailed, or when he'd return. The chances of him missing important events in her life was high.

Not many significant others could handle the uncertainty. Dating an operative sounded exciting. The reality was more difficult than people realized. The divorce rate in black ops work was high. He didn't want to be a statistic or set up Rachelle to be one. "I know."

"Do you think she can handle it?"

"I do. The question is whether she wants to. This life isn't for everyone. Books and movies glamorize it. The reality is difficult."

Jackson's phone buzzed with a text. He checked the screen and grunted.

"Problem?"

"Looks like one is brewing."

"What's up?"

"Maddox says to call him when we're in a secure location."

His hands tightened on the steering wheel. Their boss must have information that he knew Cal wouldn't like. Great. Not what he needed on top of his burning desire to keep Rachelle safe.

They lapsed into silence again. Cal frequently glanced over his shoulder to check on Rachelle.

An hour later, Rafe took the exit for Maple Valley. They wound deep into the countryside and finally turned left into a long, meandering driveway.

When the driveway ended, Rafe, Cal, and Eli parked in front of a large two-story house. Max stepped out on the porch and came down the stairs. He came around to Cal's door. "Need help?"

"Grab my gear while I carry Rachelle inside." Cal opened the back door as his teammates gathered their gear and transferred everything to the house.

He scooped Rachelle into his arms and straightened. When she jerked into wakefulness, Cal said, "You're safe. We're at the safe house, and I'm carrying you inside."

"I can walk," she murmured as she snuggled close.

He tightened his grip. "Not a chance. I like holding you." When she kissed the side of his neck, Cal shivered. "You're a serious distraction," he muttered.

"Just reminding you of your promise."

"I haven't forgotten." He'd hardly been able to think of anything else during the past three hours of driving. After her injury, though, he might have to wait to feel her mouth under his.

Cal angled Rachelle through the doorway and walked into the large living room filled with two recliners and a sectional sofa.

Jesse walked into the room, concern in his eyes when he saw Cal carrying Rachelle. "Is she worse?"

"I'm fine," Rachelle insisted. "Cal is spoiling me."

"Ah." Texas team's medic sent him a knowing glance before returning his attention to Rachelle. "How's the head?"

"Hurts. I'll live."

Max descended the stairs. "Brody called. He and the others will be here in 30 minutes."

Cal sat beside Rachelle on the sectional. "What did Jon learn from our attacker?"

"Brody said Jon wanted to talk to you and Rachelle in person."

"That's not a good sign, is it?" Rachelle turned her worried gaze toward him.

Unable to help himself, Cal wrapped his arm around her shoulders and tucked her closer. "We'll handle it." He'd shield her from anyone and anything intent on harming her.

CHAPTER TWELVE

"How's Eric?" Cal asked Jesse. He wanted to insist that Rachelle go to bed, but that would be a futile battle. She'd want to know every scrap of information about Eric and Amy. He didn't blame her. Besides, if she fell asleep in his arms, he'd have an excuse to hold her, a definite win in his estimation. His body heat might lessen her pain from the accident.

"Holding his own. He'll sleep for a few more hours."

"What about Amy?" Rachelle asked.

"Sleeping in the room next to his. Eric's in a suite. The doors to both sides of the bathroom are open so she can hear what's happening in his room."

He understood. Cal would sleep tonight with his door open to hear if Rachelle needed him, too.

"How did you transport Eric to the house?" Rachelle asked.

"The county sheriff arranged transport and provided protection until we were set up here."

Cal frowned. "He left?"

"He was called to a murder scene. He volunteered to leave a deputy until the rest of the team arrived, but we didn't want him short-handed. The crime scene is two miles away. If we had a problem, backup was two minutes away."

Eli sat on a recliner as Rafe kept watch out the front window. "Time to call the boss. We need to report in."

"He has news?" Cal asked.

With a nod, Eli made the call.

A moment later, a gruff voice answered. "Yeah, Maddox."

"It's Eli. You're on speaker."

"Sit rep." When Eli finished his report, Maddox said, "How's your head, Rachelle?"

"Aside from a massive headache, I'm fine."

"Jackson."

"Ten stitches near her hairline along with cracked ribs. She's on pain meds and antibiotics. I'll tape her ribs in a few minutes so she's more comfortable. Rachelle will be back to normal in a few days."

"Excellent."

"You told us to call." Cal stroked Rachelle's arm with his thumb. "You have new information?"

"Someone broke into Rachelle's apartment."

She gasped. "Oh, no. What did they take?"

"As far as we can tell, nothing."

Cal frowned. Stealing her belongings wasn't the point. Was someone hunting for clues to her location? "Did they search her home?"

"No. That wasn't their purpose."

"What did they want?" Rachelle asked.

"To leave behind evidence that you're plotting to kill President Martin."

Her hands fisted. "It's not true."

Ice water flowed through his veins. "Rachelle would never threaten Martin," Cal insisted.

"We know. The Secret Service, however, would take the threat seriously if they learned of it."

"Fortress investigated when the alarm was tripped?"

"I responded with a team. If it was a simple B & E, I would have called Metro PD."

"Good thing Metro's finest weren't called." Eli's voice was grim. "They would've reported the threat to the feds."

"I didn't threaten the president, sir," Rachelle said, voice shaking.

"I believe you. I'm concerned about what will happen when the person who planted the information realizes the plan didn't work."

"They'll try again."

"Be prepared."

"What happened to the planted threat?" Cal asked.

"Confiscated and removed from her apartment."

"Destroyed?"

"Not yet. We might need it as proof of a frame. No one will find the information."

"Let me know what the crime scene team uncovers."

"Copy that. Doubt they'll find anything, though. Rachelle?"

"Yes, sir?"

"We'll discover what's going on. Your job is to remain safe and heal. Follow the orders of your bodyguards."

"I will."

"Eli."

"Yes, sir?"

"Watch your backs. Whatever you need, you'll get. We protect our own. The person who targeted Rachelle will pay."

"Copy that." He ended the call. "When the rest of our team arrives, we'll set up guard rotations. In the meantime, I'll check on the food supplies. If we have enough for tonight, I'll go to the grocery store in the morning. Rachelle, do you need a drink or snack?"

"I'd love hot tea or a soft drink."

Jackson studied her face. "Do you feel queasy?"

"A little," she admitted.

Cal watched her, unsure if the nausea stemmed from a concussion, reaction to the latest news, or something else.

When she started to rise, Jackson motioned for her to stay put. "If we don't have tea bags or a soft drink, I'll place an anti-nausea patch behind your ear."

The medic and Eli walked to the kitchen together. Jesse crouched in front of Rachelle. "Is there anything I can do to help you?"

"No, but thanks for offering." Rachelle's voice sounded thick.

Oh, man. Rachelle's eyes glistened with unshed tears. Gut clenching, he glanced at the medic, feeling helpless. He could fight the enemy all day, but how did he combat this woman's tears?

Jesse patted her hand. "My best advice is rest. The terrorist attack, traveling through several time zones, and the accident exhausted you. Your body's been through the ringer in the past 36 hours. Have Cal whisper sweet nothings in your ear for a few minutes, then call it a night." After another pat on her hand, he returned to the second floor.

Jackson walked in carrying a coffee mug. "We're in luck. I found mint tea." The medic handed her the mug. "We also have enough food to feed an army when you're ready to eat."

Cal threaded his fingers through Rachelle's hair, the texture like silk. He'd wondered for months how her hair would feel. Now that he knew, Cal would have a difficult time keeping his hands from her soft tresses.

"I'm grabbing a snack," Jackson said. "Tell me when Rachelle's ready for me to tape her ribs."

Cal remained silent while she sipped her tea. When she finished, he set the mug on the coffee table. "You can sit with me for a while to see if the tea works, go upstairs to prepare for bed, or sleep here."

She stared. "Where will you be?"

"Wherever you are."

"Even if I choose to sleep on the couch?"

"Yes, ma'am. I'd sleep on the floor or one of the recliners."

"That sounds painful."

"I've slept on worse. You'll be more comfortable on a bed. My room is next to yours. If you need me, call out. I'll hear you." He'd also be checking on her throughout the night.

"Will you take a guard shift?"

"We all will."

"I'll sleep upstairs. I want to sit with you a while before Jackson tapes my ribs. Do you mind?"

"Of course not." Only one thing came to mind that he'd like more. The kiss he'd promised her. "Jon and the others will be here soon."

Cal settled deeper into the cushions. "Close your eyes and relax." He tugged a blanket from the back of the couch and draped it over Rachelle.

"I still want a kiss," she murmured. "I've wanted one for months."

"Me, too." Kissing her tonight depended on how she felt when he escorted her upstairs. Within minutes, Rachelle was asleep.

Rafe glanced over his shoulder. "You're a lucky man."

"Not lucky. Blessed beyond belief." Something he wouldn't forget.

Ten minutes later, Rafe opened the front door to admit their teammates.

While the operatives unloaded the SUVs, Cal woke Rachelle. "Jon and the others are here."

Once Jon dropped his gear in his assigned room, the sniper returned to the living room and sat in the recliner across from Rachelle and Cal. "How are you, Rachelle?"

"Not bad."

He shifted his attention to Cal, his eyebrow raised.

"Ten stitches in her forehead and cracked ribs on the right side."

With the exception of Jesse, the operatives ranged themselves around the living room.

"What did you learn, Jon?" Eli asked.

"Nothing good. His name is Ray Phillips. He's an independent operator with a record a mile long."

Cal frowned. "He planned to cash in on the reward for the women?"

"He wasn't after the women." Jon inclined his head toward Rachelle. "Phillips and the others came for her."

A ball of ice formed in Cal's stomach. "Why?"

"Rachelle is the target."

CHAPTER THIRTEEN

Rachelle stared at the operative who'd dropped the bombshell that blew apart the foundations of her world. Jon must be wrong. If not, then she was responsible for the deaths of many people over the past thirty-six hours, some innocent, some not. She drew in a shaky breath. "Are you sure?"

Jon nodded. "I'm sorry."

"I'm not important to anyone except my family and Fortress."

Cal tapped her nose gently. "And me. I'm hoping I have my own place in that list."

Her cheeks burned at the gentle tease from the handsome operative at her side. "A very personal place," she said, voice so soft only he could hear her response.

He winked at her. "That's what I wanted to hear."

Eli rolled his eyes. "If you're finished flirting with the lady, we have plans to make."

Rachelle dragged her attention away from Cal. "What kind of plans?"

"Once we confirm the information from Phillips, we have to separate you from Amy and Eric."

Wise move. If she was the target, she endangered them. "Another safe house."

"The Texas team needs backup," Jackson said. "Moving Eric in an emergency will be next to impossible with a five-man team tasked with transporting a critically-ill patient, protecting Amy, and fighting off attackers."

"I have an idea on that."

"Plan to share with the class?" Cal asked.

"After I've consulted with Maddox and the county sheriff. If they reject my idea, we'll move Rachelle to another town."

If Eric needed Wolf Pack's help, who would protect her? The idea of being separated from Cal made her stomach twist. She looked at Cal. "If I have to relocate, who will be on my protection detail?"

He bracketed her chin between his thumb and forefinger. "Where you go, I go. I'll ask to be assigned to your detail. If Maddox won't give me permission, I'll take a leave of absence. I won't leave your side until you're safe."

Jon said, "We've been assigned as your protection detail, Rachelle. Maddox has options if another team can't assist Texas."

"Sounds great until you take into account the number of men sent to attack her," Cal said. "Anyone get a body count?"

"Nine dead plus Phillips." Brody folded his arms. "All heavily armed."

Nine men dead and possibly more if the terrorists were after her in Antigua instead of Amy.

Cal scowled. "Who sent them?"

"That's the million-dollar question," Eli said. "Jon contacted Zane on the way here. Our resident tech wizard is working on it. Uncovering the culprit will take time."

"What should we do in the meantime?" Rachelle asked. "I don't want to endanger Eric and Amy."

"As soon as we confirm you're the target, we'll execute Plan B."

"Which is?"

"Relocation. For now, we proceed according to the current plan. You rest and heal while the teams set up guard rotations and stay alert for trouble." He grinned. "In other words, we circle the wagons."

Sawyer snorted. "You've been watching old cowboy movies again, haven't you?"

Eli shrugged. "Can't beat the classics. We need to decide the guard rotation for the next 24 hours."

Jackson turned to Rachelle. "You look like you're ready to crash. If you agree, I'll follow you upstairs and tape your ribs while Eli and the rest decide shifts."

Cal assisted Rachelle to her feet. "I'll walk you up. Be back in a minute, Eli."

"If you take too long, we'll assign you the worst shifts," Max threatened.

"Yeah, yeah." Cal wrapped his arm around Rachelle's waist, offering support and strength as she climbed to the second floor. At the end of the hallway, he steered her into the corner bedroom.

"Stay away from the windows, and leave the curtains closed." After seating her on the edge of the bed, he crouched in front of her. "If the wrong people track us down, we don't want to pinpoint your location."

"All right." All Rachelle wanted to do was go to sleep. In a perfect world, the person targeting her would be uncovered by morning.

"We'll get your life back, baby," he murmured and kissed the corner of her mouth. "I'll check on you soon." After a pointed look at Jackson, he left.

"I want to check your ribs before I tape them."

She remained motionless while Jackson ran his fingers along her ribs, yelping when he touched a sore spot. When he reached into his bag, she asked, "Nothing worse than cracked ribs?"

"That's all." Jackson glanced at her. "I have to raise your shirt on one side. Would you feel more comfortable if Jesse or Cal is in the room?"

"Go ahead, Jackson. We don't know how long Cal will be, and I don't want to disturb Jesse."

"Tell me if you change your mind." He held up two rolls of tape. "Blue or black?"

"No pink camouflage?" she teased.

"Wolf Pack would have my hide if I packed anything girly in my mike bag."

"I'll take blue."

Jackson tossed the black tape back into his bag. "Lift your shirt to your bra line on your right side." He worked quickly to tape her ribs. When he finished, he tugged the bottom of her shirt down and sat back. "Take a breath, and tell me how you feel."

Rachelle drew in a breath, expecting the same stabbing pain. To her surprise, the pain was tolerable. "That tape is amazing. Thanks, Jackson."

"The tape will loosen after a few days. Don't try to remove it unless the tape is wet. Otherwise, you'll pull off a layer of skin, too. It's time for another round of pain meds."

Rachelle wanted to refuse, but she wouldn't sleep if she did, and that would worry Cal and the others. "All right."

Jackson handed her a packet of capsules and a small bottle of water. "Two capsules every four to six hours. This is a mild pain reliever that won't knock you out."

"I'm a lightweight when it comes to medicine."

He chuckled. "I'll keep that in mind for the next time I have to treat your injuries."

"No offense, but I hope I keep you out of work for a while."

He closed his bag and stood. "A shower or soak in the tub will help with soreness. Want me to start one of those for you?"

"I'd love a shower, but I don't have clothes to change into."

"I'll find something." He returned to the room with a black t-shirt and sweatpants. "These belong to Cal. He won't mind if you sleep in them."

She frowned. "Won't he need them to sleep in?"

"Nope. He'll sleep fully dressed as will the rest of us."

Rachelle stared at the medic as reality sank in. "In case we're attacked again."

"That's right. We won't take your safety for granted, and neither should you."

Not a great way to live. "Will you sleep with your shoes on?"

Jackson grinned. "Not tonight. We leave our boots on if we sleep outdoors on a mission. Leave your shoes beside the bed. If anything happens, you'll have time to put on your shoes."

He strode into the bathroom, laid Cal's clothes on the bathroom counter, and started the shower for her. When he returned, Jackson gripped her upper arms and helped her to her feet. "Take your time. I'll stand in the hallway with your door cracked. If you need help, call out."

"Join the discussion downstairs. I'll be fine."

The medic shook his head. "Your man wouldn't be pleased if I did."

"Why not?"

"He asked me to keep you safe until he returned. I won't break his trust."

Her mouth gaped. "When? I didn't hear him ask you to do that."

"He gave me The Look."

"The Look?"

"Yeah, the one that said, 'Look after my woman. If you let anything happen to her, you're toast.' I don't want to be on the wrong side of that SEAL, especially when it concerns someone he cares about." Jackson moved to the hallway and left the door ajar.

Thirty minutes later, Rachelle emerged from the bathroom. She pulled up short when she saw Cal leaning one shoulder against the hall door jamb, his back to her.

Without turning, he straightened. "Is it okay for me to turn around?"

"Yes."

He spun and took in her appearance at a glance. His eyebrows rose. "Those look familiar."

"They're yours. Jackson brought them to me since I don't have clothes to change into."

Cal closed the door behind him. "Tell me your sizes, and I'll have clothes for you in the morning."

"How? Maple Valley isn't a thriving metropolis. I doubt the town has a store open 24 hours a day."

Amusement filled his gaze. "Chesapeake Falls has several stores that are open."

"You already checked out towns in the area, didn't you?"

"I told you. You're my first priority." He studied her expression. "How do you feel after the shower?"

"Better."

"Did you take pain meds?"

She nodded. "Jackson's orders."

"Good." Cal shifted closer to Rachelle. "You ready to turn in for the night?"

"After."

"After what?"

"The kiss you promised me."

A slow smile curved his mouth. "You want a goodnight kiss?"

"I don't want one. I need one as long as it's yours."

Cal's gaze dropped to her mouth. "You're killing me, Rachelle." He cupped her nape. "Tell me if anything hurts."

"Shut up and kiss me."

"Yes, ma'am." Cal eased closer, bent his head, and brushed his mouth over hers. When Rachelle's breath caught, he paused.

"Cal, please," she whispered.

"Shh." He wrapped his free arm around her waist and drew her closer as his mouth settled on hers.

The next few minutes passed in a blur of heat and silk. Rachelle's heart rate rocketed into the stratosphere as Cal asked for and received permission to deepen the kiss.

Good grief! Cal Taylor's kisses were magic. Fire sizzled along her nerve endings, making her forget that all her muscles were sore from the accident.

When he broke the kiss and eased away, Rachelle rose on tiptoe and pressed her mouth to his, unwilling to give up the addicting taste of him. "Not yet," she murmured against his mouth.

He groaned and wrapped both arms around her. Capturing her mouth, Cal's blistering kisses made her head spin and her knees grow weak. If he hadn't held her up, she would've melted into a puddle on the floor.

Minutes later, the operative eased his mouth from hers and urged Rachelle to rest her head against his shoulder. Cal continued to hold her in silence for a few minutes. Finally, he threaded his fingers into her hair. "I should go."

"Do you have to?"

"If you knew how hard I fought to break the kiss, you'd toss me out on my ear. My control is razor thin. Your kisses are addictive."

She pressed a gentle kiss to his throat. "You have definite skills."

He shivered. "You aren't helping my control."

Taking pity on him, Rachelle stepped out of his hold. "Do you have a shift?"

"I'm on shift now. That's why I was standing in your doorway." He winked. "And maybe I hoped for a goodnight kiss. Tell me your sizes. I'll pick up clothes for you after I'm off shift."

"Wouldn't it be easier for me to go with you?"

"While I would love your company, I don't want your face on security cameras. If the person hunting you has computer hackers in his employ, we could give away your general location."

She told him her sizes. "I'm not picky."

He dropped a fast, hard kiss on her mouth and put more distance between them. "I need to go while I still can. I'll leave your door open. If you need something or can't sleep, come find me."

"Will you tell me when you leave?"

"If you want me to."

"I want to know." She worried about his safety. Although he could protect himself, Cal wasn't invincible. The person after her might have a hacker scanning for the faces of the men who rescued her from Antigua.

"All right." Another hard kiss. "I have to get out of here before I can't leave you at all," he muttered. "I'll be close if you need me, Rachelle." He strode from the room without looking back.

CHAPTER FOURTEEN

Jon turned from the window as Cal descended the stairs. "How is she?"

"Better." He scowled at his friend. "You could have been more diplomatic delivering the bad news to her."

"That's Eli's department, not mine. I don't do smooth."

"You wouldn't have won Dana's heart if you didn't have some gentleness inside you."

"Only for my wife and daughter."

Jon could tell himself and anyone else that. Cal knew better. His teammate had a soft spot for women and children, especially those from abusive situations. "Thanks for covering for me. I'll take the watch. Get some sleep."

A nod. "Eli's in the kitchen brewing coffee."

Cal flinched. "Thanks for the warning." That brought a snort from Jon as he left the room.

Cal headed for the kitchen. Although fumes from Eli's coffee could peel paint off walls, the caffeine-laden drink would keep him awake during his shift.

Eli turned when Cal walked in. He inclined his head toward the mug filled with steaming liquid. "I'll keep us supplied during our shift."

Great. His disdain for Eli's coffee-making skills must have shown on his face because his teammate rolled his eyes.

"Suck it up, Buttercup. My coffee's not that bad."

"Ha. Your coffee's lethal."

"Aww. Now you've hurt my feelings." He sipped from his own mug. "Jon's coffee is worse. The fumes alone will kill you."

True. "Doesn't make yours any easier to swallow."

"Wuss."

"Yeah, yeah." He preferred to keep his stomach lining intact. "Any news from Zane?"

"Nothing definitive, but he and Brent believe moving Rachelle is best for Eric's sake."

"Location?"

"Ten miles to the east."

"Another safe house?"

"Not officially. The sheriff is letting us stay at his family's ranch. He and his brothers, all deputies and former military, will provide backup for both teams until Brent can make other arrangements."

Cal sipped his coffee and manfully held back a shudder at the bitter taste. Man, Eli must have tripled the amount of grounds he dumped in the basket with this pot. He swallowed and congratulated himself for maintaining his composure. "How soon?"

"Tomorrow morning, as soon as Rachelle is ready to leave."

"I need to buy clothes for her in Chesapeake Falls after my shift."

Eli's eyebrows rose. "She trusts your taste in clothes?"

"I didn't give her a choice. I don't want her face on security cams." He returned to the living room and took a position near the large window.

During his shift, nothing moved aside from two cats, a dog, a family of deer, and a raccoon. When Jon and Rafe took over the watch, Cal climbed the stairs two at a time. He knocked and nudged Rachelle's door open wider. "Rachelle."

A rustle of movement from the bed. "What's wrong?" She moved to the doorway, eyes heavy-lidded. She looked cute in his t-shirt and sweatpants.

He cupped her cheek. Her skin was so soft. "I'm ready to leave for Chesapeake Falls."

"I wish you would take me."

His lips curved. "You don't trust my taste in clothes?"

"It's not that. I want you to have backup."

Cal stared. "You want to risk yourself to watch my back?"

She nodded. "Let me go with you."

His heart squeezed. "You don't know what your offer means to me." He kissed the top of her head. "Although I appreciate the offer, I won't risk your safety."

"Because of me, you're in danger, too. Take someone with you."

He brushed her mouth with his. "Jon, Jackson, and Rafe are on duty, and Eli is sleeping. The Texas team has the watch in a few hours."

She hugged him tight. "All right. I want you back in one piece, so be careful."

"Always." Another kiss, this one longer and deeper, a silent testament to his vested interest in her. "I have the best reason to watch my back."

"What's that?"

"You. I have you where I need you, in my arms. Do you think I'd do anything to mess that up?"

A beautiful smile curved her lips. "Excellent reason to remain safe." She stepped back. "See you soon."

Cal hurried down the stairs and out the front door. He suspected Rachelle wouldn't rest while he was gone.

On the trip into Chesapeake Falls, he called Fortress for an update. Zane answered his call. Cal frowned. "Don't you ever sleep?"

"My wife had an early-morning photoshoot two hours from Nashville. I helped her pack the SUV with her photo equipment, baby stuff, and our son. Since I don't sleep when they're on the road, I came in early."

"Any updates?"

"I have independent confirmation from one source that Rachelle is the target. I'm chasing the thread of another."

"But?"

"I'd move her away from Eric and Amy."

Cal's gut agreed with his tech-savvy friend. "Still no idea who's behind the contract?"

"Sorry, man. I'm working as fast as I can to run down leads. Trace's wife, Bridget, will be here in three hours. I'll hand off the search for a money trail to her. She's incredible."

High praise for the fellow operative's wife. "Sounds like your protege is spreading her wings." Zane had insisted on expanding the research maven's role in Fortress.

"I'll pat myself on the back later for blackmailing Brent into letting me train her the right way."

Cal chuckled. Zane, a fellow SEAL injured in the Sand Box, was an extraordinary hacker. If he praised Bridget for her hacking skills, she must be scary good. "Care to share Brent's vulnerable spot?"

"No way. Find your own leverage. So, Taylor, what's the latest news on your end?"

He scowled, recognizing that tone. Zane knew about him and Rachelle. "Who tattled?"

"Doesn't matter. Two things. First, I'm happy for you. You've been mooning around here for too long without making a move on the lady which shows what an idiot you were."

Couldn't argue with that. He should have manned up and asked her out sooner. "Second?"

"If you hurt her, I'll personally make your life miserable."

He flinched. That wasn't an idle threat. Zane's wicked hacking skills meant all kinds of headaches, not to mention his pull with the boss meant Cal would be assigned the worst duties known to man. "You know me better than that. We're former teammates, Z. I would never hurt Rachelle intentionally."

"I like the lady. A lot. Even if you hurt her unintentionally, I will make you suffer."

Ouch. Serious intent filled his friend's voice. "I hear you."

"Good. That's the only warning you get."

Wow. "Message received. I'm headed to Chesapeake Falls to purchase clothes for Rachelle."

"Copy that." Zane ended the call.

Fifteen minutes later, Cal parked in front of a big box store that remained open 24/7. With Rachelle's sizes and clothing tastes in mind, Cal made quick work of purchasing clothes and toiletries for her.

Wasn't the first time he'd purchased basic necessities for a woman. Growing up with sisters, Cal had learned to power shop for them when necessary. Thank goodness his sisters' husbands took care of clothes and toiletry emergencies these days.

He paid for his purchases with a credit card in an alternate name sanctioned by Fortress. If a tech geek connected the name to Cal, he'd shift to the ID he'd commissioned in a back-alley shop in Nashville. Stewart was a genius with false identification.

An hour later, he parked the SUV in front of the house with the rest of the Fortress fleet, grabbed the bags from the backseat, and let himself into the house.

He nodded at Jon and headed for Rachelle's room. His soft knock was answered immediately. "Special delivery for the most beautiful woman on the planet."

She smiled, relief shining in her eyes. "You need your eyes checked, but thank you."

Cal brushed her mouth with his. "I speak the truth. I bought what you asked for and a few other things that caught my eye. If you don't like what I chose, I'll exchange it."

"I'm sure what you chose is fine." She kissed him. "Go rest."

"If you need me, come to me."

"You need sleep."

"Rachelle." He had to know she'd come to him or he wouldn't be able to rest.

A sigh. "I'll come if I need you. But I won't."

He had to smile. Good enough. "I'll be awake in three hours."

She frowned.

"I've operated on less sleep in the field. Don't worry." Knowing she cared so much felt good. No, her concern felt like a miracle. With a squeeze of her fingers, he went to his room and laid down. Within seconds, he was out.

At the three-hour mark, he woke, fully alert. He listened for movement from Rachelle's room. Not hearing anything, he rolled out of bed and showered.

When he emerged from his room dressed in black cargoes and t-shirt, Cal stepped into the hallway and started to turn toward Rachelle's room to check on her when he heard her laughter coming from the first floor. He also caught the scent of food. Who was cooking? Jon and Eli were decent cooks.

Brody turned from the front window and nodded in greeting as Cal passed through the living room on the way to the kitchen.

His eyes widened when he saw Rachelle pulling a baking dish from the oven, then grabbing the second one a moment later.

Eli clapped him on the shoulder. "About time you woke up, sleeping beauty."

"Who got two extra hours of sleep?" he reminded his teammate. "Oh, yeah. That would be you."

"Feels amazing, too. My first decent night's sleep since my daughter's birth."

"And you don't regret one minute of lost sleep, either."

A grin. "Nope."

A twinge of envy hit Cal. He loved Eli and Brenna's daughter. Thank goodness she looked more like her gorgeous mother than her SEAL father. Seeing the three of them together made him want the same for himself.

Cal's gaze slid to Rachelle. Did she want a family? A conversation for later. He had no intention of talking about that with his teammates within hearing distance. He gathered her against him and dropped a light kiss on her mouth. "Good morning."

"Again." She smiled. "I made a breakfast casserole if you're hungry."

"Smells great." Not as good as her, though. If they didn't have an audience, he'd be tempted to nibble on her neck. "All of us cook a little. We're not chefs like Nate Armstrong on the Durango team, but we hold our own. You don't have to cook."

"I enjoyed having something to keep my hands and mind busy." She glanced around at the other men in the room who stared at them with grins on their faces. "Don't let the food grow cold."

Cal frowned at them. What was their problem? Nosy parkers.

Eli squeezed her shoulder. "Thanks for making breakfast, sugar. You should eat, too. We need to leave soon."

She looked at Cal. "Where are we going?"

"A ranch not far from here."

"All of us? Eric and Amy, too?"

He shook his head. "Wolf Pack and you. The rest are staying here."

Her expression sobered. "Zane confirmed I'm the target."

"I'm sorry."

She rested her head on his chest. "I wish I knew why a terrorist group wants to kill me."

"We'll figure out who's behind the threat and why."

She sighed. "When?"

Cal cupped her nape. "I don't know, but we're working as fast as we can," he murmured as the rest of his teammates gathered around the stove to fill their plates.

"I'm sorry," she whispered. "I sound ungrateful, and I'm not. I know the sacrifices you're all making to keep me safe. But I'm leaving Micah in a lurch."

"Micah understands the threat and he agrees with Maddox on this. With the encryption on my computer, you can work from here while we deal with your problem."

Cal's phone signaled an incoming text message. He checked the screen. His stomach twisted into a knot. What was this about?

"Something up?" Rafe asked.

"Maddox wants me to call him."

Eli paused with a forkful of food halfway to his mouth. "Find out what he wants and report back."

Code for calling the boss out of Rachelle's hearing. Good idea. Based on his wording, Maddox's news had to do with Rachelle, and it wouldn't be good.

He released her. "I'll be back soon." After stepping outside onto the deck, he called Brent.

"Maddox."

"It's Cal."

"Can you talk?"

"Yes, sir. I'm outside, alone. What's going on?"

"Plenty. The State Department wants to interview Rachelle and Amy."

"They can do it by phone or video chat."

"They agreed to a phone conversation with Amy."

"But not Rachelle."

"I'm sorry, Cal. They insist on a face-to-face with her."

"No. I'm not allowing the feds to lead the enemy to the safe house."

"They're playing hardball, threatening to blackball Fortress from future government contracts if we don't allow them access to Rachelle."

He analyzed what Brent said and what he hadn't. "What alternatives do we have?"

"None. They want her to come to Washington, D.C. for formal interviews."

"I'm not taking her into that viper nest."

"While I understand your reluctance, we don't have a choice. President Martin needs Fortress on the A list."

"Brent..."

"I made it clear that you and your team would be granted full access to Rachelle at all times, or we'd make her disappear and they'd never have their questions answered."

"She's mine to protect." He'd kill anyone who was a threat to her safety, including feds.

A pause, then, "I see. Does she know how you feel about her?"

"She does, and she's okay with it. If you're not, we're going to have a problem."

"There's no problem as long as the relationship doesn't interfere with the mission."

"Then there's no issue because she is my mission."

"Even if you have to take her to D.C. for questioning?"

"Since when do we play ball with the feds?"

"We don't," Brent snapped. "Not unless the president asks me to cooperate. He knows what's at stake, Cal. He trusts Fortress to keep Rachelle safe. Are you telling me you can't do the job? Because if that's the case, I'll pull you from her detail and replace you with someone who can."

"Forget it. I'll deal." Somehow. "Fair warning, though. If anything happens to her, you and I will be going one-on-one."

"Understood."

"I won't take her today or tomorrow. She needs to heal before we throw her to the lions."

"I'll be in touch with details." Maddox ended the call.

Cal dragged a hand down his face, frustration eating a hole in his gut. Why were the feds insisting that Rachelle answer questions in person? While he'd preferred face-to-face when he was a cop, Cal had utilized phone interviews along with video chats.

He didn't understand the feds throwing their weight around. No one had challenged their authority. The sole reason Fortress had stepped in to rescue Amy and Eric without prior authorization was because they were with Rachelle and were fellow Americans in danger.

He shoved his phone into his pocket and braced his hands on the deck railing as he took a moment to bleed off the sharpest edge of his temper.

When the door behind him opened, Cal didn't turn. He knew without looking who had followed him outside.

"What's wrong?"

Rachelle's soft voice soothed him as nothing else had ever done. "We have a problem."

Her face paled. "You changed your mind?" she whispered.

His heart skipped a beat as he realized what she referred to. Cal wrapped his arms around her. "Not about us as a couple. The problem is with the feds."

She blinked. "What about them?"

"They insist on interviewing you in Washington, D.C. about the terrorist attack in Mexico."

"Why is that a problem?"

"Keeping you safe in D.C. is more of a challenge for a team of five operatives. Second, despite assurances that we'll be able to do our jobs, I don't trust the feds as far as I can throw them." If the State Department could get by with it, they'd wrest control of Rachelle from Fortress.

CHAPTER FIFTEEN

Rachelle studied the sign over the ranch's entrance. The letter M balanced on a rocking chair. Sweet and whimsical, a great combination.

The Rocking M Ranch was a beautiful parcel of land. Cows grazed in one pasture on this bright, sunshine-drenched day while horses occupied another. Rolling hills covered with grass were a colorful sight after staring at four walls and jet cabins for days.

Cal squeezed her fingers as he drove through the gated entrance. "What do you think?"

"I love it. This is a beautiful place to hide."

"Know anything about ranching?"

"If romantic suspense novels with cowboy heroes don't count, then no."

"You don't go for the black ops or military heroes?"

"Of course I do. I also favor law enforcement heroes." She slid him a pointed glance. "Don't knock romantic suspense novels until you try them, Taylor."

He held up a hand. "I'll take your word for it. I'm happy my profession is on your list."

"It's at the top."

"Good to know." His lips curved.

"Why are we here instead of another city?"

"Sheriff Montgomery and his brothers are former military as well as local law enforcement. They'll backup both teams until Maddox sends more help. On top of that, the Rocking M employs several hands who can be called upon in an emergency."

"The area is wide-open fields with fences easy to crawl through."

"People might sneak onto the land, but they can't break into the house without triggering alarms. The Montgomerys have sensors throughout the property, multiple ways to escape the house, and a safe room." Cal wrapped his hand around hers. "You'll be safe. I wouldn't bring you here otherwise."

He'd told about her traveling to Washington, D.C. to answer the State Department's questions regarding her experience in Mexico. Her stomach knotted. "When do we leave?"

"I asked Maddox for two days, but the State Department is anxious to interview you."

Rachelle dreaded the trip and the heightened danger to Wolf Pack. Cal and his team would risk their lives to keep her safe. She didn't want them to be targets because of her.

Cal parked in front of a large two-story white house with a wraparound porch, then circled the SUV and opened her door. The front door of the home opened as they approached.

An older woman met them, an easy smile on her face. "Welcome to the Rocking M," she said as they drew near. "I'm Mrs. Grady, the housekeeper, but the Montgomerys call me Mrs. G." She gestured for them to go into the house, then greeted the other members of Wolf Pack who walked onto the porch, gear bags on their shoulders. Cal returned to the SUV for their bags.

Mrs. Grady led the Wolf Pack and Rachelle up the sweeping staircase. "David said you'd prefer your rooms grouped together." She paused in front of a set of double doors. "This is a suite with two bedrooms and a shared sitting area." She threw open the doors and walked inside. "I thought you'd like this arrangement, Rachelle. You'll have your own room and so will your bodyguard."

Rachelle smiled. "It's perfect. Thank you."

The housekeeper looked at the others in the group. "The remaining three rooms are across the hall. Do you think this will work?"

Eli said, "This is exactly what we need."

"David will be home as soon as he can. Lunch will be served at noon and dinner at 7:00. If you aren't ready to eat at those times, you're free to rummage through the kitchen when you are. The kitchen is down the stairs and to the left. It's large enough to accommodate all of you plus the hands who arrive in shifts to eat. If you need anything, let me know."

Cal opened the suite doors and deposited their bags inside the door. He turned to Jackson. "Bunk in the second bedroom."

Rachelle's heart sank. Cal didn't want to stay in the suite with her. "Where will you sleep?" she asked him.

"The couch outside your door." He kissed her knuckles. "The second bedroom is too far away from you. If someone breaks in, he'll have to go through me to reach you."

"No problem." Jackson set his bags inside the door. "Check the rooms and tell me which one you want me in."

While Eli, Jon, and Rafe dropped their bags in the other rooms, Cal examined the suite. When he returned, he motioned for his teammate to take the room on the right. "A tree is too close to the window."

The medic scooped up his bags. "I'll rig something to alert us if an intruder comes in that way."

Cal walked Rachelle to her room.

"Oh, wow. This is incredible." A large blue-and-green quilt covered the king-size bed. Matching quilted pillowcases covered two large decorator pillows, the bed frame a gorgeous pine. The windows sported white curtains plus sheers to block direct view into the bedroom.

Cal set her bag on the foot of the bed. "Same rules apply as in the safe house. Don't open the curtains. We need to familiarize ourselves with the house. Want to explore?"

Who wouldn't? "I'd love to."

By the time lunch was served, Wolf Pack and Rachelle had toured the rest of the house. "This place is amazing," she said as Cal seated her at the dining table in the kitchen.

Mrs. Grady beamed at her. "I think so. I'm glad you do, too."

"How long have you worked here?"

"My whole life. My mother worked for the family and, when I was sixteen, Mrs. Montgomery offered me a job. I've worked here ever since. My husband is the ranch foreman."

From her expression, the Montgomerys were family to Mrs. Grady. "You must love it here."

"I wouldn't work for another family. The Montgomerys are special."

She understood Mrs. Grady's sentiment and loyalty. Rachelle loved working for Fortress Security, in particular for Micah Winter. Her boss was a good man who adored his wife, Sophie, and their children. A former Secret Service agent, Micah was as fierce a protector as the operatives. She wasn't surprised Micah insisted she go to a safe house.

Ranch hands came and went in shifts, the conversation focusing on their jobs. They sent curious looks in the direction of the operatives, but no one asked why they were on the ranch and Wolf Pack didn't offer explanations.

Rachelle received the lion's share of curiosity from the hands. Cal regarded them with suspicion. Since she doubted any of them were in Mexico, he must view the interest as a threat to his claim. If Cal knew how deep her feelings for him went, he wouldn't be concerned.

Under the table, Rachelle threaded her fingers through Cal's. The tense lines of his body relaxed.

Three men entered the kitchen, badges and guns hooked onto their belts. Each man kissed Mrs. Grady's cheek. The tallest of the three looked at the ranch hands. They six men carried their food and drinks into another room without protest.

The man held out his hand to Eli. "David Montgomery, sheriff of Morgan County."

Eli shook his hand. "Eli Wolfe." He motioned to each person as he introduced them. "Jon Smith, Jackson Conner, Rafe Torres, Cal Taylor. The pretty lady beside Cal is Rachelle Carter, our principal."

David nodded at each in turn, then said to Rachelle, "I understand you were in the middle of a terrorist attack in Mexico."

"And she outsmarted them." Cal squeezed her fingers.

"Good job, Ms. Carter."

"Call me Rachelle."

"Yes, ma'am. These are my brothers, Caleb and Levi. You'll meet my other brothers, Elliot and Owen, later."

David shifted his attention to Eli. "Elliot and Owen are at the Watts crime scene. If you give me your number, I'll send you my contact info as well as that of my brothers."

"Appreciate it. We'll let you know as soon as Maddox sends reinforcements."

"As long as the principals don't go into town, you'll remain off the grid."

Cal frowned. "The ranch hands saw Rachelle. How do we know they won't run their mouths about the five men loaded down with weapons and a drop-dead gorgeous woman on the ranch?"

Cal saw her as drop-dead gorgeous? Nice.

David stared at Cal. "With the exception of a few, the hands have been with the Rocking M for years. My men won't sell out Rachelle. She's safe here."

"Cut Cal a break," Eli said with an easy smile. "He has a personal interest in protecting Rachelle."

Surprise flashed in the sheriff's eyes. "I'm surprised you're on her protection detail," he said to Cal.

"The commander has mellowed out," Rafe said.

Jon shook his head. "You need a dictionary. He'll allow Cal to remain on the detail as long as he's focused."

"The heart messes with the head," Levi said.

"What happens if you don't stay focused?" Mrs. Grady asked Cal.

"The boss sends someone to replace me on Rachelle's protection detail, and I take a leave of absence to stay with her."

"He'll allow that?" Caleb asked.

"Brent won't have a choice unless he wants me to resign. I can return to MNPD as a homicide detective if he cuts me loose."

The Montgomery brothers exchanged glances, then relaxed their stances. David gave a short nod. "Military?"

"SEAL, a teammate of Brent's. All of us are SEALs."

"So was I. I was stationed on the west coast when Brent was in DEVGRU," David said.

"What's DEVGRU?" Rachelle asked.

"Another name for SEAL Team 6," Cal said.

She stared. Good grief. Although she didn't know much about SEALs, she'd heard plenty about the types of missions that particular team carried out. She couldn't imagine the horrors he'd witnessed while protecting innocents and hunting down terrorists.

When Cal's face lost all expression, she realized he had mistaken her surprise for rejection. She needed to repair the damage, but couldn't do it in front of an audience. She glanced at Eli. "Is it safe for Cal and me to sit on the porch for a few minutes?"

Eli looked at David.

"Should be safe enough," the sheriff said. "Trees block long-range shots."

Oh, man. She hadn't considered a sniper. "We won't be long."

Cal stood and held out his hand to Rachelle. She gripped his hand tight and headed for the front door. On the porch, she led him to the swing. "Sit with me."

"If you plan to tell me you want out, get it over with."

Rachelle tugged on his hand until he sat beside her. When he stared straight ahead as though waiting for the ax to drop, she turned his face toward her. "This is where I tell you how much I appreciate your service in the military and in law enforcement."

He stared. "You don't want out of this relationship?"

She shook her head. "I was surprised to learn you were a member of SEAL Team 6. I shouldn't have been."

Cal wrapped an arm around her shoulders and drew her against him. "What do you mean?"

"Operatives talk at Fortress. Since I'm interested in all things Cal Taylor, I listened to everything about you. You're a legend around Fortress. The less experienced operatives view you as Superman."

He snorted. "Hardly. I have miles on me and experience."

"They look good on you." Rachelle kissed him, slow and sweet. When she eased back, she said, "I'm tougher than I look, Cal. I won't run because you accepted a difficult job and rose to the top of your profession as a SEAL. In fact, I'm honored to have a chance to be with you."

"I'm the one who is honored. You're much too good for me."

"We'll have to agree to disagree. I'm sorry to worry you."

"I'm just glad you're not kicking me to the curb."

The front door opened, and Eli poked his head out. "Brent will call soon. He wants you and Rachelle to be there."

They followed Eli into the kitchen.

At the two-minute mark, Eli's phone rang. He swiped his screen. "It's Eli. You're on speaker with Wolf Pack, Rachelle, David Montgomery, and two of his brothers."

"Thanks for providing a safe haven, David."

"I'm glad to help."

"What's the latest news?" Eli asked.

"First, Zane has confirmation from two more sources that Rachelle is the target."

Cal's hand tightened around Rachelle's. "What about Amy and Eric?"

"The goal is to reacquire Rachelle."

He frowned. "Reacquire, not kill?"

"Affirmative."

"Why do they want her?"

"Unknown. You'll know as soon as we do."

"Next?" Eli asked.

"The State Department isn't happy about the delay, but I pulled in a favor to get them to agree. Rachelle, you're due in D.C. day after tomorrow at the Harry S. Truman Building at 2:00 p.m."

She leaned her head against Cal's shoulder, dreading the interview to come. "Yes, sir."

Cal kissed her temple, then said, "I know that tone of voice, Brent. What else is going on?"

"Bridget is following the money."

"Progress?"

A pause, then, "Will you go into another room for a few minutes, Rachelle?"

She narrowed her eyes. "If this concerns me, no."

Fortress Security's CEO snorted as the men around the table exchanged amused glances. "You remind me of my wife, Rowan."

"That's quite a compliment, sir."

"Yeah, it is. Like you, she's strong. All right. The money trail is bouncing all over the globe, but more and more rumors are surfacing that the origination is closer to home than we want."

"What does that mean?" she demanded.

"The source of the money is coming from Washington, D.C."

She froze. When she went for the interview at the State Department, she'd be walking into an avalanche of trouble.

CHAPTER SIXTEEN

Cal scowled. "D.C. is a snake pit of politicians and lackeys who'd sell their own mothers to get ahead. Can't you narrow down the possibilities?"

"You think I haven't tried?" Brent snapped. "Rachelle is as important to me as you and the rest of my people."

"Then we have a problem because I'm not taking her into an unknown situation where I can't control the risks."

"No choice, Taylor. This interview isn't an option. If she doesn't show up, federal law enforcement will get involved. The president doesn't want us on the wrong side of the law."

He clenched his jaw. Aside from the unspoken warning from his boss that he was crossing a line, Cal didn't want Rachelle on federal law enforcement radar. "Would you take Rowan into that kind of danger?"

Eli groaned. "Ignore that, boss." He glared at Cal. "Wolf Pack will deliver Rachelle on time. No one will touch her on our watch."

Cal refused to contemplate the fallout should they fail in their mission.

"Are you in agreement, Taylor, or do I send your replacement?" Brent asked.

His gut warned that trouble was coming and Rachelle would be caught in the crossfire. However, Wolf Pack was a new team. Cal trusted the men on his team. Anyone new brought the potential for discord and ineffectiveness. Cal would suck it up and deal if it meant staying with Rachelle until she was free from danger.

"Cal, please," Rachelle whispered. "I can't do this without you."

"One way or another, I'm not leaving your side." Heart warmed by her trust, he turned to Eli and gave a short nod. "We'll make it work," he told Brent. "However, my gut says trouble is coming."

"Same," Eli said.

"On that, we're on the same page. I understand your reluctance to take Rachelle to D.C., Cal. We don't have a choice. I'll keep searching for someone to talk to me off the record about the money. You have your own sources. Call in the favors. Same with the rest of you."

Cal frowned. "All right. I'll see what I can learn. I want to know who will be in that interview room with Rachelle, Brent. Make it clear that I'll be with her."

"Copy that. Keep me updated. I'll contact you soon." Brent ended the call.

Levi whistled. "I'd hate to cross that man. He plays hardball."

"It's not a wise move," Jon agreed. He looked at Cal. "You want me to trace the money pipeline?"

He wasn't a cop any longer. The restrictions of the law no longer hamstrung him like it once did. "Do it." Rachelle's life was at stake. He'd do anything to save her because she'd slid deep into his heart. What would he do if she didn't feel the same way about him?

He glanced her way. SEALs were mission driven. Rachelle was his. End of story.

"I'll do what I can," Jon said.

"Do I want to know how far you'll go?" David asked the sniper.

He smiled.

"That's what I thought." His eyes narrowed. "Wait. You're Jon Smith, the sniper, aren't you?"

He inclined his head.

"Holy cow," Caleb muttered. "I don't think your team will need us for anything except mop up."

Rafe's expression darkened. "Until we discover who's after Rachelle and why, she'll continue to be a target. Someone wants their hands on her bad enough to send multiple teams. They didn't count on Fortress defending one of their own."

Jackson shook his head. "Cal had a major role in saving Rachelle in Antigua. I lost count of how many men he killed to reach her in time."

"Enough," Cal said, voice soft. He wasn't ashamed of his role, but didn't glory in the deaths either.

David refocused on Jon. "How many other hidden skills do you have, Smith?"

"Want me to demonstrate?"

"Not on your life. I want to know the skills at my disposal when you're in town."

A shrug. "Interrogation."

A slow smile curved the sheriff's mouth. "I'll keep your training in mind if we discover terrorists in my county."

He turned to Eli. "The safe room is behind the bookcase filled with mysteries in the library. Third shelf down from the top, pull the last book on the right. The bookcase will move, revealing a steel door with a keypad." He reeled off the six-digit code for the safe room. "Once you're inside and shut the door, the bookcase will slide back into place. The keypad inside the room allows occupants out. One wall is monitors tied to the security cameras."

"Thanks. Let's hope we don't need it."

"We need to return to work. We have a killer to catch."

Sorrow shadowed Levi's eyes. "Mr. Watts was a good man. He deserved better than to be bludgeoned to death."

"He was a friend of yours?" Eli asked.

"To all of us. He was best friends with our grandfather, but he taught us to be better cowboys and men."

Caleb chuckled. "Raising the Montgomery boys was a community affair. Mr. Watts had more influence than anyone except Dad and Grandpa." His amusement faded. "We'll do right by him."

After David and his brothers left to return to their duties, Jon eyed Eli. "I need to scout the terrain, then search the Net."

Eli rose. "I'll go with you. Jackson, Rafe, scout the grounds close to the house. Cal, you and Rachelle work on escape routes. After that, study the satellite images of the Rocking M. The rest of us will do the same once we return to the house."

When the others left, Rachelle looked at Cal, a puzzled look on her face. "Why does Eli want us to study satellite images?"

"In case you have to run."

"You said I would be safe here."

"No place is impregnable. We hope for the best and plan for the worst. You ready to plot escape routes?"

"The sooner I know where to run, the better."

They crisscrossed the house, memorizing multiple escape routes. Once Rachelle could navigate each route without hesitation, Cal led her to the suite and grabbed his laptop.

After sitting beside her on the couch, he booted up his laptop and clicked on the link of satellite images Zane had sent to his email. For the next two hours, they studied and memorized the landmarks and terrain of the ranch, deciding where she should hide if he told Rachelle to run.

Finally, Cal set the computer aside. "How bad is the pain?"

"On a scale of 1 to 10, it's a 15."

"Ouch. When did you take pain medicine last?"

She dropped her gaze. "I'm not sure."

His eyes narrowed. He wasn't buying that. "Guess."

"Last night," she admitted.

He tapped the tip of her nose. "Are you trying to be Supergirl?"

"I didn't want my mind to be fuzzy if we ran into trouble."

"Operatives use the same pain medicine when we're in the field if our injuries aren't serious. Where are the capsules he gave you?"

She patted her front jeans pocket.

Cal opened the mini-refrigerator and grabbed two bottles of water, handing one to Rachelle. Once she swallowed two capsules, he eased her against his side. With Rafe and Jackson keeping watch near the house, he allowed himself a few minutes to enjoy holding Rachelle. "Rest a few minutes while the pain medicine starts to work."

"I can help with research."

"Jon, Bridget, and Zane have the heavy lifting at the moment. Your job is to rest and heal so you can travel tomorrow."

"You're injured, too. How do you feel?"

The corners of his mouth tipped up. "Better with you in my arms." His arm ached, but he wasn't giving up this privilege.

"Sweet talker." She fell silent and minutes later was asleep.

Cal waited twenty minutes before sliding his phone from his pocket. He scrolled down his contact list until he found the name of a former teammate who might have information to end the threat to Rachelle.

He called his friend. A moment later, a clipped, deep voice answered. "Blake, it's Cal."

"Hey, buddy. Great to hear from you. It's been a while."

"Been busy." What an understatement. Cal had changed careers for a third time, gone through additional training at PSI to hone his SEAL skills, and deployed on single assignments until he was assigned to a team since he last talked to Blake Sims.

"Still working for MNPD?"

"Not anymore. I'm with Fortress Security full-time now."

A soft whistle came over the phone. "Congratulations, Cal. They're a tough outfit to land a job with. I've been hoping for an interview offer from Maddox, but no dice. Maybe you can nudge your boss to at least give me an interview."

"I'll mention your name." Chances were good that Brent wouldn't act on the recommendation. Blake had been riding a desk at the State Department for years and would require extensive retraining to be qualified as an operative.

"I appreciate it."

"I need a favor."

"Name it."

"Can you talk?"

"No. Give me five." His friend ended the call.

He settled deeper into the couch cushions and leaned his head back while he waited for Blake to go someplace more secure.

At the five-minute mark, Cal's phone vibrated with the incoming call from his friend.

"What do you need?" Blake asked.

"Information. You know anything about the terrorist attack in Antigua, Mexico?"

The other man's voice softened. "Are you kidding? Who hasn't heard about it? The ambassador's daughter escaped by the skin of her teeth." He paused. "Wait. Rumors are floating around that some black ops group rescued her. Was that Fortress?"

"My team plus another one rescued her, one of her bodyguards, and another American woman."

"What's your interest? You're not sweet on the ambassador's girl, are you?" he teased.

"No, the other American woman."

"Seriously?" A laugh. "I can't believe Ice Man Cal Taylor has fallen victim to Cupid's arrow."

"Knock it off."

Silence, then, "Uh oh. What's going on, Cal?"

"My girlfriend has a contract on her. I need a name."

"Why do you think I..." Blake stopped and groaned. "You think it's someone in the State Department. Tell me you're not serious."

"The information is pointing your way."

He growled. "Do you have any idea how much trouble I'll be in if I help you? I could lose my job, Cal."

"My woman's life is at risk. She's already been attacked in Antigua and in Tennessee. The body count is rising, and I don't want her name on the casualty list."

"She means that much to you?" Blake asked, voice soft.

"She means everything."

A sigh. "What's her name?"

"Rachelle Carter."

"I'll see what I can find out. If this goes bad, I will need a new job."

"I'll pass the word to my boss." If Blake got sacked for poking his nose into the wrong area and leaking information to Fortress, Cal would recommend Maddox train Blake as a bodyguard if he didn't make the cut as an operative. "Be careful, Blake. Whoever is after Rachelle has deep pockets and is determined to take her out."

"Why does he want her?"

"I don't know, but I'll find out."

CHAPTER SEVENTEEN

Rachelle sat near the back of the jet, dread knotting her stomach. With luck, she and Wolf Pack would return to Maple Valley tonight. If not, the power brokers in Washington, D.C. would finish grilling her about the terrorist attack tomorrow.

Cal covered her hand with his. "Everything will be all right, Rachelle."

Why did she feel as though disaster loomed in the offing? "I don't want to do this."

"I understand. Once we're in the air, I arranged a counseling session for you."

Oh, joy. She wrinkled her nose. "Do you think it will help?"

"The first time discussing a traumatic incident is the hardest. Talking to the counselor will prepare you for the State Department interview."

"Thanks for arranging the session."

He smiled. "Even though you don't want it?"

"You and the other operatives must know the benefit of Brent's recommended counseling services."

A snort. "Recommended? Try ordered. If we don't comply, he pulls us off active duty until we do."

"Good thing Micah's my direct supervisor. He's not hard-nosed."

"Who do you think ordered me to have you talk to the counselor before we land in D.C. or he'd have my hide?"

She stared. "I thought the session was your idea."

Cal squeezed her hand. "I should have insisted you talk to the counselor yesterday. I chose to give you a break from reality. Winter accused me of going soft."

She grinned at the disgust in his voice. "Got you where it hurt, didn't he?"

"He's a regular marshmallow." Eli laughed at the glare Cal sent his way. "If he's not careful, Brent and Micah will have a roasting party with Cal as the guest of honor."

Cal flinched. "Shut up, Wolfe, or I'll sic Brenna on you."

His team leader waggled his index finger. "Not nice, Taylor. Remember, I have someone as tough as Brenna to make you toe the line." He motioned to Rachelle.

Her? Tough? She felt like a scared child at the prospect of answering questions by politicians with more money than sense. What if they wanted information Fortress preferred she didn't share? She wanted to protect Wolf Pack and Texas, but if doing so required lying to the feds, the teams were in trouble. The people interviewing her would know if she lied. She was a terrible liar.

Rachelle concentrated on the feel of Cal's hand on hers. She had time before the interview at the Truman Building. Cal and the others would help her prepare for the interview. If the Washington bureaucrats threatened to throw her in jail, Fortress lawyers chewed up and spit out politicians like them every day.

"You okay?" Cal asked, his voice low.

"I will be."

Once the jet leveled, Cal pulled Rachelle to her feet. "Come on. I want you to have as much time as you need with the counselor."

"Great."

He chuckled. "Hold back your enthusiasm."

"Would you be enthusiastic in my shoes?"

Cal led her into the bedroom and shut the door. "I have been, more than once. I remind myself It's short-term discomfort for long-term payoff."

"Does that work?"

"Most of the time." He cupped her cheeks. "I'll set up the computer chat for you. I can stay with you or go back to our seats. It's your call."

"Stay."

"If you start the session and change your mind, tell me."

She wouldn't. His presence kept her grounded.

Cal logged onto the computer and contacted the counselor. "Are you ready, Marcus?"

Rachelle breathed a sigh of relief. Marcus Lang and his wife, Paige, were friends. Her cheeks burned. Paige had probably told Marcus about Rachelle's interest in Cal by now. Would he approve of them dating?

"I'm set." The dark-haired man on the screen smiled. "Glad you're safe, Rachelle. I hear you've had excitement in the past few days."

She smiled. "Hi, Marcus. Unfortunately, you're right."

"Cal, are you staying with Rachelle or waiting elsewhere?"

"Staying."

"Rachelle, do you want him to stay or leave? Choose what's best for you."

"I want him here."

His eyebrows shot up. "Do you have news to share?"

"Cal and I are dating."

Marcus smiled. "Congratulations to both of you. How's Amy?"

And so the questions began. At the end of the session, Rachelle felt more at peace, her confidence restored. Marcus and Cal had prepared her well for the interview. "Thank you, Marcus."

"Any time, my friend. I'm always available if you need me." He shifted his gaze to Cal. "Same goes for you, Cal. Day or night."

"Thanks."

"Paige and I will be in town next month. We'd love to take you and Rachelle out for dinner if you're not deployed."

"Sounds great. If we can't work it out, we might drive to Otter Creek one weekend to visit."

"Perfect. Both of you, be safe." The screen went dark.

Without a word, Cal drew Rachelle into his arms and held her.

Minutes later, she leaned back to look at him. "You arranged for Marcus to be my counselor."

"Caught me."

"You were right. The session helped. Marcus made it easier." Rachelle kissed him. "More than anything, your presence provided strength and support."

"I'm glad." He wrapped his hand around hers. "Time to return to our seats. We land soon."

After landing, Wolf Pack loaded their gear into two SUVs waiting for them at the private airstrip. Cal climbed into the driver's seat of one vehicle while Rafe drove the other.

For the next 90 minutes, they battled traffic on the journey into the city and parked several blocks from the Truman Building.

"The State Department should have arranged for parking." Jackson frowned as they began to walk.

"But that would make sense," Rafe said, scowling. "Doesn't happen often in this town."

Rachelle ignored their banter, growing more uneasy the closer they walked to the Truman Building. Cal must have sensed her distress because he wrapped his arm around her shoulders and tucked her against his side.

Fifteen minutes before her interview, Rachelle and Wolf Pack entered the building. After submitting to multiple screenings for weapons, they were issued visitors badges and escorted to the appropriate floor.

A man dressed in a charcoal suit, white shirt, and red tie met them when they stepped off the elevator. He focused on Rachelle. "Rachelle Carter?"

She nodded.

"Come with me, please."

Cal threaded his fingers through hers. "Lead the way."

The man frowned. "Not you. Just her."

"No. I stay with her, or she doesn't go. End of discussion. Your boss agreed to my stipulation."

"Who are you?"

"Contact your boss."

The man scowled at Cal as he slid his phone from his pocket. "Remain here," he snapped, and moved away to make a call.

"What if he doesn't agree?" Rachelle whispered.

"We leave." Cal squeezed her hand. "My presence during the interrogation was non-negotiable."

Rachelle made a face. "I prefer the term interview."

The expression on Red Tie's face darkened the longer he spoke on the phone. Finally, he shoved the phone into his pocket and stalked toward them. "Follow me."

She and Cal trailed Red Tie until he stopped at one door, opened it, and gestured for them to go inside.

Cal stepped into the room first, his body blocking her from the view of the occupants. A moment later, Cal stepped aside for Rachelle to enter the room.

Three men stared at her. The oldest stood, prompting the others to follow suit after a beat.

"Please, sit down," the man said, indicating two seats across from the trio. He looked at Red Tie. "That will be all, Gerald. I'll call when we're ready for you to escort them from the building."

"Yes, sir." The door closed with a soft click.

"Thank you for coming, Ms. Carter. I'm Steve Meyer. This is Roger Benson and Ken Caldwell. In light of Tim Garner's death, I'm sure you understand our need for information."

"Of course. I'm sorry for your loss. Tim was a good man. My condolences to his friends and family."

Meyer inclined his head. "Thank you." He turned to Cal. "You must be Cal Taylor. Brent Maddox speaks highly of you."

Benson snorted. "Maddox also said you were as immovable as a rock. He's right. The lady doesn't need a bodyguard."

"Ms. Carter is safe here," Caldwell said. "We have strong security measures."

Cal eyed the three men. "I don't trust anyone I haven't personally vetted. Rachelle is important to me."

Meyer frowned. "Maddox said you're Ms. Carter's bodyguard. Is that all you are to her?"

"My role in her life isn't your business."

Silence filled the room, tension thick enough to cut with a knife.

The other man blinked. "My apologies." He shifted his attention to Rachelle. "Before we begin, would you like water, coffee, or tea? I'll have Gerald bring your choice."

Under cover of the table, Cal tightened his hold on her hand in silent reminder of his earlier warning not to accept food or drink from anyone.

She smiled. "Thank you for the offer, but I don't need anything."

"If you change your mind, let me know." Meyer sat back. "Now, let's begin. Mr. Garner's family deserves answers."

An invisible band tightened around Rachelle's heart. She couldn't imagine the pain Tim's family was going through.

"Tell us what happened in Antigua."

Rachelle recounted the events, starting with the terrorist attack on the hotel. She talked about the escape to and from the hospital.

Caldwell scowled. "Why would you leave a place of safety and her security team, then strike out on your own? It was foolish."

"When Tim realized the terrorists were attacking the hospital, his first concern was protecting Amy and his wounded partner."

"Why didn't you stay with Amy's security detail?"

"Tim told me to run and take Amy to safety."

Benson slapped the table, making Rachelle jump. "That doesn't make sense. Why would he send you into the streets with the ambassador's daughter rather than stay where he could protect her?"

"I don't know."

He folded his arms across his chest. "Guess, Ms. Carter."

"He wanted Amy to be safe and to draw the terrorists away from his injured partner."

Benson snorted. "A pretty story."

"You don't believe me."

"No, lady, I don't."

Cal, who'd been silent to this point, stirred. "That's enough, Benson."

"My friend is dead because of her."

"Explain that."

"She's lying about what happened."

"You have a different explanation?"

"Ms. Carter panicked and ran. Afraid for her, Amy followed. Tim couldn't protect his partner and the women, so he chose to protect Agent Hoss." He flipped open a manila folder and slid a photograph across the table to Rachelle. "Tim took a bullet to the head to protect you."

Rachelle caught a glimpse of Tim's face with a bullet hole in the middle of his forehead before Cal tossed the picture back at Benson. She clamped a hand over her mouth, nausea bubbling in her stomach.

CHAPTER EIGHTEEN

Cal shoved away from the table. "We're finished. Other questions will be handled by video chat." While the men cursed and protested his decision, he rushed Rachelle from the conference room.

Ignoring the shouts, Cal escorted her to the women's bathroom and stationed himself outside the door, seething at the underhanded tactics used by the men. He should have known better than to trust feds to keep their word.

The person who signed off on assigning two people to Amy's security detail had contributed to Tim Garner's death. As an HVT, Amy had needed more security. Some of the areas she and Rachelle visited were hazardous for American diplomats and their families. The State Department gambled and lost one of their own as a result of their decision.

The sound of someone running toward him made Cal shift to stand directly in front of the bathroom door to block access to Rachelle.

Meyer hurried down the hall, slowing when he saw Cal. He straightened his jacket and drew in a breath. "Is Ms. Carter all right?"

"What do you think?"

The older man flinched at the rage in Cal's voice. "I'm sorry. I didn't know Benson planned to do that."

"Your colleague added to Rachelle's trauma. Worse, Benson knew the reaction he'd get and did it anyway."

"We need answers. She's the only one who can provide them aside from Amy."

"Talk to Amy. We'll arrange a video chat."

"I'd prefer not to bother her at this time."

But forcing Rachelle to go over her story multiple times was acceptable? "Rethink that plan, Meyer. Amy knew the players on the field and what was at stake. Rachelle was visiting Amy at her request."

"This isn't about Amy. Benson's assessment of Ms. Carter is correct. She's a coward and partially responsible for the death of Tim Garner."

Cal's hands fisted. "He's dead wrong and so are you. Rachelle is one of the bravest people I've met in my life."

A frown. "How can you say that after what she did?"

"She followed Tim's orders to the letter, risking her life to protect Amy. Would you go unarmed into streets filled with terrorists on the order of a security detail to save a friend's life? She and Amy ran for miles to escape the terrorists, then Rachelle found a place for them to hide until help arrived. She saved the life of the ambassador's daughter. From where I'm standing, my woman deserves a medal for bravery."

Meyer stared. "Your woman? Don't you mean your principal?"

"She's mine."

Understanding dawned in his eyes. "I see."

"I'll do whatever it takes to protect Rachelle from harm. Remember that the next time you and your cronies send someone after her."

He looked puzzled. "I don't understand."

Either Meyer was a superb liar or he wasn't the one who sent thugs after Rachelle.

"We still have questions for Ms. Carter. We'll give her a few minutes to calm down, then resume our session. I'll do my best to rein in my colleagues."

"Forget it. The rest of your questions will be answered by email or video chat."

"That's not acceptable, Taylor."

"Tough. If you have a complaint, contact Fortress."

"I can have security detain you."

"Try it." No one would stop him from taking Rachelle from this building and city. If necessary, he'd call in a favor with President Martin.

Meyer stared at him a moment, then said, "Wait here." He strode toward the conference room.

Fat chance. Cal would leave when Rachelle returned. The bathroom door opened, and he turned to see Rachelle's pale face and tear-reddened eyes. Good thing Benson wasn't close or he'd have punched the smug jerk in the face.

He spread his arms and Rachelle dived into his embrace. Cal held her a few seconds, then said, "Ready to leave?"

She nodded.

With one arm wrapped around her, he guided Rachelle toward the elevator. His team straightened as they approached.

"What happened?" Eli asked.

"Later."

Jackson punched the elevator call button while the rest of Wolf Pack closed ranks around them to prevent anyone from coming close.

Seconds later, the silver doors slid open. Cal summarized the interview for his teammates as the elevator descended to the first floor.

They exited the building and headed for the vehicles with Cal and Rachelle surrounded by Wolf Pack. Rachelle wiped a tear from her face. Cal wanted to go back and punch the men who made her cry.

Eli's phone signaled an incoming call. "Wolfe," he answered without glancing at the screen, his gaze scanning their surroundings. As he listened to the caller, his expression darkened. "No promises."

He ended the call and glanced at Cal. "Meyer contacted Fortress. He's demanding another interview tomorrow morning."

"No."

"He told Brent that Benson won't be there."

"Meyer's crazy if he thinks I'll believe anything he says. What does Brent want us to do?"

"Answer their questions, then take Rachelle off the grid until we unravel this mess. Think about it. We'll give him our answer when we're in the SUV."

Great. He had five minutes to come to terms with subjecting his woman to another round of gut-wrenching questions from men who believed her responsible for the death of one of their own.

As they continued on, Cal remained alert, scanning for trouble while he considered the request from Meyer. No way was Rachelle going back to the Truman Building. With her on their turf, Meyer and his buddies would try another power play.

At the hotel, however, Wolf Pack would be in control and would either contain the three bureaucrats or kick them out and spirit Rachelle out of town.

When they reached the SUVs, Eli pointed at Cal. "You and Rachelle ride with me. Jackson, you're with Rafe and Jon."

Suited him fine. Knowing Eli preferred to drive, Cal tossed him the remote, then climbed into the backseat beside Rachelle.

After exiting the parking garage, Eli glanced at Cal in the rearview mirror. "What's your decision? Airstrip or the hotel?"

"Hotel for now. I'll talk to Brent before I make the final call."

"Tell Rafe where we're headed, then touch base with Brent. If you're not satisfied with what you hear, we'll go to the airstrip."

Cal talked to his teammate, then called his boss.

"Yeah, Maddox."

"It's Cal."

"Decision?"

His lips curved. "What? No small talk? I'm hurt."

A snort. "You're not big on small talk."

"What accommodations did Zane arrange?"

"A suite plus two rooms across the hall."

"I have stipulations. If they don't agree, the deal's off."

"Name them."

"The only way I'll agree to allow Meyer and company near Rachelle is on our turf. Benson won't be allowed in the suite under any circumstances. I want to know the name of the person replacing Benson. Wolf Pack will be present at all times. If I think Rachelle has had enough, the interview ends. Meyer and his team will leave without argument or I'll throw them out. State Department security won't be allowed inside. Meyer and his buddies aren't to know the name of our hotel until tomorrow morning when they begin the drive."

"Done. Other stipulations?"

"No weapons on the diplomats or we'll consider them a threat to Rachelle's safety and take them down hard."

"Copy that. How bad was the interview?"

"Bad enough. They believe Rachelle's to blame for the death of their agent and upset her, hoping for a confession."

A growl. "Details."

Cal summarized the interview as well as Benson's tactic at the end using the rapid-fire reporting method they'd learned in the military.

A soft whistle came through the phone. "I'm surprised you're willing to give them another chance."

"Last one. If they play mind games again, they'll be out on their ears, and this time, there won't be a reboot of the session."

"I'll make that clear to Meyer. How's Rachelle?"

He glanced down at her, pleased that she'd relaxed enough to fall asleep against him. "The photo of Garner shook her."

"Do what you can to help her recover. Tomorrow won't be easy."

"Yes, sir."

"Any luck with your sources?"

"I contacted a friend in the State Department. He's nosing around."

"Let me know if Rachelle needs anything." Maddox ended the call.

Eli drove a winding route to the hotel in a small town an hour outside of Washington, D.C. He parked in the lot and turned off the engine. "I'll check us in while you wake her," he murmured, and exited the vehicle.

Within seconds, the rest of his teammates surrounded the SUV, facing away from Cal and Rachelle to give them privacy and protect them from potential threats.

Cal trailed his hand along Rachelle's arm. "Rachelle, we're at the hotel."

She kissed his neck.

He shivered. What he wouldn't give to spend time with this woman without fear of another attack. Soon, he promised himself. He'd discover why Rachelle was a target and eliminate the problem. After that, he'd court Rachelle as she deserved. "You're a serious distraction, lady."

She smiled. "So are you." The smile faded as she glanced around. "We're staying?"

"For the night. We're leaving tomorrow." Didn't matter if Meyer or the president himself requested they stay. Cal didn't believe Rachelle would be safe this close to Washington, D.C. for much longer.

Rachelle winced.

"If Benson comes, he won't be allowed in."

"What time is the interview at the Truman Building tomorrow?"

"Meyer and his associates will come to the hotel. I'll be with you and so will the rest of Wolf Pack. If Meyer or his buddies step out of line again, I'll stop the interview and kick them out."

He kissed her, the touch one of gentleness and comfort. Although he wanted to indulge in a longer kiss, he couldn't afford to lose focus. This SUV lacked the normal Fortress security upgrades. "Ready to go inside?" He'd relax when Rachelle was in a more secure location.

She nodded. "I'd kill for a soft drink."

"As soon as we're settled in the suite, I'll find a vending machine."

"I'll owe Fortress a ton of money after this is over."

"No cost for employees." He'd cover the bill himself if necessary.

He rapped on the window to signal his teammates that they were ready to go inside. Jon opened the door for them.

Cal exited the vehicle and assisted Rachelle to the pavement. Jackson fell into step on the other side of her as they walked toward the hotel lobby.

Inside, Eli handed Cal a key card. "Room 5638. Jackson, you're with them. The rest of us will occupy the other two rooms."

An elevator ride later, Cal unlocked the suite door and ushered Rachelle inside. "Wait here." He grabbed his signal tracker and swept both bedrooms, bathrooms, and the living room. The chaser lights remained green.

He returned to the living room. "All clear." Cal carried Rachelle's bag into her room. "I'll find a vending machine."

"Thank you, Cal." Rachelle brushed her lips over his. "For everything."

He trailed the backs of his fingers down her cheek before leaving the room, closing the door behind him.

Jackson turned from the sliding glass door. "She okay?"

"She needs a soft drink."

"I'll find something. For some reason, that otherwise intelligent woman prefers comfort from you." The medic gave an exaggerated sigh. "And here I thought the lady had better taste than that." With a grin, he left the suite.

Cal's phone rang. He glanced at the screen. Finally. "What do you have for me, Blake?"

"Nothing good." His friend's voice was hushed.

"Do you have a name?"

"Couldn't narrow it down to one." Blake's breathing roughened. "I have to go. I think someone's following me."

"Wait. When is it safe to contact you?"

"After I leave work," he hissed. "Text me your location, and I'll meet you."

"Not happening. It's too risky for Rachelle. Choose a place. I'll come to you."

"You don't trust me around your principal?"

"I don't trust anyone in this town. Someone hung a target on my woman's back."

A muttered curse, then, "I'll ditch the tail and contact you."

Cal frowned as he slid the phone into his pocket. Blake used to be one of the best on the Teams at ferreting out information. He hoped his friend hadn't made a mistake. The person after Rachelle wasn't fooling around. If he didn't balk at taking on a black ops team, he wouldn't hesitate to kill one former SEAL who tipped his hand.

CHAPTER NINETEEN

Cal turned as Rachelle's bedroom door opened. His heart skipped a beat. Man, she was beautiful inside and out.

She glanced around. "Where's Jackson?"

"Looking for a vending machine." He embraced her. "I asked a friend for information. He called a minute ago."

"And?"

"He uncovered something, but got spooked and refused to talk on the phone. He wants to meet later."

She studied him a moment. "You're worried."

He tightened his hold on her. "He picked up a tail which means he might have tipped someone off while he nosed around."

"Can Fortress protect him?"

"He won't take the offer."

"Why not?"

"Blake wants to work for Fortress. Tough to convince Brent that he'd make a great operative if he can't protect himself much less a principal."

"It's better than ending up on a slab in the morgue."

That argument carried more weight if Blake was a civilian. But a SEAL? No, Cal didn't see his friend accepting protection from Fortress.

Jackson unlocked the door and walked inside carrying four soft drinks. "What did I miss?"

"Contact by my friend at the State Department. He got spooked before he gave me anything. We're supposed to meet later tonight."

"You need backup." He handed Rachelle a green bottle.

"I'll ask Rafe to go with me."

"I want to go."

Cal's first instinct was to refuse, but Rachelle wasn't a junior operative who would follow his orders to the letter. She had great instincts, and those instincts were urging her to watch his back.

"No one knows where we are," she continued. "How would they know I'll be with you when you visit a friend?"

Jackson flashed him a look of sympathy before he unlocked the sliding glass door and stepped out on the balcony to give them privacy.

"You have a price on your head."

"Washington, D.C. is a big city. How would anyone know where we'll be to set up an ambush?"

She had a point. Eli and Rafe had been vigilant in watching for tails. No one had followed them to the hotel. "We're meeting someplace neutral, but someone could follow Blake."

"Take a teammate as backup, but please let me accompany you."

"Why would you put yourself at risk?"

"Blake might be more willing to talk if he meets me."

Cal didn't like the risk, but his SEAL buddy had a soft spot for women in trouble. "You have to promise to do everything I tell you without argument."

"Of course."

His lips twitched. "You don't know what I'll ask you to do."

"Your orders are for my safety. I'd be a fool to argue."

He noted the determined gleam in her eyes and suspected she'd find a way to meet with Blake Sims face-to-face whether Cal agreed or not.

He considered and discarded several plans in the space of seconds. He'd prefer to keep Rachelle by his side. Perhaps taking her along was for the best. That way, his team could provide protection for Rachelle and watch his back.

He understood her desire to find answers for herself. He wouldn't let someone else take the risks if his life was on the line. But Rachelle didn't have self-protection skills if something went wrong.

"All right. Don't make me regret it."

"I'll be with you. What could go wrong?"

He could think of many things, each one worse than the last, all culminating in her injury or death. "Let's hope we don't find out."

Jackson poked his head in the door. "Is it safe to return?"

"Yeah." After dropping a light kiss on Rachelle's lips, he turned to his teammate. "Wolf Pack needs to meet."

Amusement gleamed in Jackson's eyes. "I'll let them know." He returned to the suite with Eli, Jon, and Rafe.

"Did your friend make contact?" Eli asked.

"A few minutes ago. He was spooked and wouldn't talk on the phone except to say what he found wasn't good."

Jon frowned. "Cryptic and unhelpful."

"Anything else?" Rafe asked.

"Sims will contact me with a location for us to meet. He wanted to come here. I refused."

He snorted. "Hard to believe he suggested that."

Eli tilted his head. "Is your contact Blake Sims?"

Cal stiffened. "Yes. Why?"

His team leader exchanged glances with his partner. "Sims was one of the few SEALs we worked with who looked after his own hide before that of his teammates."

Rafe sat in the recliner. "You sure we can trust him, Cal?"

"He owes me. I saved his hide on more than one occasion. Also, he wants a job at Fortress. He won't screw up his only chance for a possible interview with Brent by feeding me bad intel."

Jon scowled. "I don't want him on a team watching our backs."

"He won't be," Cal assured him. "If Brent agrees to interview him, I'll be honest about his shortcomings."

"In that case, Maddox won't hire him. So, what's the plan?" Rafe asked.

"Choose a place to meet that allows us to blend into the crowd but still provide protection for Rachelle. I don't trust Blake's recommendations." Stunned silence met his statement.

"You're taking your woman to a meeting with an informant who protects himself first?" Jon's razor-sharp voice could cut glass.

"I insisted," Rachelle said. "Cal hates the idea, but I convinced him to see reason."

"What possible reason could be important enough to risk your life?"

"I think Sims will cooperate if he sees me."

"Not good enough," Jon snapped. "Grow a spine, Cal."

"Sims is a sucker for a pretty face," Eli said.

"I'll get the information out of him. Easy to do when the man in question avoids pain. You'd never allow Brenna to risk herself that way. I wouldn't risk Dana's life on the instincts of a coward."

"That comparison won't fly." Cal glared at his teammate. "You're discounting the strength of your women and mine. I can and will protect Rachelle with my life. I'm counting on Wolf Pack to have our backs."

Eli quelled Jon with a look before facing Cal. "You don't have to ask. You know we'll protect both of you."

"Then let's find a place suitable for our needs."

After another frosty stare, Jon said, "Laptop." He logged into Cal's computer and spent a few minutes searching the Net for an appropriate place to meet while the rest of Wolf Pack discussed other avenues to track the person targeting Rachelle.

Jon sat back. "The best place to meet is Derringer Steakhouse in Sharondale, Maryland." He turned the laptop around for the others to see the split screen containing a map of the area and the steakhouse.

Cal studied the layout of the restaurant. "Why there?"

"If we meet at the steakhouse at 8:00 tonight, the restaurant will be busy but most families will be home that time."

Minimizing the risk to children, a soft spot for Jon as well as the rest of them. Cal gave a slow nod as he looked at the map. "Sharondale is 90 minutes from here."

"It's further away from Washington, D.C. If Sims is worried about being seen with you or Rachelle, the risk of recognition in Sharondale is minimal."

"A good choice." Rafe enlarged the map of the area. "Easy access to interstates and highways in case we need a fast escape. We'll need to nail down escape routes before we leave."

A nod of approval from Eli. "We should be in place well before Blake is due to arrive."

"Does the steakhouse have good ratings from customers?" Rachelle asked.

Jon smiled. "As a matter of fact, it does."

"Then we have dinner plans tonight." She looked at Cal. "Is that plan acceptable?"

"Sounds perfect." He dropped a light kiss on her mouth and released her. "I'll text Blake the information." As long as his friend didn't lead a tail to Rachelle, the plan should work.

They spent the next two hours memorizing the layout of the restaurant and deciding the best escape routes. By the time they were ready to leave, Rachelle knew the information as well as the operatives.

Back in the SUVs, Cal threaded his fingers through Rachelle's as he drove to Sharondale. Jon's assessment of the restaurant was accurate. The steakhouse was filled with couples.

Cal requested a table at the back of the restaurant. Two minutes later, his teammates entered the restaurant in pairs and were seated nearby.

After the waitress took their drink orders for iced tea, Cal covered Rachelle's hand with his. "You need to eat. The stress you're under is short-circuiting your hunger signals."

"I'll try."

When the waitress returned with their glasses of tea, Rachelle and Cal gave the woman their meal order. He scanned the restaurant's patrons. No one seemed to be paying attention to them or Wolf Pack.

He refocused on the woman across from him. "How's your headache?"

"Nagging, but manageable."

"And the ribs?"

"Sore. They'd be worse if Jackson hadn't taped them. Have you had cracked ribs before?"

"More than once. It's never fun." He tapped the comm device in his ear that connected him to his teammates. "Anything suspicious?" The response was negative. "Keep an eye out. Blake should arrive in the next thirty minutes."

"Copy that," Eli murmured.

While keeping watch for his friend, Cal kept the conversation with Rachelle light and easy. Although he wouldn't count this as a date, he vowed to make that happen when this was over.

When deployed, Jon had gifts and flowers delivered to his wife every day. Eli had meals sent to his home so Brenna and Jon's wife, Dana, wouldn't have to cook. The sisters always stayed together when Eli and Jon were gone. Cal couldn't wait to surprise Rachelle with gifts while he was deployed, too.

He dragged his mind from the tantalizing possibility of a lifetime with Rachelle. Traveling too far down that road wasn't wise. They were still in the early stages of their relationship.

Rachelle laid her hand on his arm, drawing his attention. "Penny for your thoughts."

Cal smiled. "I'm dreaming about the future."

"Something good?"

"Very."

Her eyes sparkled. "Sounds intriguing. Care to share?"

"Later."

"Aww, come on, Taylor," Rafe complained through the comm system. "The suspense is killing me."

Connected to Wolf Pack with her own comm device, Rachelle laughed.

"Knock it off, Torres," Cal muttered.

His teammates chuckled. "But it's fun to give you grief instead of listening to you rag on us," Eli murmured.

"Yeah, yeah." Cal tolerated the teasing until he and Rachelle finished eating.

He glanced at his watch and frowned. "Blake's late." Forty minutes beyond the appointed time. Blake wasn't the bravest man on a team, but he was punctual. Something was wrong. "We need to recon to see if he ran into trouble outside the restaurant."

"I've already paid our tab," Rafe said. "Jackson and I will go."

Minutes later, Rafe said, "Sims isn't here, and there's no sign of trouble."

"Copy."

"What should we do now?" Rachelle asked.

If Rachelle wasn't with him, Cal would go to Blake's home. "Would you allow one of my teammates to take you to the hotel?"

Her eyebrow winged up. "What do you think?"

His teammates chuckled again.

Rachelle was as stubborn as she was beautiful. "Let's go."

After paying their bill, Cal and Rachelle met the others at the SUVs. He called Fortress for Blake's address. Two minutes later, the tech sent the information to Cal and Eli. They arrived at Blake's home two hours later.

Cal circled the block before parking a few houses away. He slowly surveyed the neighborhood.

Eli activated his comm system. "I don't see anything."

"Same."

"Give us a minute to check the back."

"Copy." He glanced at Rachelle, wondering if she considered hot chocolate a comfort food like his sisters. "After we talk to Blake, we'll return to the hotel. Would you like hot chocolate as an after-dinner treat?"

She smiled. "I'd love that. Will the hotel kitchen still be open?"

He kissed her knuckles, pleased that he'd guessed right. "I saw a coffee shop on the way here that's open 24 hours a day."

"Thank you for thinking about me." She kissed him briefly.

"Hey," Jackson complained from the backseat. "I'm feeling left out."

"You'll need medical attention if you don't knock it off," Cal muttered.

"Backyard's clear," Jon murmured. "Go, Cal."

"Copy." He squeezed Rachelle's hand. "Ready?"

She nodded. "Let's make your friend spill his guts."

He winked at her, delighted that she was his and unafraid of his world. He escorted her to Blake's home.

The small bungalow was dark inside. Blake's black sports car sat in the driveway. Cal laid his hand on the hood. "Car engine's cold," he reported to the others.

"No sign of movement inside," Eli whispered.

At the front door, Cal shifted to the side of the frame, drawing Rachelle against his back and out of the line of fire. Jackson took position on the other side of the door. Both men palmed their weapons.

Cal nodded at the medic who rang the doorbell. Chimes pealed through the house. No movement. "Nothing," he whispered to his teammates.

"Pick the locks," Eli whispered.

Jackson stood behind Cal, blocking him from view. Seconds after inserting his lock picks, the tumblers shifted. Cal stood and slid his lock picks into his pocket. "Ready," he whispered.

Eli counted down. "Go."

Standing to the side of the door, Cal twisted the knob and pushed it open. He heard a low moan. "Blake?"

"Help me."

He signaled for Jackson to cover right while he took left. Weapons up, they entered the house.

"Cal." Jackson shoved his weapon into his holster and rushed toward the figure crumpled on the floor in the living room. He crouched beside the fallen man.

Cal turned on a lamp. His jaw hardened as he took in his friend's appearance. Someone beat Blake, then shot him in the shoulder.

At Rachelle's soft gasp, he moved to her side in seconds, drawing her against him. "What do you need, Jackson?"

"Mike bag and an ambulance." The medic looked at Rachelle. "Don't leave fingerprints anywhere, but I need towels."

Rachelle blinked, then drew in a deep breath. "Towels. Right." She stumbled toward the back where his teammates had entered the house.

Cal called 911. "There's a paramedic on scene," he informed the dispatcher. Cal ended the call and motioned for Rafe to stay with Jackson while he grabbed the medic's bag.

After handing Jackson his bag, Cal searched the rest of the house, looking for signs of an intruder. One window was open, dirt smeared on the windowsill. Examination of the glass revealed a perfect circle cut out near the lock.

He returned to the living room and knelt beside his friend. "Blake."

The man opened his eyes as Jackson worked on him. "Screwed up," he whispered. "Sorry."

"I'll kick your backside later." If Blake lived. Cal wouldn't bet on that.

Blake's lips twitched. "Deserve it. Lost my touch."

"You'll blow the dust off your skills at Fortress." When the injured man reached up, Cal gripped his hand. "Who hurt you?"

A groan when Jackson applied a pressure bandage to the front of his shoulder.

"Suck it up," the medic said. "The bandages will keep you from losing more blood."

"Hurts."

"I know, buddy. You'll hurt more in a minute when I apply a bandage to the back of your shoulder."

Cal squeezed Blake's hand. "Don't make us look like wusses in front of Rachelle."

A flicker of a smile.

Sirens drew closer. Cal was running out of time to obtain answers. "Blake, I need your help. Who did this to you, and who's after my woman?"

"Ski mask. Security system." He groaned louder when Rafe helped Jackson roll the downed man to his side and apply another pressure bandage. Blake whispered the password to the system as the sirens cut off.

"Who's targeting Rachelle?" Cal pressed.

"They call him Falcon."

"Do you know his identity?"

A slight head shake. "High in the department. That's all I know."

"Why does he want her?"

"She saw too much in Mexico. He won't stop until she's dead."

CHAPTER TWENTY

On her knees by Blake's head, Rachelle stared, unable to believe what he said to Cal. When had she seen too much and where? Who was Falcon? She didn't recognize the name and longed to shake the information from him, but the police swarmed into the house with guns drawn, shouting orders at Cal and his teammates. This wasn't the time to push for answers.

"Hands on your heads, fingers interlocked," one barrel-chested policeman ordered with his gun pointed at Cal. His gray hair glistened in the lamp light.

"No," Rachelle protested. "You don't understand. These are the good guys. They didn't hurt Blake."

"Rachelle, everything will be fine," Cal said as he, Rafe, Eli, and Jon slowly complied with the order. "They don't have the facts yet. This is standard procedure until they know what's going on."

"They're treating you like criminals."

Except for Jackson, the operatives were handcuffed. When one of the younger policemen approached Rachelle with his handcuffs out, Cal shifted as though preparing to intervene.

Tension in the room escalated. Rachelle had to do something before the operatives came to her aid. "It's all right," she said and held out her wrists to the policeman. "Secure my hands in front so I can help the paramedic."

Unsure, the patrolman looked at Barrel chest for instructions. When he received a nod, he fastened the handcuffs around Rachelle's wrists.

Although angry on her behalf, Cal settled against the wall, his gaze locked on Rachelle. Even restrained, she knew he'd protect her if she was in danger.

While Barrel chest questioned the operatives, Jackson continued to work on stabilizing an unconscious Blake. Minutes later, EMTs hurried into the room with their gear bags.

"What do we have?" the blond man asked.

While Jackson reported the injuries he'd found on Blake and his treatment, the policeman who cuffed her reached for Rachelle.

Cal straightened from the wall.

"Don't move," Barrel chest ordered, hand on his weapon.

"Tell Junior to be very careful with my girlfriend," he said, voice soft.

A snort from the man. "You're not in charge here, buddy." He looked at the younger cop. "Put her in the chair against the wall and keep an eye on her. Callen, help me check these guys for weapons." He eyed the operatives. "How many weapons are you carrying?"

Eli smiled. "A lot."

"More than I can see?"

"What do you think?" Jon asked.

"What are you guys, some kind of home-grown terrorists?"

"Black ops, private," Rafe said. "Fortress Security."

The cops looked at each other, eyes wide. The fourth man who had yet to say anything looked from the operatives to Rachelle. "Is she an HVT?"

"Yes, she is," Cal said.

Fourth man's eyebrows rose. "I'm surprised you're on your girlfriend's security detail."

The EMTs brought in a gurney and transferred Blake into the ambulance. A moment later, they left to the accompaniment of flashing lights and blaring sirens.

"Weren't you Army Special Forces?" Barrel chest said to Fourth man.

"Yes, sir."

"Check for weapons while the rest of us cover you."

The man headed for Eli first. "How long have you worked with Fortress?"

"Since Maddox founded the company."

"Like it?"

A slow smile from Eli. "We're able to help people without fighting through red tape or waiting for warrants. Yeah, we like it."

"Less red tape is better. What branch of the military were you in?"

"All of us are SEALs. You?"

"Force Recon."

"What's your name?"

"Chase McCord."

"If you decide to go private, call Fortress and ask for Eli Wolfe. I'll put in a good word for you with our boss."

McCord stilled. "I heard you don't apply for jobs with Maddox."

"It's true. He trashes applications by the hundreds every month. The only way to slide a foot in the door is if he asks you to come in for an interview. As soon as the cuffs come off, I'll give you my card."

"Hey." Barrel chest scowled. "Stop recruiting my partner. I just got him trained."

"Do the weapons check," Cal said to McCord. "We need to get Rachelle out of here."

By the time McCord finished searching the operatives, a pile of weapons sat in front of each member of Wolf Pack.

Holy cow. Rachelle didn't realize they carried so many weapons on their persons.

"Check the chick, too," Barrel chest ordered.

McCord glanced at Cal.

"That's an order," the grizzled cop snapped.

"Be careful," Cal warned. "She has cracked ribs on the right side, a parting gift from thugs who tried to kill her two nights ago."

"Yes, sir."

Barrel chest frowned and motioned for McCord to do his job.

McCord assisted Rachelle to her feet. "I'm sorry, ma'am," he murmured. "It's policy."

"I understand."

"If your boyfriend thinks I'm hurting you, he'll be on me in a flash and end up in jail. I'll do my best not to hurt you."

Even if he did, Rachelle refused to show it. The least she could do was keep Cal from being arrested. She stood still as the officer patted her down for weapons, then helped her sit again.

Barrel chest swaggered to the middle of the room, notebook and pen in hand. He pointed to Wolfe. "You first. What's your beef with the vic?"

"We don't have one. Sims is a friend of Taylor's. He and Taylor arranged to meet at a restaurant for dinner."

"Name of the place?"

"Derringer Steakhouse in Sharondale."

"Never heard of the place."

"I have," McCord said. "Good food."

"Yeah, whatever." Barrel chest turned his gaze back to Eli. "What time were you at the restaurant?"

"We arrived at 8:00 and left at 9:30. When Sims didn't show, we came to check on him. Took us two hours to drive from Sharondale. We found him on the floor, beaten and shot in the shoulder. Conner is a Fortress medic and a nationally certified paramedic. He treated Sims until the EMTs arrived."

"I'm well aware of the rep for Fortress operatives. You're all highly trained. You expect me to believe you didn't do that damage to our vic?"

Jackson frowned. "Check our hands."

"Right." He glanced down at his notes. "How did you get in the house?"

Cal answered that question. "We rang the bell with no response. Sims's car was in the driveway, but all the lights were off. He didn't answer when we called out."

A frown. "He might have been entertaining a woman and blew you guys off in favor of more pleasurable pursuits."

With the favor he owed Cal and the scheduled meeting, that scenario was unlikely. Rachelle scanned the impassive faces of the operatives. How much of the truth would they volunteer?

"Sims would have called me to cancel."

Barrel chest motioned for Cal to continue.

"We searched the back of the house and discovered a raised window with a circle cut from the glass."

Barrel chest stared. "Was the door unlocked?"

"Because I feared for Blake's wellbeing, I picked the lock. We found him on the floor."

"You picked the lock." His pen tapped on the notepad. "I could arrest you for breaking and entering."

"You could." Cal stared. "You won't. The paperwork will be a nuisance when you have more important things to focus on."

Barrel chest's eyes narrowed. "What do you know about the paperwork?"

"Too much. I was a homicide cop in Nashville."

"So, you know what you did was illegal."

"I'd do it again in a heartbeat if I thought a life was at stake. Ignoring the law was the right call tonight. If I hadn't, Blake would have died."

"You brought your principal to a potentially dangerous situation."

"Not my first choice. I didn't want to leave her unprotected in the SUV."

A snort. The older cop glanced at Rachelle. "If you're smart, you'll dump this clown and find someone with your safety in mind. You could have been hurt or killed."

Rachelle raised her chin. "He saved my life more than once. I trust him."

"I hope I don't read your obituary in the newspaper because you trusted the wrong man." He turned back to Cal. "Tell me the rest."

"We called 911. You know the rest."

Barrel chest glared at him. "That's the way you want it, huh? Fine. I'll report to the judge that you were uncooperative with my investigation." He looked at McCord. "Put Taylor in the back of your patrol car. He'll be our guest for a few days."

Oh, man. This wasn't good. Since no one paid attention to her, she freed her phone from her pocket and sent Micah a text message. McCord glanced at her, but didn't stop her.

Micah requested the name of the officer in charge. Great. She caught McCord's attention while Eli protested the older cop's order. "What's his name?" she whispered.

"Gavin Soto."

She sent her boss the name. Micah Winter had deep ties in the Washington, D.C. community from his years as a Secret Service agent.

Five minutes later as McCord moved to Cal's side to escort him to the cruiser, Soto's cell phone rang. He glanced at the screen and frowned. "A blocked number?" he muttered.

"If I were you, I'd answer that call," Rachelle said.

He scowled at her, but swiped the screen anyway. "Yeah, Soto." The cop's face lost all expression as he listened, blood draining from his cheeks. "Yes, sir." More listening, then, "I understand, sir." Silence. "Yes, sir." Soto slid his phone away with a trembling hand. He looked at McCord. "Turn them loose."

One of the others protested. "We need to take them to the station for questioning, sir."

Soto gave a bark of laughter. "What we want don't matter, kid. I don't know how they did it, but the man on the phone was President Martin. He wants these guys turned loose, and he cleared it with the police chief."

McCord rubbed his jaw, amusement glittering in his eyes. "Nice work," he murmured to Rachelle as he unlocked her handcuffs. Soto's partner released Wolf Pack.

"Get your kits." Soto said to his partner and McCord. "Callen and I will take statements from the rest of these yahoos and send them on their way."

While the two policemen interviewed Jon and Rafe, Eli disappeared down the hallway. Cal crouched beside Rachelle. "You contacted Micah?"

She nodded. "I had no idea he'd call the president."

"Your idea worked."

"At least it kept you from landing in jail." She smiled. "I don't have the funds to bail you out."

Cal chuckled. "I could have posted my own bail, but I'm glad it wasn't necessary." His smile faded. "I don't want you out of my sight."

She wrapped her arms around his neck and whispered in his ear, "Will you question Blake again?"

He shook his head. "He doesn't know anything else." Cal pressed a kiss behind her ear and made her shiver. He turned to look at Eli when he eased back into the living room.

Wolf Pack's leader headed for Cal and Rachelle. "Got it," he murmured.

"Blake needs a guard." Cal threaded his fingers through Rachelle's. "Whoever beat him may try to finish the job."

"Suggestions?"

"McCord."

"I'll see what I can do."

When the interviews concluded, the operatives gathered their weapons and left the house. Rachelle glanced at her watch and sighed.

Cal glanced her way. "What's wrong?"

"It's 3:00 a.m. We have a 90-minute drive ahead of us, and Meyer and his friends will be at the hotel in a few hours."

He unlocked his SUV. "I'll delay the interview. The State Department doesn't know where we're staying and won't until I give Maddox permission to tell them."

Rachelle shook her head. "I want the interview behind me so we can leave." She felt as though someone watched every move she and Wolf Pack made.

"I'll contact Brent when we return to the hotel and have him call Meyer at 7:00. That will put the feds on our doorstep between 8:30 and 9:00."

He shut the door and came around to the driver's side. Once Jackson slid into the backseat with his mike bag, Cal cranked the engine and drove away from Blake's home.

As they drove through the dark night, Rachelle thought over what they'd learned from Blake and what they hadn't. Who was the Falcon? Try as she might, she didn't remember anyone mentioning a person named Falcon while she was in Mexico. Was he the leader of the terrorists who attacked the hotel and killed Tim Garner? Why did he want her dead, and how far would he go to achieve his goal?

CHAPTER TWENTY-ONE

After escorting Rachelle to her bedroom in the suite, Cal fed his newest addiction for a few minutes. Rachelle's taste sent him back for a kiss again and again, tilting his head until he found the perfect fit, his tongue gliding against hers in a gentle dance that stoked the flames of his need for her.

Aware of time slipping away and Rachelle's need for rest before another grueling interview with Meyer, Cal eased his mouth from hers, already mourning the loss of her taste and the feel of her lips against his. "I have to stop while I still can," he murmured. Another kiss. "Stopping might kill me, though."

Her kiss-swollen lips curved. "Same for me. Rain check?"

He trailed his fingers down her cheek. "Anytime." Cal stepped away from her, using every ounce of self-control he had left. "I'll be in the living room if you need me."

He left the room. If he glanced back, his control would turn into mist.

Cal made a pot of coffee and consumed half a mug before he could draw a full breath and focus. Rachelle

Carter torpedoed his concentration. He glanced toward her closed door, longing for more sizzling kisses.

His phone chirped with an incoming message. As he read the text, satisfaction filled him. Excellent. Eli had arranged for McCord and another former Special Forces soldier who worked for the D.C. police to be assigned to Sims' protection detail.

Cal sent Zane a text, asking the tech wizard to contact him as soon as he arrived at Fortress. Zane was his best hope of discovering Falcon's identity.

A minute later, his phone rang. Cal glanced at the screen and winced. "Sorry, Z. I didn't mean to wake you."

"No problem. What do you need?"

He summarized what they'd learned from Blake. "I need to know who Falcon is. According to Blake, this guy won't stop gunning for Rachelle until she's dead."

"We'll smoke him out before he accomplishes his goal. I'll let you know as soon as I have anything."

"Thanks. Has Bridget made progress?"

"She's digging through layers of multiple shell corporations. The trail is nearly nonexistent so it takes time."

Time Rachelle might not have. "I understand, but Rachelle's life is on the line. I can't lose her, Z."

Silence, then, "Like that, is it?"

"Maybe."

A short laugh. "Definitely. Good for you. She's a good woman. Don't forget what I told you earlier."

"Yeah, yeah. If I hurt her, you'll take me down yourself." Despite being in a wheelchair, Zane Murphy was still as much of a SEAL as the rest of them, and he would do as he'd threatened.

"Don't hassle Bridget. She's working hard to track down the information for you. If you need a contact person, come to me."

His eyebrows rose. "Yes, sir."

"Sorry. Two operatives are giving her grief for not moving fast enough on their searches."

"I'm surprised her husband doesn't have them in his rifle scope."

"He and his team are out of the country at the moment."

"Give me their names. I'll pay them a visit the next time I'm in town."

"Ha. Never mind, buddy. I'll take care of them myself by the end of the day."

Oh, boy. That set down would make the gossip circuit at Fortress pretty fast. "If you need backup, let me know."

"I won't need help." A baby's cry sounded in the background. "I need to go. Later, my friend." Zane ended the call.

Cal, on watch until 6:00, carried his refilled mug to the French doors. The idiots hassling Bridget Young were in serious trouble. Zane was very protective of his younger protege, and ticking off the man who saved the hides of operatives was not a smart move. If Z didn't get the job done, Bridget's husband, Trace, would deal with them when he returned to the US, provided Maddox didn't haul them in himself. He also had a soft spot for his new researcher.

An hour later, a light tap sounded on the suite door. Frowning, Cal palmed his weapon and checked the peephole. He opened the door to admit Jon. "Why are you awake?"

"Couldn't sleep. Decided to let you have some beauty sleep." He clapped Cal on the shoulder. "Go. I've got the watch."

He stretched out on the couch as Jon took his place at the French doors and was asleep in seconds. At 7:00, he woke to a knock on the suite door. "Room service," a male voice called.

Cal sat up, weapon in hand, as Jon looked through the peephole. His teammate unlocked the door and motioned for the bellhops to roll their carts into the suite. After tipping them, Jon sent the men on their way.

"That's quite a feast." Cal perused the dishes, glad to see yogurt, cut fruit, and bagels among the offerings. "Good choices."

"Rafe and Eli will be here soon."

Time to wake Rachelle. Even though he wanted her to sleep as much as possible, she also needed a few minutes to eat before Meyer and his friends arrived to question her.

Cal knocked on her door. "Rachelle?"

The door swung open. The woman he'd dreamed about while he slept stood in the doorway, fully dressed in jeans and a long-sleeved t-shirt, tennis shoes clutched in one hand. "Do you mind helping me with my shoes? I can't bend over to tie the laces."

"No problem." He led her to the couch and knelt in front of her. "Breakfast just arrived."

She didn't respond.

Hmm. Cal finished tying her shoe laces. "You okay?"

"I'm not hungry."

Jackson walked into the living room in time to hear Rachelle's comment. "Nausea still plaguing you?"

"My stomach's in a knot. I'll eat later."

The medic squeezed her shoulder and sent Cal a pointed glance.

He suspected the problem was the coming interview. After what they pulled the previous day, he didn't blame her for being reluctant. But delaying the inevitable would place the president in an awkward position.

An idea to distract Rachelle formed in his mind. He raised her hand to his lips and kissed her palm as his teammate joined Jon at the breakfast cart. "I need to shower and change. Shouldn't take more than five minutes."

She looked skeptical.

He grinned. "Hey, the military drummed speed into our heads. When I finish, would you like to go on a breakfast date?"

Rachelle brightened. "I'd love to." Then, her expression dimmed. "We shouldn't, though. Meyer will be here soon."

"He and his friends will wait. You're the guest of honor. They can't start the party without you." He brushed a kiss over her lips. "I'll be back soon." Cal looked at Jon, who gave a slight nod. Five minutes later, he returned to the living room, showered, shaved, and dressed in clean clothes.

Rachelle smiled. "I'm impressed. Five minutes to the second."

He'd finished his shower and dressed in three minutes, then used the other two to arrange a treat for Rachelle. "Ready?"

She nodded. "Where are we going?"

"Some things are better experienced. Jon, we'll be back in time to meet the threesome from the State Department."

"Need backup?"

He shook his head. "We aren't leaving the hotel. If something comes up, text me." Cal opened the suite door, checked the hallway, then escorted Rachelle to the elevator. Although he preferred the stairs, his lady wasn't up to it today. On the ground floor, Cal kept his hand at her lower back as he guided her toward the solarium.

She sent him a puzzled glance. "We're not going to the restaurant?"

"I planned something else for you." He continued through the maze of greenery until he reached the secluded area where one of the staff waited for them beside a table draped with a white cloth. A simple flower arrangement sat in the center of the table. Beside the table was a cart identical to the ones the bellhops brought to the suite.

Rachelle gasped. "Cal, how did you arrange this? You were gone for five minutes."

"Superpowers are supposed to be a secret." Since the food he'd requested had been on the breakfast bar in the main dining room, a promised large tip had persuaded the waitstaff to accommodate his request. Cal slipped the tip to the waiter who returned to his regular duties with a promise to check on them soon.

Turning to seat Rachelle, Cal froze when he saw tears on her face. Oh, man. Dismay knotted his gut. Had he hurt her? He cupped her cheek. "I didn't mean to upset you, baby."

She kissed him. "These are happy tears because you went to so much trouble for me."

He relaxed. "Thank goodness. I have four teammates upstairs who will lay me out flat if I hurt you."

"You're a SEAL and a big, bad black ops soldier. You can't be afraid of your teammates."

He snorted. "Those men are as tough as nails and I don't want to be on their bad list. They'll take it personally if I make you cry."

Rachelle gave a watery laugh. "You're safe, Cal. I'll vouch for your intentions."

"I appreciate that." He seated her, removed the plate covers, and set Rachelle's breakfast in front of her. A blueberry bagel, cream cheese, and cut fruit for her. A full traditional breakfast for him along with coffee and a clear soft drink for Rachelle.

She bit into the bagel and sighed. "This is perfect. How did you know what to choose?"

"I've seen plenty of operatives with appetite problems from PTSD. They all needed something light to entice them to eat." He covered her hand with his. "What's upsetting you, Rachelle?"

She gave a rueful laugh. "Everything. Meyer's visit, Blake, the Falcon, being on the run, the attacks, the pain in my ribs that prevents me from sleeping. They all contribute to my lack of appetite."

"If you can't sleep again tonight, tell me. Jackson might add more tape to give you relief or use ice packs. He can also give you stronger pain meds."

"Since I'm a lightweight, I'm likely to run into a tree or a wall if Jackson gives me heavy-duty pain medicine."

Cal chuckled. "I'll have to remember that." He kept their conversation light, telling her funny incidents from his childhood that kept her in stitches. She consumed a whole bagel, part of the fruit, and finished her soft drink. He counted that as a win.

Aware their time was gone, he raised her hand to his mouth and kissed her palm. "We need to go."

"Thank you for taking me on a breakfast date. When we return home, I'd like to cook breakfast for you."

He didn't have the heart to tell her that his mornings started two hours or more before hers. The day she chose to cook breakfast for him, he'd shift his workout to the afternoon. "I'd like that."

Cal walked with Rachelle to the elevator, his hand on her waist. "Meyer and his crew will arrive soon. Would you like to sit on the balcony with me until they show up?"

He'd checked the lines of sight. Too many trees for a sniper to have a shot at her. Being outside would give her a sense of normalcy and push back reality for a few more minutes.

"I'd enjoy the sunshine and the company."

"Coffee or tea and fresh air with my girl counts as a date." As he'd intended, she laughed.

"I'll have to come up with interesting date ideas, too." When he didn't say anything, she looked at him, her smile fading. "You don't mind, do you?"

"I'm glad you want to plan things for us."

"But?"

He shrugged. "No other woman planned dates for me. They expected me to plan and cater to their needs and wants."

"They were stupid and selfish."

He chuckled. "Tell me how you really feel."

"Letting you slip through their fingers was a colossal mistake."

Cal stilled. "You won't do that?" Would she commit to dating him long term?

A smile curved her lips. "I've wanted to date you since I first laid eyes on you. I don't know who you dated before me and prefer not to know their names, but they were selfish. Relationships are two-way streets. For a relationship to work, we have to give one hundred percent. One person can't carry the load. My parents and grandparents were great examples of full partnerships. From the way you talk about your family, I bet they operated the same way."

True. Some of the women he dated came from families with stable marriages as examples to emulate. They still focused on themselves and what Cal could do for them.

The elevator arrived at their floor. "Would you like coffee or tea on our balcony date?"

"Tea. We'll call room service."

"I have it covered." He'd slipped tea packets into his Go bag for Rachelle in case they stayed overnight. He inserted his card into the lock.

Jackson turned from the French doors and studied Rachelle's face a moment before sending Cal a nod of approval. "All quiet so far."

"Things will liven up soon. Rachelle and I plan to sit on the balcony for a while."

"I'll let you know when our guests arrive."

Cal nuked water and a tea bag, then joined Rachelle on the outdoor couch. He handed her the tea, then wrapped his arm around her shoulders. He sipped his coffee and enjoyed a time of peace.

When Rachelle finished her tea, Cal set the mug beside his empty one. "Meyer and his friends will have one hour to ask questions, then it will be my turn."

"You're turning the tables on them."

"You bet."

A knock sounded on the glass behind them. Cal glanced over his shoulder as Jon headed toward the suite door.

"Are they here?" Rachelle asked.

His teammate checked the peephole, looked at Cal, and nodded.

"Yes. Remember, if you need a break, tell me and I'll make it happen."

"They won't be happy about that."

"I don't care how they feel. The only person who matters to me is you." He stood and held out his hand. "We're in control, not them."

"You don't know how happy that makes me." Rachelle squared her shoulders. "Let's go. I want to leave this town."

He couldn't agree more. Cal admired Rachelle's strength and calm demeanor.

The trio protested when Eli ordered the men to place their hands on the wall while he searched for weapons. "This is outrageous," Meyer snapped. "We're not criminals."

Cal led Rachelle to the couch. "Our rules, Meyer. If you want the interview with Rachelle, you'll comply. This is your last chance to ask Rachelle questions in person."

The new man with blond hair and ice-blue eyes scowled. "Who are these jokers?" he asked Meyer. "Do they know who we are?"

"They're with Fortress Security and have friends in high places," Meyer said, his tone sour. "Don't tick them off."

Once Eli completed the search, he stepped back. "They're clean."

Cal directed them to the loveseat and recliner. "Have a seat, gentlemen." He turned to the new member of Meyer's team. "You must be Russell Stokes."

"And you are?"

"Cal Taylor. This is Rachelle Carter."

A nod. "Ms. Carter."

"Why were you included in this interview?" Cal asked.

Stokes frowned. "We're the ones asking questions, not you."

"Meyer and his friends distressed Rachelle yesterday. That won't happen again. You have one hour for questions. If Rachelle needs a break, she'll get one."

A scowl from Stokes. "I don't care who your friends are, we have a responsibility to the Secretary of State and Tim Garner's family to obtain answers. Ms. Carter is the only one who can help."

"Amy Morales was with Rachelle every moment in Mexico. While a face-to-face interview isn't possible, she can answer questions via video chat."

"We spoke to her late last night. Ms. Morales was helpful, but she's been traumatized enough."

And Rachelle hadn't? Cal stared at Stokes whose cheeks flushed. "Be careful how you ask Rachelle questions. She's here as a favor. If you badger her, the interview ends."

"You can't do that," he snapped.

"Try me." Cal threaded his fingers through Rachelle's. "You're wasting time. The one-hour clock starts now."

For a moment, the State Department employees froze as though unable to believe he was serious about the time limit. If they tested him, they'd find out how serious he was.

Stokes's gaze dropped to Cal and Rachelle's intertwined hands. "Not very professional behavior for a bodyguard."

"You've used two minutes posturing and jockeying for power, Stokes," Cal warned. "You're not in control here."

The other man glanced at Wolf Pack stationed around the room. He frowned, then said, "Ms. Carter, I want to hear what happened while you were in Mexico with Ms. Morales."

Rachelle drew in a deep breath and began. At various points during the interview, the men asked clarifying questions.

When she finished, Stokes said, "So-called terrorists attacked the hotel the only night you stayed there. When you fled to the hospital with Agent Hoss, the gunmen showed up and killed Agent Garner."

Rachelle's grip on Cal's hand tightened. "Yes, sir."

"What's your point, Stokes?" Cal asked, voice hard.

Ignoring him, Stokes said, "Ms. Carter, do you have anything else to tell us?"

"Like what?" she asked.

"You weren't at Ms. Morales's side the entire time you were in Mexico. Where did you go when you were alone?"

She frowned. "I walked around the neighborhood in two cities when Amy gave her speech."

"Walked around the neighborhood, huh?" Stokes reached into his jacket pocket.

Cal and the rest of Wolf Pack had their weapons out and leveled at Stokes in seconds.

The State Department trio froze.

"I'm grabbing a picture from my pocket," Stokes said. "Your friend patted us down for weapons."

"Take your hand from the jacket slowly," Cal said.

When Stokes removed a folded picture, Cal took it from him. He unfolded the paper and glanced at the grainy photograph.

Frowning, he studied the scene that showed Rachelle in a dingy, dirty alley. The photo could have been taken anywhere, including Mexico.

He recognized the man with her. Keeping his expression neutral, he returned to Rachelle and handed her the paper.

She didn't look. "What's wrong?"

"Look at the picture, sweetheart."

She tore her gaze from his and glanced down. Rachelle gasped. "No! I didn't do that, Cal. I've never seen him before."

"You appear to know that man very well, Ms. Carter," Stokes snapped. "You might convince your bodyguard that you're innocent of fraternizing with a known criminal, but you won't convince me."

"I don't know him."

"Funny thing about that. I have several pictures of you and this stranger taken in different places that say otherwise."

CHAPTER TWENTY-TWO

"I want to see the pictures." Rachelle glared at the odious Russell Stokes. She waggled the photo. "This is a copy. I want to see the originals."

"They were sent to my email." Stokes inclined his head toward the paper. "Explain that."

"I can't. Yet. But this picture is fake. While I don't know this man, it seems you do. Who is he?"

The man turned his cold gaze to Cal. "Ask your bodyguard. I'm sure he will answer your question. Won't you, Taylor?" His expression shifted to smug satisfaction. "Isn't he in your deck of America's most wanted criminals?"

"I'm not with the military."

"Once a SEAL, always a SEAL."

How did Stokes know Cal was a SEAL? The information wasn't common knowledge.

Cal said, "His name is Clint Nichols."

Her gaze dropped to the picture again, stomach churning at the news. "My boss has mentioned the name. Nichols is into drugs and human trafficking."

"So, you do know him." Satisfaction gleamed in the depths of Stokes's eyes. "Perhaps you'd like to change your story now."

"I know the name, but I haven't met him."

"Evidence says otherwise."

"Evidence can be manufactured." Cal looked at Jon. "My bag is on the bed."

His teammate returned with Cal's laptop in his hand. After Jon sat at the table and booted up the laptop, Cal keyed in his passwords. He returned to the couch and wrapped his arm around Rachelle's shoulders.

She relaxed, grateful he believed her. The person who sent the photo to Stokes doctored it. But would everyone who saw the photo believe she told the truth?

"Log into your email, Stokes," Cal said. "My friend will forward the emails to our tech department to analyze."

Stokes frowned. "How do I know he won't delete them to protect a woman who is more than a client to you?"

"Save them to your cloud drive as soon as you forward the emails," Jon said.

While his colleague was on the laptop, Meyer's gaze locked on Rachelle. "I want an explanation, Ms. Carter."

"Your hour is up," Cal said. "No more questions."

"We'll force her compliance," he threatened.

"A wise man would rethink that plan." Cal's voice sent a shiver up Rachelle's spine. "You'll bring yourself nothing except trouble if you press ahead."

"Your objectivity is questionable."

"No doubt. My warning stands." Cal glanced at Jon who nodded.

Rachelle breathed easier. Thank goodness. Jon or Zane would get to the truth about the pictures.

"Who sent the photos?" Cal asked.

Stokes snorted. "I'm not revealing my source, and you won't learn the identity from those emails, either. They came from an account that was closed as soon as the emails were sent."

"But you know who it is."

"It's someone I trust."

Cal's eyebrow rose. "I hope your trust isn't misplaced because another person who asked questions about Rachelle landed in the hospital with life-threatening injuries."

Thankfully, Blake's doctor worked fast enough to save his life. Barring complications, he should fully recover.

A glare from Stokes. "Are you threatening me?"

"Stating a fact."

"Who was injured?"

"Blake Sims. Someone broke into his home, beat and shot him. Whoever is running this operation isn't joking around."

Another snort. "Sims is a flunky, hardly a threat to anyone."

Why would Stokes, a man higher in the ranks, know a flunky like Blake? He was one of thousands employed by the State Department. Stokes knew more than he was saying.

"Asking questions about Rachelle was enough to draw the wrong attention. Blake might work for the State Department now, but he was a Navy SEAL and capable of protecting himself."

Not as capable as Cal and Wolf Pack, but better prepared than a typical government employee. For the first time, Stokes appeared uncertain. Good. He needed to show discretion when he asked questions. The man's smug attitude wouldn't stop bullets. Rachelle ought to know. She'd been dodging plenty of metal projectiles in the past few days without the attitude.

Stokes rose. "We're finished for now. I trust Ms. Carter will be available for follow-up questions." He turned to Rachelle. "I assure you, we'll have plenty. Your actions cost one of our men his life. You won't be the cause of more deaths on my watch."

"That's enough," Cal said. "Sit down, Stokes. I have questions for you."

The man scowled. "You're joking."

"Sit."

"I don't think so." He pivoted and saw Rafe and Eli blocking the suite door. "This is outrageous. You can't stop us from leaving. Our security is in the hallway. If I raise my voice, they'll break in here. I'll be thrilled to have you arrested for unlawful detainment."

Cal's eyebrow rose. "You tossed questions around like candy at Mardi Gras. Are you afraid to answer a few questions yourself?"

Meyer sighed. "Sit down, Russ. He's doing his job, like we are. What do you want to know, Taylor?"

"Who decided a two-man security detail was sufficient for the ambassador's daughter?"

Ken Caldwell rolled his eyes. "Come on, Taylor. Ms. Morales was on a goodwill tour. She didn't need a full security detail."

"In light of the attack on Amy, Rachelle, and the security team, it's obvious she did. Your decision endangered Rachelle, something Fortress doesn't take lightly."

Stokes made a rolling motion with his hand. "What else? We have real jobs to return to."

Rachelle's eyes narrowed. And Wolf Pack didn't? What an arrogant jerk.

"What do you know about the Falcon?" Cal asked.

For the first time since he'd stepped into the suite, Stokes remained silent while his friends exchanged puzzled glances with each other. "Why are you asking about birds of prey?" Meyer asked.

"Falcon is a person, not a bird. What do you know about him?"

"Never heard of him. I'm sure your computer support people will investigate Falcon for you unless they're incompetent."

"Who is Falcon?" Caldwell asked.

"You tell me."

"I don't know him, either."

Cal shifted his gaze to the stone-faced Stokes. "What about you?"

"This isn't about me." He inclined his head toward Rachelle. "It's about her role in a colleague's death."

"You're lying. Why?"

"I'm not. This is ridiculous. I'm not on trial." Stokes stood again. "I don't know anyone named Falcon. Satisfied?"

Without waiting for an answer from Cal, he turned to his companions. "We've wasted enough time today. Since Ms. Carter isn't cooperative, I suggest we turn our own investigators loose and bring her in for an interview without her guard dog."

Cal stood, placing himself between Rachelle and the men from the State Department. "That's not going to happen. If you insist on questioning her again, I'll be inside the room with Rachelle along with her legal counsel."

Stokes glared at him before turning to Eli and Rafe. "Move or I call our security detail to deal with you."

"Did you provide yourself with a full security detail?" Rafe asked, his tone mocking.

That earned the operative a scowl. "Move."

"I'll take that as a yes. Guess protecting your own hide takes precedence over safeguarding your people."

Eli glanced at Cal and received a slight nod in agreement. He and Rafe shifted to either side of the door.

"You'll hear from us soon," Meyer said to Rachelle. He held his hand out to shake Cal's hand. "No hard feelings, Taylor. We want the truth about our colleague's death as you would do if you lost a teammate or your girlfriend."

When Cal didn't reply, Meyer extended his hand to Rachelle. When she accepted, he sandwiched her hand between both of his. "I didn't know Benson would show you Garner's picture yesterday. Please accept my apologies for causing you distress."

When Rachelle gave a slight nod, Meyer released her. Caldwell and Stokes shook hands with her and Cal although neither said a word.

Stokes retained possession of her hand too long, his fingers sliding over her wrist. She frowned and freed herself from his hold. Stokes smirked and stalked toward the door. A moment later, they were gone.

Cal wrapped his arms around Rachelle. "Great job. You gave them straight facts without volunteering information."

Jackson went to the small kitchenette. He filled a mug with water and a tea bag. "Very impressive, Rachelle. Maybe you should talk to Maddox about becoming an operative."

"Bite your tongue," Cal said. "I like Rachelle working in a safe environment."

Rachelle smiled at the medic. "Thanks for the vote of confidence, but I'm happy with my job."

When the microwave's heating cycle ended, Jackson removed the tea bag and added sugar. He gave the mug to Rachelle. "I know you don't add sugar to your tea, but you've been through a lot."

"Thanks for taking such good care of me."

He cleared his throat. "Yes, ma'am."

That made her laugh despite the ball of ice in her stomach. "Have you looked at the pictures Stokes sent?" she asked Jon.

"Not with the feds in the room."

"Let's see them. I need to know what I'm facing." Why was she in danger? What did she see that made her a target of Falcon?

Jon looked at Cal. "Now or wait?"

He cupped her cheek. "We need to wait, Rachelle. I want to see the photos, but I want you in a secure location. Too many people know your location."

Although disappointed with the decision, she appreciated his logic. She didn't want to endanger Wolf Pack. "When do we leave?"

"As soon as you're packed."

"I'm ready. I never unpacked my bag." Her lips curved. "I was afraid we might have to leave the suite in a hurry overnight."

"Smart," Jackson commented. He poured her hot tea into a to-go cup and covered the top with a plastic lid. "You can drink your tea on the way to the airstrip."

While Eli checked out, Cal and the others gathered the bags and brought them to the suite. Twenty minutes later, they rode the elevator to the garage. Cal escorted her to the SUV and slid behind the wheel. He cranked the engine and pulled a signal detector from his pocket.

Rachelle's eyes widened. Why check the SUV? The chaser lights went from green to red. Oh, man.

Cal held up the gadget for Jackson to see, then sent a text to one of his teammates. He glanced at Rachelle and pressed his forefinger to his lips to indicate the need for silence.

She nodded. Who gained access to the SUV and planted a bug?

The ride to the airstrip was silent with Cal and Jackson watching for signs of trouble. By the time Cal parked near the tarmac, Rachelle's muscles ached from tension.

Would she and the operatives be prevented from leaving? Meyer, Caldwell, and Stokes wouldn't be happy when they realized she was gone. Would she be labeled a fugitive?

The operatives exited the vehicles. When Cal was satisfied the area was secure, he opened her door, tucked her against his side, and moved quickly to the Fortress jet.

In less than a minute, Wolf Pack had boarded the jet with the bags. As soon as the door was secured, Eli instructed the pilot to take off.

Worry gnawed at Rachelle. They had too many questions and not enough answers. How would they find the necessary information to track down their quarry? She wanted her life back and a chance to date Cal without wondering if Falcon would get her before the feds did.

A hard, warm hand covered her clenched fist. "You okay?"

"Not even close."

"What do you need?"

"Answers."

"We're working to find them as fast as we can. We want answers as much as you do."

She leaned her head against his shoulder. "I'm sorry," she whispered. "I know you're doing your best, but I'm frustrated and afraid."

His hand tightened. "I'll protect you with my life, Rachelle."

The reserve in his voice filled her with dismay. "I'm not afraid for myself. I'm afraid for you and your teammates. I don't want you hurt on my account."

"Baby, we're SEALs and highly trained black ops warriors."

"You can still be hurt and I don't want any of you injured."

Cal kissed her. "Thank you."

"For what?"

"Thinking of us. Most of our principals are only interested in protecting themselves."

Jon unbuckled his seatbelt and reached into the overhead bin for his laptop. He glanced at Cal and walked to the conference table.

"Ready?" Cal asked Rachelle.

Not really, but how else would she know what she was facing? Rachelle walked up the aisle with Cal, followed by the other operatives.

Sitting beside her, Cal nodded at Jon. "Let's take a look."

"Based on the way Stokes gloated, this won't be good," Rafe muttered.

No kidding. "That's what worries me."

Jon's fingers flew over the keyboard. Seconds later, the screen on the wall flickered to life, showing a picture of Rachelle with her back against a brick wall, Clint Nichols caging her in, a sleazy smile on his mouth.

"That never happened," Rachelle insisted.

Cal pressed a gentle kiss to her palm. "We'll examine the photos more closely after we view them all." He motioned for Jon to show the next one.

Each picture was worse than the one before. The worst photo appeared to be her on a bed with Nichols. "Oh, no." Tears burned her eyes. "That never happened, Cal." What must he think of her?

He didn't respond to her statement. "Is that all of them, Jon?"

His teammate nodded. "Want me to send them to Fortress or handle this ourselves?"

"We'll deal with it in-house." Cal stalked away from the table.

CHAPTER TWENTY-THREE

Needing to regain his control before he did something stupid and scared Rachelle, Cal walked into the bedroom. Bone-deep fury at the perp who made Rachelle's life miserable ate a hole in his gut along with frustration that he seemed incapable of helping her.

Who had set up Rachelle for a hard fall, and why? She was the least likely person to be the target of a criminal.

He crossed the room until he stood at the window, hands braced on either side. Was she a target because of him?

Pain speared him. As a SEAL and an operative, he protected his friends and family. Had he made a mistake and endangered Rachelle?

A soft noise behind Cal warned him that he wasn't alone. Rachelle. His teammates wouldn't have made a sound. He closed his eyes a moment. Although he loved being with her, he still hadn't reined in his temper.

"Cal."

If he'd drawn the attention of his enemies to Rachelle, he should walk away from her to keep her safe. Cal turned to face her. One look in her eyes, and Cal knew he couldn't let her go. She was already too deep in his heart. Losing her would leave him a shell, going through the motions without a purpose.

Rachelle hovered in the doorway, unsure of her welcome.

His heart squeezed. She thought he didn't want her. Never. He held out his hand. "Close the door," he murmured. Her face lost all color. When she turned back after doing as he asked, Cal said, "Come here." She moved to him, and he wrapped her in a tight embrace.

"I didn't meet Nichols in Mexico," she said. "I longed to be more than a friend to you. Hooking up with Nichols would be a betrayal. I've been a hundred percent honest with you from the day we met."

"Rachelle." He waited until her gaze lifted to meet his. "You don't have to explain. I know the pictures are a lie."

A tear slipped down her cheek. "I was afraid you didn't believe me, and that's why you came in here."

"I needed a minute to regain my control." His lips twitched. "Wouldn't be wise to punch a hole in the wall at 20,000 feet." He swiped the tears from her face and covered her mouth with his.

His kiss was gentle, offering comfort and a hint of how precious she was to him. Did she understand what he was telling her without words, what he'd discovered himself the minute she stepped into the bedroom?

He changed the angle of his head and deepened the kiss. Falling in love with Rachelle had blindsided him, and it was too soon to tell her. Wasn't it? They'd shared coffee dates for months. Did she suspect his feelings went deeper than he'd admitted?

Cal eased back and stared into her beautiful eyes, longing to tell her that he loved her. Would she reject him? He wasn't a good bet in a relationship. His job was unsafe, his schedule erratic.

"Is something wrong?"

Nothing, except the timing. Knee-knocking scary? Oh, yeah. He shook his head. "We should study those photos."

She grimaced. "Do we have to? Looking at them turns my stomach, especially the last one."

Seeing the photos tied his gut into knots. Even though they were fake, he didn't want his teammates seeing Rachelle that way. "Don't look at your face in the photos. Look at everything else. If we can't pinpoint something to prove the photos are fake, we'll have to turn them over to Fortress for assistance."

"I don't want to walk the halls every day and wonder if the people I pass saw the photos and believe I'm a two-timing cheat and liar who doesn't deserve to be with an honorable man like you."

"If we have to ask Fortress to help, I'll request that only Zane and Brent have access to the photos. Come on. We have work to do before we land." He led her into the main cabin where the others continued to examine the photos on the wall screen.

At the table, Cal seated himself beside Rachelle and threaded his fingers through hers in silent support. "Jon, show one photo at a time, full screen."

A moment later, the photo of Rachelle with her back pressed against a brick wall appeared on the screen. She flinched at the sight.

No one spoke as they studied the photo. Finally, Rafe said, "Looks like the photo was taken from the street. Enough of the storefront is visible to see the building is old and appears to be in Mexico."

"Could be photoshopped to look like it's in Mexico, but I agree with you." Jon zoomed in on the visible portion of the store window.

Cal frowned. "Enlarge the reflection on the left side."

Jon's fingers flew over the keyboard and the picture shifted to focus on the window reflection. A figure stared at Rachelle and Clint Nichols. The figure, a man, held a cell phone in his hands, taking a picture of the couple. "Focus on the man's face."

Jackson's brows knitted. "The cell phone blocks our view of his face."

"Should be enough for our facial recognition software to obtain a positive ID on him. Don't you recognize him?" Jon split the screen. One half showed the man with the cell phone. The other half was a clear photo of Clint Nichols.

Rachelle gasped. "It's Clint Nichols. If Nichols took the photo, he can't be in the alley."

"There's proof the man with Rachelle isn't Nichols." Eli inclined his head toward the screen. "Look at the woman against the wall. What do you see besides your face, sugar?"

She studied the screen, frowning. "I don't have an outfit like that."

"Someone could say you ditched the clothes," Rafe pointed out.

"That's not Rachelle," Cal said, voice soft. "The woman against the wall is taller than she is. Nichols is six feet two. That woman must be at least five feet ten where Rachelle is at least five inches shorter."

"Six," she muttered.

He smiled. "The point is, that can't be you, Rachelle."

Eli stared at the screen. "But Nichols isn't in the alley. We can't know how tall he is."

Cal waved his comment aside. "Jon can run the photo through our analysis program to show the woman's body type is wrong. If you look at the woman's hand, you'll see it's not Rachelle's." He ought to know. He'd dreamed about those hands trailing over his chest and shoulders for months.

He glanced at Rachelle who continued to stare at the screen with a puzzled expression on her face. "What did you notice?"

"I saw a woman in Mexico wearing those clothes."

"Do you know if the outfit is off the rack or designer?" Rafe asked.

"A fashionista, I am not. However, I only saw one woman wearing those clothes."

Cal squeezed her hand. "Do you remember who?"

"A young woman, I think."

Jackson frowned. "Jon, change the focus to zoom in on the couple." When he did, the medic was silent for a long minute, then glanced at Eli. "Rachelle's right. The girl is young enough to be jailbait."

A scowl. "Underage?"

"Based on what I'm seeing in the photo, yes."

A ball of ice formed in Cal's stomach. "She could be 18."

"Maybe." The medic didn't sound convinced.

Cal turned to Rachelle. "Do you remember where you saw her?"

She shook her head. "Amy and I traveled to so many cities, they blurred together."

"Think about the day you saw her in relation to the terrorist attack. What day did you see her?" Narrowing the time frame might spark her memory of the place where she'd seen the girl. Whether the girl was important or a convenient tool to frame Rachelle remained to be seen. Cal believed the girl was important.

Her eyes widened. "I saw her the afternoon before the attack."

"Where?" he prompted.

"Antigua. Amy delivered two speeches the day of the attack, the first one at noon, the other at 6:00 that evening."

"Excellent. Ignore the faces in the photo. Do you remember seeing a couple in an alley in that position?"

She bit her lower lip. "Something about them is familiar, but I'm not sure."

"Close your eyes. Take a deep breath. Good. Again. Relax and let your mind drift back to the day before the attack." When the lines of her body softened, he murmured, "Tell me what you did from the time you arrived in Antigua."

Rachelle frowned. "Why do you want to know all that?"

"I'm interested in your day."

She looked skeptical, but recounted her movements with Amy, beginning with the check-in to the hotel. As she continued to describe her movements in the afternoon and into the early evening, Rachelle stopped in mid-sentence and tightened her grip on Cal's hand. "I did see them."

"Where and when?"

"A block from the hotel as we were going out for dinner."

"Close your eyes again. Focus on the man in the alley. Picture his face. Can you see him?"

"Not well. I was on the other side of the street. Amy and I were walking with Tim and Eric to the restaurant."

He frowned. "Why didn't they drive you?"

"Amy wanted fresh air and the restaurant was two blocks from the hotel."

"Do you recognize the man in the alley?"

"I don't think so."

"Did Amy see the couple?"

Rachelle opened her eyes, a smile curving her lips. "Are you kidding? She only had eyes for Eric. And before you ask, I don't think Eric saw the couple either."

"What about the woman? Can you see her face?"

She remained silent for a while, then sighed. "I'm sorry. I saw them for a second in passing. I remember thinking his behavior was inappropriate in public."

"Did she behave the same way?"

She blinked. "No. That's odd, isn't it?"

"Not if she's underage and under duress," Rafe murmured.

"You're amazing, Rachelle." Cal raised her hand to his mouth and kissed her knuckles. He glanced at Jon. "Go to the next picture."

When the new photo popped onto the screen, Jackson's eyes narrowed. "Zoom in on the couple." The perspective shifted to bring the couple into focus. "Same girl. Different clothes."

Rafe growled. "No convenient window reflection this time."

"If the girl is the same, chances are good this is photoshopped as well. I bet Nichols is the photographer for this picture, too."

"Too bad he's not in the States. We could send someone from Fortress to question him."

"Still can." Jon looked at Cal. "Our operatives cross the globe all the time. Maddox could dispatch a team to do a grab-and-go."

Cal considered it, then shook his head. "Not yet. Nichols is well guarded and I don't want to risk a team if we can unearth the information by other means."

"Jon, zoom in on the lower right-hand corner." Rafe studied the design on the wall of the building in the background. He frowned. "That's Rosita's, a bar and grill in Antigua."

"You've been to Antigua?" Eli asked.

"Once with the FBI." A muscle in his jaw twitched. "Rosita's is a known meat market."

Rachelle stared. "Meat market?"

"Girls and women auctioned off to the highest bidder for as long as you want them. You pay a higher price for longer entertainment. Returning them alive is preferred, but not required."

"You couldn't shut it down?" Cal demanded.

"The mayor and chief of police are clients at Rosita's. What do you think?"

"You should have torched the place," Jackson said.

"Wasted effort. Nichols and his cronies would have set up somewhere else in town. Besides, the feds take a dim view of agents who go off the reservation. The US would like to maintain good relations with Mexico. Burning down a building wouldn't be conducive to good public relations."

"Nichols is a human trafficker." Rachelle looked at Cal. "Would the Shadow unit know him?"

"I'd be surprised if they didn't." Most of Shadow unit's missions involved taking down human traffickers. "I'll see if Nico is available to talk." Cal grabbed his phone and sent a text to Nico Rivera, Shadow unit's leader.

His phone rang a minute later. Cal put the call on speaker. "It's Cal. You're on speaker with Wolf Pack and Rachelle Carter."

"Hello, Rachelle. I hear you had some excitement on your vacation."

"That's the understatement of the century."

"I'm glad you escaped without injury. So, Wolf Pack, huh?" Nico laughed. "Has to be Eli's choice."

"Hey, it's a good name," Eli protested.

"It has a ring to it," Nico agreed. "What do you need?"

"Anything you have on Clint Nichols."

A growl came over the speaker. "He's a thorn in our side although we haven't crossed paths with him yet. If we had, we would've taken care of him. That man is pure evil."

"How so?" Jon asked.

"He's connected to the movers and shakers in Mexico. His sister married a heavy hitter in Mexican politics and that gave Nichols his introduction into the halls of power. He's made bank on the connections. Doesn't hurt that he's a slick charmer who fools people into believing he's a decent human being until his true colors show."

"Blackmail?"

"That's part of it. He's an all-purpose sleaze, but Nichols' main source of income is special requests."

Cal's gut clenched. "Special requests?"

"He provides companions for wealthy and powerful politicians who prefer underage girls. Tell Maddox if he wants us to do a grab-and-go with Nichols, Shadow will do it for free."

Had Rachelle seen a powerful politician with the girl in the photo?

CHAPTER TWENTY-FOUR

Cal's gaze shifted to Rachelle. "Do you remember what street you were on when you saw the couple in the alley?"

"Avenida Juarez."

"Jon, can you access street or security cams in that area?"

"If the cameras are active, yes. Rachelle, what time did you go to dinner?"

"Eight o'clock."

"I'll see what I can find. Might take a while."

Eli smiled. "You don't have anything to do for the next hour. Should be a breeze for a man who types faster than the speed of sound. Go to the next picture."

They analyzed each photo. When the final one appeared on the screen, grim expressions settled on the faces of Cal's teammates.

"We know that's not you." Cal squeezed Rachelle's hand. "How do we prove it with this photo?"

"The girl has two tattoos, one on her ankle and one on the inside of her wrist. I don't have any."

"Could be explained as a temporary tattoo. Do you notice anything else?"

She shook her head.

Rafe pointed at the screen. "Zoom in on the man's right shoulder blade. What is that?"

The view shifted to an enhanced view of the shoulder blade. "Tattoo."

"Can you clean that up?" Cal demanded.

Jon's fingers flew over the keyboard. Seconds later, a clearer view of the tattoo filled the screen.

Rachelle stared. "That's a bird."

Cal's free hand fisted. "A falcon."

"This man is the reason you have a price on your head, Rachelle," Eli said. "You saw a heavy hitter with an underage girl in that alley."

"I saw them for a second," she protested. "I can't identify him."

"He thinks you did," Jackson said. "Worse, he got a good look at you."

She paled. "He recognized Amy and figured out who I was by association."

Rafe frowned. "Anyone looking at this picture wouldn't be able to tell the man is Clint Nichols. All we see is his back. Does Nichols have a falcon tattoo?"

"I'll ask Maddox to send Shadow to grab him and find out," Eli said. "Do the feds want Nichols?"

"Oh, yeah. He's slippery, though. Every time we sent a team after him, Nichols was conveniently absent."

"I'll bet no one knew where he was, either," Jon said.

Rafe's lips curled. "How did you know?"

The sniper snorted. "My gut says this man is Falcon, not Nichols. Since he's into blackmail, Nichols would love to wave this picture in Falcon's face and demand a payout to remain quiet."

Eli made a call, putting it on speaker.

Maddox answered seconds later. "What do you need, Wolfe?"

"Clint Nichols. He's involved in an attempt to frame Rachelle and hand her to the feds."

"Explain."

Eli told Maddox about the photos and the proof that they were photoshopped. "Nico volunteered his team to grab Nichols and check his back."

"The feds want Nichols," Rafe said. "They'll be happy to have him gift wrapped and left for pick up. An anonymous tip should take care of the rest."

"That's not enough to send a team to nab this guy."

"Nichols heads a human trafficking operation that specializes in providing minors for hire, especially for the rich and powerful," Cal said. "We think Rachelle saw a man known as Falcon the night before the attack at the hotel, a client of Nichols."

"Proof?"

"Thin," he admitted. "That's why we need Nichols. If he doesn't have a falcon tattoo, then he knows who this man is. He's probably using the photos for blackmail. It's what he does."

Maddox said, "If we do this, the feds will owe us a favor. I like them in our debt. All right. Done. I'll reroute Shadow to Antigua."

"Tell them to be careful," Rachelle said. "The terrorists might be in the area."

"We need to talk about the gunmen."

Cal frowned. "What about them?"

"Zane has camera footage of the men involved in the attacks at the hotel and the hospital. They aren't terrorists. They're connected to human traffickers in the area."

"In other words, they're connected to Clint Nichols."

"You got it."

"Human traffickers again." Jackson scrubbed his face with his hands. "Why come after Rachelle? She's not a threat to their operation."

"If she connects Clint Nichols and the girl in the photos to Falcon, their whole operation is in jeopardy," Cal said. "He won't go down alone. He'll take Nichols and his operation with him. Yeah, Rachelle is a definite threat."

"Especially if this man is a well-known power broker," Maddox added. "Rachelle, what are your thoughts?"

"The man knows Amy. How would he identify me otherwise?"

"Nichols is American," Jon said. "Falcon could be American as well."

"I was thinking the same thing. If you connect Nichols to the gunmen who attacked the hotel, shot Hoss, and killed Garner, he'll leave the federal penitentiary in a body bag."

"Nichols is well protected," Rafe said. "Shadow might need help."

"Copy that. Need anything else, Wolfe?"

"Keep the feds off our backs," Eli said. "Meyer and company had more questions for Rachelle. They won't be happy when they discover we left town. They'll send law enforcement after Rachelle if her location is leaked."

"Rachelle, do you need anything?"

"No, sir." She glanced at Cal. "I have exactly what I need."

His heart skipped a beat. If they didn't have an audience, he'd kiss her senseless for saying that. He prayed she meant what she said.

"We land in Maple Valley in an hour," Eli told Maddox. "I'll check in when we're at the Rocking M."

"Copy that." Maddox ended the call.

Eli stood. "Rest until we land. We'll need it."

Rachelle walked with Cal to their seats. "Why did Eli say we should rest?"

"Eli's gut is telling him this mission is heating up."

"How does he know?"

"He feels it." Just like Cal. "We've been on enough missions to know when something is ready to break. Falcon is afraid you'll identify him and is desperate to silence you before you expose him as a murderer and pedophile."

"I saw his face for a split second, not long enough to recognize him."

"Falcon doesn't know that. To him, you're a threat."

Rachelle sighed. "He must have money at his disposal if he persuaded human traffickers to attack a hotel and hospital in their hometown. Wouldn't Antigua law enforcement recognize them?"

"If enough money greases their palms, they'll develop convenient amnesia."

"Oh, man. Shadow shouldn't go to Antigua."

"Don't worry. Shadow is the best at what they do. If any team has the ability to snatch Nichols from under the noses of his bodyguards, it's Shadow."

Cal grabbed a blanket from one of the overhead bins. When she snuggled against his side, he spread the blanket over them. "Relax for a few minutes."

"We should be doing research."

"Give your body time to recharge. Besides, I need to hold you."

She smiled. "You won't hear me complain."

"Sleep, baby. You'll remember more when you're rested and relaxed."

"I doubt I'll be able to sleep. I'm almost vibrating with adrenaline and tension."

She'd crash soon. "Close your eyes. Let me enjoy holding you."

Within five minutes, Rachelle was asleep. Cal dozed, waking when the jet's airspeed and altitude changed. Nearby, his teammates prepared for landing.

Cal kissed Rachelle's forehead. "Rachelle."

"Mmm." She snuggled deeper into his arms.

"Wake up. We land soon."

She blinked. "I can't believe I fell asleep again."

Cal chuckled. "You were warm and safe. Adrenaline dump did the rest."

When the jet landed, the operatives grabbed their gear and headed for the SUVs, alert as they crossed the tarmac. After helping Rachelle into the vehicle, Cal stored their gear in the back. He got behind the wheel and Jackson slid into the backseat.

At the Rocking M, Mrs. Grady greeted them. "Welcome back," she said, beaming. "Was your trip successful?"

"We learned a few things," Cal said.

She laughed. "You sound like David, giving me an answer that tells me nothing but satisfies most of my curiosity."

"It's for your own safety, Mrs. Grady," Eli said. "Sometimes, less knowledge is safer."

"I understand. Store your bags in your rooms. Lunch is ready."

When they arrived in the kitchen for their meal, Cal's mouth watered at the feast of chicken pot pies with banana pudding for dessert. He'd have to run extra miles when his team resumed training.

"Mrs. Grady, this is fabulous," Rachelle said after eating a bite. "I hope you'll share your recipe."

"Of course, dear."

After lunch, Eli checked in with Maddox. When he ended the call, he told the others, "Shadow's been diverted with Zane providing tech support. Rafe, Jackson and I will guard the perimeter of the house. Jon, are you making progress?"

"Should have something soon."

Wolf Pack's leader rolled his eyes. "Cryptic much?" He glanced at Cal. "Stay with Rachelle. Check in with Amy and Eric. I'll touch base with Brody."

"Copy that." He also had a friend who was a tattoo artist and well known in that community. Artie might know who created the falcon tattoo.

After the rest of Wolf Pack scattered, Cal and Rachelle helped Mrs. Grady clear the table. When they finished, Cal led Rachelle to the library. "Check on Amy and Eric. I want to call a friend who's a tattoo artist."

After Rachelle curled up on the couch and called Amy, Cal moved to the far end of the library to talk to Artie.

"Artistic Ink," a bass voice growled into the phone.

"It's Cal."

"Been a while, buddy. Where you been?"

"Here and there."

A chuckle. "Still as talkative as always."

"Got a minute?"

"Hold." Artie's voice became muffled, then the background noise disappeared. "What do you need?"

"Email address still the same?"

"Yep."

Cal sent a cropped picture of the tattoo. "Check your email. Have you seen this tattoo?"

"I've seen it. In fact, I created the design."

He stilled. "Did you give the design to another artist to use?"

"No way, man. You know how proprietary I am. This business is competitive. I'm not about to hand over one of my specialty designs."

"Do you know who chose that design?"

"I used it twice. Hang on a sec." Artie set the phone down with a thunk. A minute later, he said, "Got it. A woman and a man chose the design."

"Are they Americans?"

"Yep. Why?"

"Might be important." He already knew what Artie would say to his next question. "What are their names?"

"You know I can't tell you that. They're clients, Cal. If I revealed names, I wouldn't have a business for long."

"My woman's life is on the line. I believe the man wearing your tattoo is involved with attempts to kill my girlfriend. I need his name."

"Are you playing me?"

"As one SEAL to another, I'm telling you the truth."

"I don't know, Cal."

"You owe me."

"Aww, man. Are you serious?"

"Try me."

Artie blew out a breath. "Your girl means that much to you?"

Cal glanced over his shoulder at Rachelle. "She's everything."

"We're square after this, right?"

"Yeah, buddy. We're square. I need a name."

"Don Hale. He's some bigwig in D.C."

He froze. "Are you telling me the Under Secretary of State is wearing that tattoo?"

"Yep. Fine piece of craftsmanship."

"Yeah, it's a work of art, buddy. I should have recognized your handiwork."

"I gotta get back to work. Got customers waiting. Need anything else?"

"No. Thanks, Artie. You might have saved my girlfriend's life."

"I don't know what you've gotten yourself into, Cal, but watch your back. Crossing Hale isn't healthy. He don't mind throwing his weight or money around."

"Thanks for the warning." He ended the call, gritting his teeth. Brent wouldn't be pleased when he learned the truth. He should abort Shadow's mission. No need to risk Nico and his team.

Since Rachelle was still engrossed in her conversation with Amy, Cal walked outside and called Brent.

"Maddox."

"We have a problem."

A snort. "What else is new? Talk to me."

"I know the identity of the man with the tattoo."

"How? Eli sent the pictures to my email. You can't see Falcon's face."

"I called a SEAL teammate who is a tattoo artist. Turns out he's the one who designed the tattoo, and he's only used the design twice. Once on a man, once on a woman."

"Definitely not a woman in that picture. What's his name?"

"Don Hale."

"Under Secretary of State Don Hale?"

"The same."

"He has deep pockets with connections in every branch of government and has aspirations to be President of the United States."

"Call off Shadow's mission."

"No. Capturing him will strike a blow to the human trafficking operation in that region and make our job easier on future missions."

"Until another sleaze takes over Nichols' operation or starts one of his own."

"One battle at a time, Cal. First, we need proof Don Hale is the man in the photos."

"We're working on it. Jon's scouring the cam footage on Avenida Juarez at the time Rachelle saw the couple in the pictures."

"To find the right angle for a clear picture will be a stroke of luck."

"We have a name. That's more than we had before my call to Artie."

"I haven't talked to Artie Hammond in a long while. Is he sure the man with the tattoo is Hale?"

"Afraid so."

"What do you want to do?"

"Take Rachelle on a nice, long vacation to a deserted island somewhere in the Caribbean."

"How can I help?"

"I need alternate ID for Rachelle."

CHAPTER TWENTY-FIVE

Rachelle settled deeper into the couch. "I'm glad Eric is improving. Jesse is a great medic."

"He's dedicated. Every time I look in on Eric during the night, Jesse is awake, watching over Eric. I don't think the man sleeps at all."

"The operatives are like Superman. They don't quit until the job's finished."

"So, how are things going with your friend?" Amy asked. "You and Cal looked pretty cozy before you left us."

She smiled. "We're officially dating now."

"That's great! Too bad you can't go on real dates instead of hiding."

"We squeezed in a few dates."

"Were they good ones?" Amy teased.

"They were perfect." She lowered her voice, aware of Cal standing across the room. "He's the most thoughtful man I've ever had the privilege to know."

"You sound as though you're smitten with the handsome operative."

Smitten didn't come close to describing how she felt about Cal Taylor. "You could say that."

A gasp. "Rachelle, are you in love with him?"

"Maybe." Head over heels.

"How long have you known him?"

"A year." The best day of her life was the day he walked into her office to speak to Micah.

"For coffee dates. Come on. You can't be that serious about him this soon."

She laughed. "And how quickly after you met Eric did I start hearing about the hot DSS agent assigned to guard you?"

"The next day," Amy admitted.

"Two weeks after that, you told me you were in love with him." Her smile faded as she watched Cal leave the room by the French doors. He seemed upset. What had he learned? "My feelings for Cal have grown for a year."

"Are you sure, Rachelle?" Worry filled her friend's voice.

"Why wouldn't I be?"

"He's in black ops. The work is dangerous. He could be injured or die on a mission."

"He could be an accountant and die in a car accident or plane crash, too. Every minute I have with him is a blessing." She'd regret walking away and losing the chance to create something wonderful with him.

"I hope you know what you're doing."

When Rachelle ended the call, she shoved her phone into her pocket and walked outside in time to hear Cal request an alternate ID for her.

She stilled. Oh, man. The news Cal learned must be terrible for him to consider sending her off the grid under a new name.

Cal turned and held out his hand. When she went to him, he wrapped his arm around her and pulled her close. "Let me know when you have everything ready. Thanks, Brent." He shoved the phone into his pocket.

"How bad?" she asked, voice soft.

"Enough to warrant a backup plan."

"Tell me."

"I called a former SEAL teammate who's a tattoo artist. Artie's lives outside of D.C. He recognized the falcon design."

Her brows knitted. "A lot of tattoo artists might use that design."

"Artie created the design and won't share it. He used the design twice, once on a man, once on a woman."

Her breath caught. "If he knows the identity of the man in the picture, that's good news. Why are you upset?"

"The man wearing the tattoo on his back is Under Secretary of State Don Hale."

"He's not above the law."

"We need absolute proof he's guilty, Rachelle. No one will arrest Hale on your word alone."

"We'll find the proof."

"Until he's behind bars, Hale is a danger to you. He has influence and money. Going after him will create a firestorm with you in the center. You'll be a target of the media, Hale's political cronies, and hitmen unless we find a way to lift the contract."

"What do you want to do?"

"Take you to a deserted island for an extended vacation where I can treat you like a princess and concentrate fully on you."

Her eyes burned. Sounded like a dream come true. "You can't, though. You have an important job to do. Why is Brent creating a new name and background for me?"

"If we can't find a way to bring down Hale soon, we'll disappear until Wolf Pack finishes the job."

He would hate leaving Hale to his teammates. "You're talking about the Fortress witness protection program for both of us?"

"I won't send you into a new life without me."

"What about your family?"

He smiled. "I'm a SEAL and an operative. We'll see our families."

"I can't let you give up your life." Her voice broke. "The sacrifice is too great."

"You are my life." Cal's voice was gentle. "I wouldn't survive without you."

Rachelle's breath caught. He couldn't mean that. Could he? "I don't understand." But she wanted to.

He lowered his head and captured her mouth with his. Molten heat shot through her veins at his possessive touch.

Long minutes later, Cal lifted his head, his eyes glittering with desire and another emotion she couldn't name. He drew in a slow, deep breath as though steadying himself. "I love you," he said simply. "I've waited a lifetime for you, Rachelle. If you go into witness protection, I'll go with you."

Stunned, she couldn't form coherent thoughts. Her heart raced in a mad rhythm. "I don't know what to say."

He cupped her cheek with a trembling hand. "If it's the truth, tell me you love me. I don't want a lie to spare my feelings."

Rachelle kissed him. "I love you so much I can hardly breathe at times, Cal."

He closed his eyes for a second. "Thank God. If you'd rejected me, I would have launched a campaign to win your heart."

She smiled. "I fell for you on our first coffee date. I didn't believe I had a real chance with you, though."

"When I walked into Micah's outer office and saw you behind that desk, no other woman held any interest for me."

"I heard the women at work talking about their plans to ask you on a date."

"They asked. I turned them down. I haven't dated anyone but you in the past year."

"Why didn't you ask me to dinner or a movie?"

"Every time I worked up the courage, Brent sent me for more training or on a mission. When I returned, the cycle started over again with the coffee dates."

"I would have said yes."

"Good to know. The pace gave me the opportunity to know you better without the pressure of dating expectations." He smiled. "You didn't realize I was courting you slow and easy. SEALs excel at stealth."

"Mission accomplished. You stole my heart."

Cal sobered. "You own mine."

At that moment, Eli jogged around the corner of the house. "We've got trouble."

Cal straightened. "What is it?"

"Brody called. A team of men triggered the safe-house sensors at the half-mile mark. They're closing fast. Texas needs backup."

"Could be a diversion."

"I know. You staying or going?"

"Going," Rachelle said. "Your team needs you, Cal."

"So do you." He rubbed the back of his neck. "Let's move you into the safe room. Don't come out for any reason until I come for you."

Cal gripped her hand and led her to his bedroom first. He dug into his bag. When he stood again, Cal showed her two small skin-colored patches. "These are trackers. For my peace of mind, will you wear them until I return?"

"Of course." Whatever he needed to be able to concentrate on his job instead of worrying about her.

He placed one patch behind her ear where she'd worn the anti-nausea patch. Cal looked into her eyes. "Trust me?" When she nodded, he lifted the back of her shirt and pressed the second tracker to the small of her back. "If anything happens, don't touch the trackers. If you do, the wrong person might notice."

Goosebumps surged across her skin. "All right."

"Come on." He grabbed his bag and ran with her to the first-floor library. In seconds, she was inside the room. He pressed a hard kiss to her mouth. "I love you." He closed the door and left.

Rachelle turned to the wall of monitors and sat at the desk. Every screen showed a different view of the house, inside and out, and various parts of the ranch.

She watched Wolf Pack gear up in less than a minute and run with their Go bags to the SUVs. They left in a cloud of dust.

Rachelle shifted her attention from screen to screen. Although she longed to call Amy, she didn't want to endanger or distract her friend. Wolf Pack would arrive at the house in minutes. They already knew the lay of the land, an advantage the visitors didn't have. Eric couldn't run and Amy wouldn't leave without him. She didn't blame her friend. If Cal was injured, Rachelle wouldn't leave him.

A short while later, movement on two screens caught her attention. Rachelle frowned. A group of hands were moving closer to the house. Were they coming for a late lunch?

She started to turn her attention to another screen when Lefty, one of the cowhands Rachelle recognized, moved to intercept the group of men. One of them raised his weapon and slammed the butt of a gun onto the side of Lefty's head.

She gasped as the cowhand sank to the ground, unmoving. Rachelle grabbed her phone. Afraid to alert the enemy to his location with a phone call, she sent Cal a text to tell him what happened. He'd been right. The attack on the Texas unit was a diversion to lure Wolf Pack from the ranch.

She didn't know how soon Wolf Pack could return. There were many real cowhands on this ranch and a few fake ones. Hopefully, Wolf Pack would arrive in time to prevent a disaster.

Her phone chimed. Cal. Help is coming. Stay in place. Thank goodness. All they had to do was hang on until help arrived.

She shoved her phone back into her pocket and scanned the screens again. The strangers had disappeared from view, and that worried her. Cal had complained about the gaps in camera coverage when they memorized escape routes and chose safe places to hide. Looked as though he was right.

On one of the screens, she watched Mrs. Grady return to the kitchen and remove a bag of potatoes from the pantry to start dinner preparations. A ball of ice formed in Rachelle's stomach. She should warn Mrs. Grady that trouble was closing in on the ranch house. But she'd promised to stay in this room until Cal returned.

Before she decided what to do, the back door to the kitchen burst open. The group of strangers rushed into the room. One grabbed Mrs. Grady and forced her to one of the chairs at the kitchen table. He pressed a gun to Mrs. Grady's temple, his gaze locked on the security camera in the corner of the room. He mouthed the words, "Come out, Rachelle, or she dies. One minute."

Rachelle pressed a hand to her mouth. No, no, no. She couldn't let them kill that sweet lady.

She sent Cal another text. "They captured Mrs. Grady and have a gun to her head. They said if I don't come out, they'll kill her."

His response came seconds later. "On my way. Stall, baby."

"I love you," she texted, then slid her phone away. She entered the code to open the door to the safe room.

Rachelle closed the door behind her and walked toward the kitchen.

One of the strangers emerged from the shadows and clasped her upper arm in a tight grip. "Hello, Rachelle Carter. We've been looking for you," he murmured, voice low. He propelled her into the midst of the group of armed thugs.

Tears filled Mrs. Grady's eyes. "Rachelle, you should have stayed hidden."

"I couldn't let them hurt you."

The man with the gun to Mrs. Grady's head glanced at his friend standing a few feet away from Rachelle and the man gripping her arm. "Do it."

Do what? She turned, eyes widening when she saw him step forward with a hypodermic needle in his hand. Rachelle tried to tear her arm from the thug's grasp. "No!"

"Shut up," he snapped. The man grabbed her hair and wrapped the strands around his fist to hold her immobile. His compatriot uncapped the hypodermic and plunged the needle into her neck.

Mrs. Grady cried out in horror.

Seconds later, Rachelle sank into darkness.

CHAPTER TWENTY-SIX

Cal tracked his quarry through the woods near the safe house where Amy and Eric were holed up with the Texas team. At last count, ten men were roaming the woods, moving closer to the house by the minute.

Eli ordered Texas to stay in place to protect Eric and Amy because his gut said something was wrong. This might be a ploy to draw them from the house and leave the ambassador's daughter and her boyfriend vulnerable to attack.

The knots in Cal's stomach indicated his team leader was right about one thing. Something was wrong. He worried this was an elaborate smokescreen to lure Wolf Pack from the Rocking M and Rachelle. Amy wasn't the target. Rachelle was. But Wolf Pack couldn't afford to ignore Brody's call for backup.

Rachelle was in the safe room until he and his teammates returned to the ranch. Attackers couldn't touch her. Still, he wouldn't breathe easy until the woman he loved was in his arms again.

Twigs snapped ahead of Cal. He shifted his angle of approach, hugging the shadows. The sooner they took care of these troublemakers and returned to the Rocking M, the better. Eli's famous gut was never wrong.

A minute later, he spotted his target, stalking through the underbrush, a weapon clutched in his hand. The man wore jeans and a cowboy shirt similar to the ones used by the ranch hands at the Rocking M. A frisson of uneasiness slithered up his spine.

"One down," Rafe whispered through the comm system.

"Two down," Jackson murmured.

Cal moved behind the man who turned at the last second. He slammed his elbow into the man's jaw before he uttered a warning to his comrades. An audible crack sounded in the air as the man fell to the ground, motionless.

Cal kicked away his gun, rolled him to his stomach, and cinched his wrists with a zip tie. One of the Montgomery boys could scoop him up. "Three down."

Jon and Eli reported one down for each of them.

Cal continued through the woods, moving closer to the house. Five tangos down. Five to go. Urgency pushed him to quicken his pace. Discipline drilled into him through years and hundreds of missions as a SEAL reined him in and forced him to move with caution.

At the edge of the clearing where the safe house had been built, another intruder crouched with a weapon in hand, aiming at the living room window. A second one hunkered fifteen feet away with his Sig aimed at the bedroom window where Eric lay.

Cal changed direction and worked his way toward the second man. The guy waited beside a large rock. Cal checked the angle. Good. He could work with that.

"You see anything?" the first man called softly to his buddy.

"No."

"I think those bodyguards are a bunch of cowards or just plain stupid."

"Shut up," the second man hissed.

The two fell silent again until a shout on the other side of the clearing was cut off in mid-yell.

"What was that?"

"Trouble."

Cal smiled. More trouble than those men knew.

"Six down," Rafe murmured over the comm system.

Closing in on his target, Cal clamped one hand over the man's mouth and wrapped his arm around the man's throat, choking him out in seconds. Had to love a good sleeper hold, he thought, as he lay the man on the ground and cinched his wrists together. "Seven down," he whispered.

Retracing his steps, Cal came up behind the first man. Something must have warned the cowboy that danger was near because he turned at the last second. He scowled, rose, and pivoted to aim his weapon toward Cal.

Cal kicked the weapon from his hand and tackled him. Cowboy landed a roundhouse punch to Cal's jaw, threw him off, and dived on top of him to wrap meaty hands around his throat. Cowboy grinned as he squeezed, constricting Cal's throat, cutting off his ability to breathe.

Cal slammed his fists against the crook of the man's elbows, yanked him down, and wrapped his leg around the other man's. He used his hip to buck Cowboy off, reversed their positions, and slammed his fist once, twice, three times into the man's face. The thug's eyes rolled back in his head.

After Cal secured Cowboy's hands, he activated his mic. "Eight down." His phone vibrated in his pocket. Scanning to be sure no threats were near, Cal checked the screen. Rachelle.

He read the short message, fear for her exploding in his gut. Cal activated his mic. "Trouble at the Rocking M. Armed gunmen heading for the house."

"Copy," Eli whispered. "Contact David. I'm on nine."

"Roger that." Swallowing hard, he called David Montgomery. "Trouble at the ranch. Armed gunmen are headed toward the house."

"We're already headed that direction, but we're on the other side of the county."

"ETA?"

"Fifteen minutes."

An eternity when you stared down the barrel of a gun. At least, Rachelle was in the safe room. The gunmen wouldn't get their hands on her as along as she stayed put. "Copy that."

He ended the call and sent Rachelle a text. "Help is coming. Stay in place."

Sliding his phone away, Cal resumed the hunt for the tenth man, fighting every instinct he had to stay on task rather than race to the ranch to protect Rachelle.

"Nine down," Eli whispered. "Jon?"

"Nothing," came the soft response. "Ten is out here. I feel him."

"Let's find him and get back to the ranch."

"Copy that."

The next few minutes were spent combing the woods near the house. Finally, Jackson whispered, "Ten down."

Thank God. "Eli."

"Go. I'll contact Brody, tell him we took down ten tangos. David can send a cleanup crew to collect the trash out here. Our priority is Rachelle."

No longer concerned about stealth, Cal ran to the SUVs and stored his gear in the backseat as Jackson sprinted from the cover of the trees. The medic climbed into the passenger seat, dropping his mike bag beside Cal's gear.

Cal started the engine and shoved the SUV into gear as his teammates raced for the second SUV.

His phone vibrated. Cal tossed it to Jackson. "Read it."

"It's Rachelle. The gunmen breached the house and are threatening to kill Mrs. Grady if Rachelle doesn't give herself up in the next minute."

Cal floored the SUV.

"What do I tell her?"

He longed to order Rachelle to remain in the safe room, but knew without asking that she wouldn't comply. Cal didn't blame her. "On my way. Stall, baby."

Seconds later, his phone buzzed again. He glanced at Jackson whose eyebrows shot up. "What did she say?"

"I love you." The medic looked at him. "Is there something you want to tell the class, Taylor?"

"I'm going to marry that woman one day soon."

Jackson reached over and squeezed Cal's shoulder. "Congratulations, Cal. You're a lucky man."

"A man blessed beyond measure." His stomach twisted into a knot. "I can't lose her."

"You won't. She's smart and resourceful. These men don't know who they're going up against. We'll take them down."

Of course they would. But would they reach the ranch in time to spare Rachelle's life? Cal wouldn't let himself think of the worst. She had to be alive when they reached the Rocking M. He honestly didn't know how he would react if she wasn't.

Driving well past the speed limit, Cal slid around curves and floored the accelerator on the straightaways, praying every mile.

Finally, the entrance to the ranch came into view. Since the gates stood open, Cal barreled through the opening and raced to the ranch house. Police SUVs with lights still circling were parked in front of the house. Cal bailed from the SUV with his Sig in hand and raced toward the front door.

The knob turned easily under his hand. Stepping to the side of the frame, he eased the door open. He heard David's voice, then the voice of one of his brothers.

"It's Cal and the rest of Wolf Pack," he called out. "We're coming in soft."

"Kitchen," came the response.

He and Jackson hurried toward the back of the house. Cal stopped when he saw Mrs. Grady weeping in David's arms, the side of her face streaked with blood.

His gaze swept the room, breath stalling in his lungs. No Rachelle. Cal turned back to David. "Where's Rachelle?"

"They took her before we arrived. I'm sorry, Cal. We have a BOLO out on them, but they're driving black SUVs and have a head start on us. They could be anywhere by now." The sheriff tossed him a phone. "Found this on the floor. Is it Rachelle's?"

Rage swelled inside him. "Yeah, it is." Whoever these men were, they'd regret the day they laid their hands on his woman.

"Tracking her phone is out, then."

"Got it covered." Thank God he'd thought ahead to this possibility. He called Zane.

"What do you need?" his friend asked.

"Activate my trackers. Rachelle is wearing two of them. A group of armed men kidnapped her."

After a flurry of typing, the tech wizard said, "Done. I sent the link to your phone. How else can I help?"

Cal glanced at David. "License plates?" The chief of police raised his eyebrows but rattled off the tags which Cal relayed to Zane.

"Got it."

"Probably rentals, but see what you can find." He glanced at David again. "If you want Fortress to assist in identifying the perps, give us access to your security camera footage. We'll send the footage to our head tech."

David frowned. "We have our own system."

"Ours is better and faster," Jon said. "We're wasting time. Do you want our help or not?"

The policeman exchanged glances with Levi, then gave a tight nod and led Jon to the safe room.

Cal said, "Jon is accessing the Rocking M's security system. You should receive footage soon."

"Copy that. I'll watch the tracker signal. You'll get her back, Cal."

Yeah, he would. His hand tightened around the phone until his knuckles were white. "Thanks, Z." He ended the call and checked his text messages. His heart squeezed at seeing Rachelle's last message. He loved her so much he could barely breathe at the thought of what she might be going through at that moment.

Cal tapped the tracking link Zane had sent him. A blinking red light showed Rachelle moving quickly to the east. He frowned. Where were the men taking her?

Cal checked the map and sucked in a harsh breath. No. If he didn't catch up to Rachelle soon, it might be too late.

"What's wrong?" Levi demanded.

"Rachelle is headed toward the airstrip. I think they're going to fly her out of here."

CHAPTER TWENTY-SEVEN

Rachelle opened her eyes and frowned. Where was she? The familiar sound of an engine filled her ears. A plane? Why was she on a plane again?

Uncomfortable and unable to move, she glanced at her hands in the dim light. Adrenaline poured into her bloodstream. Handcuffs that bound her hands were attached to a chain connected to the headboard of a bed. Her arms stretched taut over her head.

How did she end up in this place? Her mind cleared in a rush. A thug pointed a gun at Mrs. Grady's head and threatened to shoot her if Rachelle didn't give herself up. She'd complied, unwilling to let the sweet housekeeper suffer. Her memory was blank after one of the thugs jabbed a needle in her neck. Whatever he'd shot into her system had knocked her out within seconds. She prayed the drug wasn't habit forming.

Rachelle tugged experimentally on her wrists again and grimaced. She wasn't escaping these cuffs on her own.

She snorted. As if escaping handcuffs at 20,000 feet would do her one bit of good. She couldn't escape from the plane. Rachelle needed to conserve her strength in case she had a chance to escape once this bird was on the ground.

Determination grew inside her. Rachelle had to escape. If she didn't, she'd never see the man she adored again. This was probably the handiwork of Falcon, and he didn't have a reason to let her live. She was too dangerous to his aspirations to live in the White House.

When she couldn't ignore the pain in her shoulders any longer, Rachelle glanced at her ankles. No restraints. Excellent. She wiggled further up the bed and was able to lower her hands by propping herself against the headboard.

Rachelle tried to listen to the conversation in the cabin and minutes later admitted defeat. She overheard a handful of words, none of them confirming Cal's identification of Falcon.

A spot behind her ear heated. Rachelle's eyes widened. Fortress must have activated the tracker. Relief swept over her in a tidal wave. Cal was coming for her. Her job was to stall and hold on until he arrived.

She could almost hear Cal's voice telling her to rest while she had the chance. Rachelle closed her eyes, drifting until a change in engine noise brought her to full wakefulness. Soon, landing gear dropped, and the jet bumped along the tarmac.

Rachelle's gaze locked on the bedroom door, waiting. Heavy footsteps sounded as someone approached. Seconds later, a man opened the door, turned on the light, and strode inside. The man was large, taller and broader across the chest than Cal.

Black eyes assessed her. Seeming satisfied that she was fully awake and alert, he shoved his hand in his pocket and pulled out a key that he shoved into the lock on the handcuffs. A quick twist and she was free. "Let's go," he growled. "He's waiting."

"Who sent you for me?"

A hard, calloused hand clamped around her wrist and jerked Rachelle to her feet. "Move." Black eyes shoved her toward the door.

She stumbled up the aisle to the exit on shaky legs. In the fading light, she scanned the area. A private airstrip. But where? They could have landed anywhere, even a foreign country. She didn't know how long she'd been unconscious.

Black eyes gripped her upper arm in a bruising hold and propelled her down the stairs, righting her when she stumbled on the tarmac. "Don't even think of running." He inclined his head toward the group of men standing guard around the jet. "You won't make it ten feet without being captured again."

Since an escape attempt would be futile at the moment, she walked to a waiting SUV. Rachelle would have a chance to escape. She'd be ready.

The gunman opened the back door and shoved her inside. He crowded in beside her, forcing Rachelle to scramble across the seat.

Another gunman climbed behind the wheel and drove the SUV from the airstrip. Neither said a word to her or each other.

She looked for road signs and realized the airstrip was on private property. No roads with signs.

Fantastic. Not only was she in the company of hired gunmen heading toward a meeting with the man who had commissioned them to kidnap her, she had no idea where she was. That was all right, she reminded herself. She might not know her location, but Fortress had activated the tracking tag. Cal knew where she was. He'd find her.

The SUV turned into a long, winding driveway that led to a large mansion of gray stone. Instead of stopping at the front of the house, the driver drove to the back.

After he parked, both men hopped out. Black eyes yanked Rachelle from the vehicle and pushed her toward the rear entrance of the mansion.

A cook and her helper paused in their meal preparation to glance over their shoulders. After a look at Rachelle, they resumed their work. She wouldn't have help from them. If Falcon was behind the abduction, this probably wasn't the first time someone entered his home under duress.

They walked through the kitchen and along several hallways until Black eyes stopped in front of a closed door and knocked.

"Come," came a curt reply from inside the room.

Her captor opened the door and dragged Rachelle into a large library with a high vaulted ceiling, heavy wooden bookcases, and a matching massive desk at the right side of the room.

Behind the desk sat a distinguished-looking man with silvery blond hair and ice blue eyes. A middle-aged Ken doll.

Black eyes pushed her forward until she stood in front of the desk. "Rachelle Carter, sir."

The man rose, his gaze raking over her, eyes glittering. "So, you're the cause of so much trouble."

"Who are you?" But she knew. Rachelle recognized his photo. Don Hale, Under Secretary of State, the political heavy hitter. Cal told her to stall. She'd follow his order.

A cold smile curved his mouth. "You don't lie well, Ms. Carter. I don't like liars. You should remember that for the sake of your health."

"What do you want with me?"

"You don't have anything I want."

Her stomach lurched. No, she supposed she didn't since Hale preferred underage girls instead of consenting adults. "Then why kidnap me?"

"Such an ugly word, kidnap." His tone came out silky. "You're bait for a deadlier problem."

Bait? Her heart skipped a beat. Oh, no. Bile rose into her throat. Cal and Wolf Pack. The trackers would lead Cal's team into a trap.

"Your friends have cost me a lot of money and favors to cover my tracks."

"You sent men to attack the ranch."

He inclined his head. "I also sent a second group to the safe house where the ambassador's daughter is hiding with her injured lover. If you'd had the decency to die in the hotel attack, I wouldn't be in this mess." Despite his silky tone, Hale's hands fisted. "Too many people are questioning the incident in Antigua. You and Fortress are to blame."

"You know about Fortress."

"I know everything about my enemies."

"No matter what happens to me and my friends, Fortress will continue to ask questions until your role in the deaths of so many people is exposed."

"If you're dead along with the team who rescued you, who will testify against me?"

Don Hale was an arrogant jerk who believed himself invincible. If he truly believed that Fortress would drop this investigation, he was fooling himself. Brent Maddox and Micah Winter wouldn't stop until they brought down Under Secretary Hale and ousted him from power.

"How five men rescued you, Morales, and Hoss despite the number of men hunting you is a mystery. Care to enlighten me?"

She breathed easier with the knowledge that Texas unit's work in Antigua had been attributed to Cal and Wolf Pack. Cal's team would have to be superheroes to pull off being in two places at once. Then again, the men sent to kill her and Amy were dead against all odds. Fortress didn't miss their targets. "You plan to kill Amy."

A snort. "The Morales girl saw me with my companion. She was in the wrong place at the wrong time." He frowned. "Her security detail should have driven you to your destination. Walking in Antigua isn't safe."

"So I've been told. Walking was Amy's idea."

"A poor one. As I said, I'll regret causing her parents pain. I like Mr. And Mrs. Morales. However, I have a future to protect, and no one will stand in my way."

"Turn yourself in, and leave us alone."

"My destiny awaits. You're an obstacle I'll deal with permanently."

Stall. She needed to stall. "How did you know where to find Amy?"

"Through her parents. She called her mother and mentioned Maple Valley. My men located the safe house in less than thirty minutes."

As long as Don Hale remained free, Amy and Eric were in danger. She had to warn them and Texas of the threat. "Did Amy tell her mother about the Rocking M, too?"

Hale chuckled. "My men followed you there."

She stared. Cal and the others would've noticed a tail. "How?"

"Russ Stokes slid a tracker under your watch. Any deaths on the ranch are on your head."

"Why do people call you Falcon?" Rachelle removed her watch. When she escaped, she'd leave her watch behind.

"Ah." He smiled. "You heard that, did you? Very good, Ms. Carter. I raise falcons and have since I was a boy. That's why I commissioned a falcon tattoo designed only for me. The artist tattooed the design on my back. Would you like to see?" Hale raised his hand to his tie.

"No, thanks." Nausea bubbled in her stomach. "I saw a picture of it."

"How?"

"I saw a picture of you in bed with a girl in Antigua. Your tattoo was visible and recognizable. The tattoo artist community is a small, close knit one and his style is unique."

A scowl. "Clint Nichols is a liability. The man is a blackmailer who has outlived his usefulness. I should have realized Nichols might try to drain money from me."

"If you knew about his blackmail schemes, why go to him?"

"He provides quality merchandise." A shrug. "He's easily replaced. I'll find another supplier to run the organization."

Stunned realization hit Rachelle. "You own the human trafficking organization?"

Hale's smug expression returned. "The perfect way to feed my addiction, wouldn't you say?"

Disgusting man. "What happens now?"

"We wait for your boyfriend and his friends to figure out where you are and ride to the rescue. If they haven't located you by tomorrow night, you'll call Taylor in my presence. Once they arrive, I'll end my problems once and for all."

CHAPTER TWENTY-EIGHT

Rachelle glared at Black eyes as he forced her to the basement stairs. When she jerked against his hold, he tightened his grip on her arm and scowled.

"Knock it off."

"Or what?" she snapped, tired of being treated like a sack of potatoes and dragged from one place to another.

"I can knock you out again."

She lowered her head and walked as though defeated. She didn't want to be incapacitated again. An escape from the mansion would mean a chance to contact Cal and prevent his team from walking into an ambush.

"If you behave, I might bring you food tomorrow."

Jerk. She didn't react, refusing to give him a response.

At the bottom of the stairs, Black eyes shoved a key in the lock of a door and twisted. He pushed her inside the cavernous space toward an interior door. Unlocking the second door, Black eyes shoved her inside without following. "Scream all you want. With these thick walls, no one will hear. Besides, no one who wants to live will help you. Take a nap or something."

With that insulting comment, Black eyes closed and locked the door, leaving Rachelle in the dimly-lit room.

She looked around her small prison. Large plastic storage bins were stacked along three of the four cement walls. On the fourth wall, free-standing utility shelves held cleaning supplies. High on the wall was a window.

She frowned at the odd placement. Curious, she found boxes light enough to scoot under the window.

Rachelle climbed on top of the boxes and peered out the window. Satisfaction filled her when she realized the ground wasn't far from the window sill.

The room appeared to be on the side of the house. A stand of trees was near. Stretching, she could reach the window lock.

Although she longed to run now, doing so with this much light would be foolhardy. If they caught her, she'd be restrained or knocked out again. When full dark fell, she'd escape and warn Cal and the others. Too bad she didn't have her phone. She'd checked on the jet. They must have taken it from her when they transported her from the Rocking M.

Rachelle descended her makeshift ladder and sat on the floor with her back against the wall to wait for nightfall.

When the sun had set, she climbed to the window again. This side of the house was poorly lit with no visible guards. Hale must have them, though. Where were they?

She reached for the lock and hesitated. What if the windows had alarms? She'd bring Black eyes down here in a hurry. Rachelle flipped the latch and raised the window two inches.

She listened for an alarm or a shout and running feet. Nothing. After a minute, Rachelle believed she was safe for the moment.

She dropped her watch to the ground. Time to leave. After she was safe, she'd figure out a way to get word to Cal. She checked one more time for anyone passing close to the basement. Still no one around. Excellent. Rachelle pushed the window up all the way, hoisted herself up and over the sill, and rolled to the ground.

Scrambling into a crouch, she hugged the wall and scanned the area. No guards in evidence yet. At that moment, clouds blocked the moon's rays. Now or never.

Rising, she crept to the corner of the house, ducking under windows as she went. She paused, peering around the corner and barely stopped a gasp as she spotted a guard standing at the other corner with his back to her. Oh, man. Not good.

While she debated what to do, another man at the front of the house hailed the guard near her. He looked to his left and abandoned his post to talk to the other man. Rachelle ran for the trees, expecting a bullet in her back or a football tackle to prevent her escape. But no one stopped her. Unable to believe she'd escaped notice, she hurried into the wooded area, doing her best to move like Cal and avoid sounding like a rampaging elephant stomping in the tree-covered strip of land.

Conscious that a clock ticked down the time until Black eyes discovered she'd escaped, Rachelle moved as fast as she dared. Although she wanted to run, the moonlight wasn't enough illumination to see all the tree roots and depressions in the earth in those shadow-drenched places the light didn't reach. She couldn't afford injuries.

She picked her way through the brush and trees, angling away from the airstrip. At a distant shout, Rachelle spun, straining to listen. More shouts. No gunfire. One of the guards must have discovered her escape, and this wooded area was the obvious place to look.

She plunged ahead, her pace faster. If Black eyes recaptured her, she would end up back in Hale's hands. The Under Secretary would make sure she didn't escape a second time.

As she hurried through the woods, Rachelle searched for a hiding place. She'd have to hide if Hale's men got too close.

Reaching a clearing, she hesitated. In the large open space, the moon's rays lit the area like a spotlight. Although she didn't see Hale's men, one of them might be watching the clearing. Not only that, her ribs ached with every breath she dragged into her lungs.

Nearby, twigs snapped, and a low male voice cursed. Not Cal or his teammates.

Rachelle glanced around, hunting for a place to hide. Trees. More trees. No convenient caves or huge rocks to hide behind. The sounds of thrashing grew louder. She was out of time.

Her gaze stopped on a huge tree that had fallen in a dark pool of shadows. Out of options, she climbed over the tree's rough wooden surface and scrambled to the other side. She dropped to the ground and scooted close to the tree, wincing at the heightened pain in her ribs. She'd love one of Jackson's pain killers.

Rachelle froze when heavy footsteps and ragged breathing alerted her to the presence of one of Hale's men. She waited and listened.

The footsteps paused.

She bit her lower lip, praying the darkness would conceal her. She wanted a future with Cal, one including a home and family. That dream wouldn't become reality if she was discovered and taken back to Hale.

"You see anything?"

Rachelle's eyes widened. At least two men were nearby.

"Nope. The boss can buy any woman he wants. Can't figure out why he wants this one so bad. I heard her boyfriend is a military hero. Why does the boss want a woman already taken by a guy like that?"

"Don't know and don't care. The only thing I want is to be sure he doesn't blow my head off losing the broad. Letting his prize escape would set him off."

A loud sigh. "I shouldn't have accepted a job with this nut case, but the money was too good to pass up."

The second man snorted. "Now you know why." A pause. "We got no way out, you know."

"What do you mean?"

"The only way out of this job is in a pine box. Come on. Let's keep looking. The woman can't have gotten far."

Their footsteps faded away along with their low-voiced conversation.

She frowned. Why were they talking? She'd be an idiot to go near them. Had they seen her or suspected she was in this area and pretended to leave in order to draw her out?

Rachelle started to move, but remained in place when she heard a soft noise that reminded her of fabric brushing against something. The two talkative thugs might have left a friend behind to catch her if she left her hiding place. Until she was positive the area was clear, her best course of action was to do nothing.

Rachelle remained tucked close to the log, listening. A short time later, another brushing sound reached her ears. Her hand fisted, preparing to defend herself. She didn't stand a chance in a one-on-one confrontation, but she might escape the hold of one man.

An eternity passed before footsteps crisscrossed the area. Could it be a member of Wolf Pack? She had to know one way or the other. She didn't want the Fortress team to miss her in the darkness of the woods.

Slowly, Rachelle angled her head to peer through the branches of the fallen tree. The man's back was to her, but she knew he was one of Hale's men.

She lowered her head again and waited. The longer this guy hung around, the greater chance Cal and the others would arrive and infiltrate Hale's home, looking for her.

Finally, the third man growled in frustration and muttered some uncomplimentary things about Rachelle and her mother. Gunfire rang out from the direction of the mansion. Swearing, the man pivoted and raced toward the sound of the shots.

After he left, Rachelle sat up and glanced around. She didn't see anyone, but her skin prickled as though someone watched her.

Not good. She couldn't return to the mansion because of the gunfire. Cal would tell her to steer clear of the battle. While the third man had backtracked to the mansion, Rachelle suspected some of the thugs would continue to scour the woods for her. The trackers would tell Cal where to find her if she continued on her current trajectory.

Rachelle stood and set out again. Minutes later, she'd skirted the large clearing. She stumbled and would have fallen except a strong hand grabbed her arm to steady her while another hand clamped over her mouth to stifle her cry of surprise. Between one heartbeat and the next, she was pulled against a broad chest.

A soft, familiar voice murmured in her hear, "It's Cal."

Relief swept over Rachelle. She nodded. When Cal loosened his hold, she twisted, threw her arms around him, and kissed him.

He drew back too soon. "We can't stay here. The woods are filled with Hale's men."

"Don't you need to help your teammates?" Although she wanted him by her side, Wolf Pack would be shorthanded without him.

"Texas came with us. The Montgomerys are protecting Amy and Eric until Texas returns. My job is to take you to safety."

"But Wolf Pack and Texas will be outnumbered." She'd lost count of the number of men milling around the mansion and the grounds.

"They can handle themselves," he said, sounding confident in his teammates' abilities.

They probably could handle Hale's men without too much difficulty. Still, unexpected things could happen.

Rachelle did her best to keep up with Cal's fast pace, but his long legs left her taking two strides for every one of his. When the pain in her ribs became unbearable, she tugged on Cal's hand. "Wait," she whispered, her free hand pressed to her ribcage. "Sorry."

"We'll rest a minute. I could use the break."

She rolled her eyes. "Liar. You haven't broken a sweat, and I'm all but a puddle on the ground."

"You're doing great, sweetheart." He wrapped one arm around her waist, allowing her to rest against him. "Did Hale hurt you?"

Rachelle shook her head. "He was waiting for Wolf Pack to arrive. He planned to kill us."

"Not going to happen."

A familiar voice chuckled as two men emerged from the shadows of the trees with weapons pointed at her and Cal. "You shouldn't lie to the lady, Taylor." Russell Stokes strode into a beam of moonlight with Hale at his side.

CHAPTER TWENTY-NINE

Cal tightened his hold on Rachelle. He figured Stokes had been covering for Hale but had underestimated his involvement. No wonder Stokes was hostile toward him and Rachelle. "Stokes."

"Surprised?" A smile curved his mouth. "Some detective you are. You and your pretty girlfriend have been nothing but trouble to our operation. I'm looking forward to getting rid of our problem."

Rachelle's breath caught. "You're part of the human trafficking ring? How do you look at yourself in the mirror?"

Stokes shrugged one shoulder. "It's business, not personal."

"I'm sure the women and kids you victimize feel differently."

Hale gestured with his weapon. "Throw down your gun, Taylor, or I shoot your lady and rid myself of a problem now instead of waiting until later."

Cal calculated the distance between him and the two men. Not close enough. He released Rachelle and laid his

Sig on the ground. When he straightened, Cal shifted to put his body between Rachelle and the two men.

He wrapped one hand around his wrist and pressed the side of his watch to signal Fortress to send assistance. If one of his teammates was free, he'd have help soon. If not, he'd find a way to save himself and Rachelle. On his own, Cal wouldn't hesitate to take on the two men. With Rachelle in the line of fire, his options were limited.

Stokes snorted. "A big, bad Navy SEAL, huh? I always thought those men were extraordinary. You're anything but extraordinary. You're a coward hiding behind a title."

Cal ignored him. "What now, Hale?"

"We kill you before we dispose of Ms. Carter."

"What about his friends?" Stokes demanded. "We can't leave them alive."

"My men will kill the remaining four."

When Cal felt the slight vibration from his watch, he relaxed and released his grip. Help was coming. He spread his hands. "You plan to shoot us?" His lips curved, mocking their choice. "That will draw too much attention."

"Get real." Stokes scowled. "Listen to the gunfire from our men. What's one more gunshot?"

"The shots aren't coming from the woods."

"Doesn't matter, does it? Your buddies won't be alive long enough to save your worthless hide."

Cal didn't react when he felt Rachelle's hands on his lower back. What was she doing? After a slight tug, he realized she'd pulled his Ka-Bar from the sheath. He eased his hand behind his back and gripped the hilt. In the shadows, he hoped no one would notice the black blade and hilt. "You willing to take that chance, Stokes? When my teammates and I aim at targets, we don't miss."

"You're lying," he snapped. "No one's that good."

Hale's eyes narrowed. "He's stalling." The Under Secretary motioned with his hand and four more men appeared. He glanced at a man large enough to be a linebacker on a football team and inclined his head toward Cal and Rachelle. "Take the woman to the basement. I'll deal with her when I'm finished with Taylor."

Rachelle gasped.

Cal glanced over his shoulder in time to see Linebacker drag Rachelle deeper into the woods. "Rachelle!"

"Focus," Eli whispered through the comm system. "Thirty seconds."

The order was enough to shift his focus back to Hale and Stokes. Hale's thug wouldn't get far with Rachelle fighting him every step of the way. Cal would deal with Hale and his remaining band of mercenaries, then go after his woman. "You don't want to do this, Hale. My team and I aren't the only ones who know your identity."

The Under Secretary's eyes narrowed. "Another lie."

Cal smiled. "You sure?"

At that moment, a red laser light appeared on Stokes's chest. Cal adjusted his grip on the hilt knife. "Now," he ordered. Shots rang out, one of them a rifle shot. Stokes flew backward. His back slammed against a tree. He slid down the trunk and keeled over onto his side, a bloodstain growing on his shirt.

Cal threw the Ka-Bar at Hale. The blade sank deep into Hale's chest. With a stunned looked on his face, the Under Secretary sank to the ground, weapon falling from his hand as he reached for the knife.

"No, Hale," Jackson shouted from behind Cal. "You'll bleed out."

The other man ignored the order and yanked the blade from his chest with a loud groan. The stain on his shirt grew at an alarming rate as Jackson closed the distance between them.

A minute later, he looked up from where he knelt beside Hale and shook his head, then went to Stokes to check for signs of life. Another head shake.

A glance around the area revealed the rest of Hale's men were down. Enough. Time to find Rachelle. "Eli."

"Go. Rafe, watch his back."

Cal scooped up his Sig and ran in the direction Linebacker had taken Rachelle without bothering to wait for his teammate. Rafe either caught up with him or he didn't. Nothing would stop Cal from rescuing the love of his life.

The bright moonlight highlighted the signs of Rachelle's fight to escape her captor, making the trail easy to follow. A scream shattered the silence of the woods.

Cal leaped over a fallen tree and dodged a boulder.

"No! Don't!" Rachelle yelled.

Two hundred yards further, he broke through the tree line to see his woman fighting Linebacker on the bank of a swift-moving river.

When Hale's man noticed Cal racing toward him, he cursed, punched Rachelle in the face, and shoved her over the bank into the water.

"Go after Rachelle," Rafe snapped. "I'll handle the garbage."

Linebacker grabbed Cal's arm as he ran past. Cal threw off his hold and leaped into the river. He surfaced seconds later and swam with the current, scanning ahead of him for Rachelle. When he didn't see anything, his gut tightened. Maybe he missed her.

What if she hadn't surfaced? After Linebacker hit her, Rachelle had gone limp. She might be unconscious. He had to find her. Now. He swam on, using every ounce of skill he'd learned during his SEAL days to move faster.

The current swept him around a bend. His heart skipped a beat. There. Dismay filled him. Rachelle was face down in the water, making no attempt to turn onto her back.

Pushing himself harder, Cal covered the distance between them and snagged her by her arm. Flipping

Rachelle to her back, he wrapped his arm around her and swam at an angle, towing her to shore.

Clambering up the bank with Rachelle in his arms, Cal laid the woman he loved on her back. He checked for signs of breathing. Nothing.

"Stay with me, baby." He tilted her head back and started CPR. "Come on, Rachelle. Breathe." He alternated chest compressions with blowing air into her lungs.

Nothing. Bone-deep terror nearly paralyzed him. He couldn't lose her. She owned him, heart and soul. "Come back to me, sweetheart. Don't leave me."

After what seemed to be an eternity, Rachelle coughed and expelled water. Cal rolled her to her side while she got rid of the rest of the river water.

Thank God. Cal gathered Rachelle into his arms and held her close. "You're all right. You're safe. I've got you."

"Love you," she whispered.

"I love you, Rachelle."

"You okay?"

He smiled, holding her tighter. "I'm fine now that you're in my arms." After a quick, gentle kiss to her lips, Cal rose with Rachelle cradled in his arms. "Let's get out of here."

She shivered. "Sounds good. Cold."

"You'll be warm soon."

He headed toward his teammates at a fast clip, alert for more of Hale's men. No one intervened, and the gunfire had ceased. The Fortress teams had taken care of business.

When he returned to the place where Linebacker shoved Rachelle into the water, Rafe was standing guard over the man. The jerk had become acquainted with Rafe's fists. The man cast a hate-filled gaze Cal's direction.

Cal glanced at Rachelle. "Okay if I put you down for a few seconds?"

Rafe's eyebrows rose.

"I'm all right. I can walk." She hesitated. "Maybe."

"You're not walking anywhere." Cal set her on the ground. When she was steady, he eyed the man who hurt Rachelle. "Get him up," he told Rafe.

His teammate hauled the man to his feet without a word.

Cal slammed his fist into the thug's jaw in the exact place where he'd punched Rachelle. The audible snap told Cal he'd broken his jaw. The man's eyes rolled back in his head. He would have fallen to the ground if Rafe hadn't kept him upright.

Rafe rolled his eyes. "Now I'll have to carry him to his buddies. Want to trade?"

"Not on your life." Cal scooped Rachelle into his arms again. "Tell Eli we're clear." His comm system had stopped working after being submerged in water.

A moment later, his teammate said, "I'll dump this guy off with the others, then intercept the feds. They're swarming over the grounds. An ambulance is waiting to transport Rachelle to the hospital."

"I'm fine," she protested. "Cal, I don't want to be separated from you."

He tightened his grip around her. "I'm going with you."

"Won't the FBI want to talk to you?"

Definitely. He'd be lucky to stay out of jail. He planned to contact Maddox and have him send one of the company lawyers to D.C. "They need to interview both of us."

"Won't you be in trouble if you leave the scene?"

He shrugged. "They'll know where to find me. I'm not leaving you."

"No hospital. I'll be fine with a heated blanket."

"We'll let a doctor tell us you're healthy. I need the peace of mind, Rachelle. You almost drowned."

After a long look into his eyes, she gave a short nod and laid her head on his shoulder.

When he reached the ambulance, Jackson was waiting for them. He inclined his head toward the rig. "You're riding in the back with Rachelle and one of the EMTs. I'll be up front with the driver."

"How did you swing that?"

"Maddox called in a few markers."

Of course he did. "Let's go. I want her checked out as soon as possible."

Minutes later, the ambulance stopped in front of the ER entrance at Longview Hospital. The EMTs wheeled Rachelle into an exam room with a warm blanket covering her.

Cal followed her into the room and wrapped his hand around hers. Jackson took up a guard position outside the door while they waited for the doctor. Although the nursing staff coming in and out cast questioning looks at Cal, they didn't insist he leave. Good thing. He wouldn't budge from Rachelle's side.

A knock sounded on the door. Jackson peered into the room. "Doc's here."

A middle-aged woman entered the room. She held out her hand to Cal. "I'm Dr. June Watson. You must be Cal Taylor. Brent Maddox called our chief of staff and requested that I check Ms. Carter."

He'd owe Brent a boatload of favors, favors he would gladly pay. "Thanks for agreeing to see Rachelle personally."

"Hey, it's not often my boss asks for a favor. Wait in the hall, Mr. Taylor. I'll bring you back in as soon as I'm finished."

Cal glanced at Rachelle. "You okay with this arrangement?"

She nodded.

"I'll be outside the door. If you need me, call out."

Dr. Watson smiled at Rachelle. "We won't take long, my dear. You'll soon have that handsome man by your side again."

After a quick kiss, Cal left the room and took up watch directly across from the door. Dr. Watson opened the door fifteen minutes later and motioned him inside.

A glance at Rachelle's face told him she was unhappy. Cal shifted his attention to the doctor. "What's the verdict?"

"She looks good considering what she's been through. No concussion. Since she was drugged, I ordered a blood draw to see if we can determine what the kidnappers used on her. I want to keep her overnight for observation but plan to release her tomorrow morning. Ms. Carter explained about the athletic tape which needs to be replaced. She prefers that your medic take care of it. An orderly will be in soon to transport Ms. Carter to her room. You're welcome to stay with her overnight, of course."

He would have insisted. Cal didn't think Hale's men would track them to the hospital to exact revenge, but he wouldn't risk Rachelle's safety.

Forty minutes later, Rachelle was settled in her room with Cal at her side. Jackson had once again taken up guard duty at the door.

"How soon will the FBI arrive?" Rachelle murmured. Her eyes were heavy.

"Shouldn't be long. Sleep while you have the chance."

"Don't leave."

He kissed the back of her hand. "No worries. I'll be here." Between one breath and the next, she was out. Cal settled back to watch over Rachelle.

An hour passed before Jackson tapped on the door and stepped inside the room. "Feds are here to interview you and Rachelle."

"Has anyone else from Fortress arrived?"

A snort. "Nope. They're dealing with the feds themselves."

"Then the feds interview us together. I won't leave her."

A slow smile curved Jackson's mouth. "I'll pass the word."

"Give me a minute to wake her."

With a nod, the medic returned to the hall.

Cal trailed his fingers down Rachelle's cheek.

She stirred. "What's wrong?"

"The feds have arrived."

Rachelle groaned. "Great. At least we'll get this over with. Maybe we can go home soon. I owe you a homecooked breakfast."

"Looking forward to that."

Two men in black suits, white shirts, and black ties walked inside. Both had sour expressions on their faces. After introducing themselves, the one named Bryant scowled at Cal. "You left the scene. You're a former homicide detective. You know better."

He caught the gleam of a wedding band on Bryant's finger. "Would you let your wife go to the hospital alone after she was kidnapped?"

"Of course not." He blinked. "Wait. You're married?"

"Not yet. Soon." He needed time to court the lady first.

"I'll interview you while Hicks interviews Ms. Carter."

"No. You boys interview us together."

"That's not how this works," Hicks snapped.

"Until Hale's organization is dismantled and his men are behind bars, Rachelle's life is still in danger. My team is tied up with your FBI buddies. I'm not leaving her. Ask your questions or you'll have to do it by video chat after we leave the hospital."

"We can arrest you for obstruction. We already suspect that you murdered the Under Secretary. Shouldn't be hard to find proof."

"Good luck proving it. Ask your questions or get out. Last chance, boys."

After exchanging a glance, they slid notebooks from their pockets.

CHAPTER THIRTY

Rachelle walked into the Rocking M's kitchen ahead of Wolf Pack, anxious to see Mrs. Grady for herself. Yes, the sheriff told Eli that the woman was a little banged up. She wanted to see for herself that the housekeeper was all right.

The older woman glanced over her shoulder. She dropped the knife in her hand and spun to face Rachelle. Her eyes widened. "Oh, Rachelle. Your poor face." She scowled at Cal. "How did that happen?"

"A thug slugged her. I didn't reach her fast enough to prevent the injury."

Rachelle's heart melted at his words. Her warrior had taken the bruise to her face hard, angry with himself for allowing the injury to happen.

"I hope you taught him a lesson on how to treat a lady."

He chuckled. "Yes, ma'am, with help from Rafe."

Mrs. Grady gave Rafe a nod of approval. "Good job."

With a grin, the handsome operative gave the housekeeper a light kiss on the cheek, making her blush. "Thank you, Mrs. G."

The older woman hugged Rachelle and led her to the kitchen table. "Would you like a cup of tea? I baked blueberry scones a few minutes ago."

"That sounds wonderful."

Mrs. Grady motioned for Wolf Pack to sit. "Coffee and scones for you boys?"

"Yes, ma'am," came the chorus of male voices.

"Are you all right, Mrs. Grady," Rachelle asked. Her gaze strayed to the bandage on the other woman's temple.

"Nothing a couple of stitches and over-the-counter pain medicine couldn't fix." She hustled around the kitchen brewing tea and coffee for her guests, and filling three plates full of scones and muffins before setting out smaller plates and napkins. "How long will you be able to stay at the Rocking M?"

"We're not sure yet," Eli said. "Depends on how long the feds take to do their jobs."

"We'll probably be here two days," Cal said, his fingers threaded through Rachelle's. "If I think Rachelle is still in danger, we'll go on a vacation out of the limelight."

"Somewhere sunny with sand," Rachelle muttered. "I'm still cold from the river."

"That sounds like a story," Mrs. Grady said. "I want to hear every detail."

An hour later, the housekeeper shook her head. "I can't believe the Under Secretary of State was responsible for so much evil and death. You sure he's dead?"

"Yes, ma'am," Cal said. "We're sure."

"Can't say I'm sorry. Now, do you want the same rooms?"

"If you don't mind." Rachelle squeezed her hand. "I like being surrounded by a bunch of handsome, fierce men."

"Hey," Cal groused, eyes twinkling. "The only man's face you're supposed to notice is mine."

The rest of Wolf Pack chuckled.

"I don't blame you for wanting to be surrounded by security specialists, especially after the harrowing experiences you've been through." Mrs. Grady shooed them out of the kitchen. "Relax and enjoy yourselves. You've earned the time off."

Except Wolf Pack wasn't off duty. Rachelle walked with Cal to the living room. "Is it safe to go outside now?"

"I think so. Want to go for a walk?"

"I'd like to sit on the porch swing with you."

Cal snagged a blanket from the back of a couch. On the swing, he draped the blanket across Rachelle's lap and wrapped his arm around her shoulders. "So, Ms. Carter, which beach would you like to visit?"

"One busy, but not packed with people." Hopefully, Cal would be able to enjoy the sand and surf, too.

"Perfect. Do you swim?"

She grinned. "You couldn't tell after the river rescue?"

He snorted. "Floating face-down in the water doesn't count."

"I can swim although I'm not in the same league as you."

"Ever gone snorkeling?"

She shook her head. "I've always wanted to, though."

"I'll set up a snorkeling expedition for us."

Her smile faded. "Will we have to hide, Cal?"

"We might. I'm considering this a vacation to relax with the woman I love, not dodging bad guys with a penchant for revenge."

"What about my job?" Having just passed her first anniversary at Fortress, she didn't have much vacation time built up.

"Don't worry about that."

"Easy for you to say. You're not an hourly employee."

He kissed her forehead. "Things will work out."

His cell phone signaled an incoming call. Checking the screen, Cal took the call on speaker. "You're on speaker with Rachelle."

"How are you, Rachelle?"

She smiled at the sound of her boss's voice. "Other than cold and bruised, I'm fine," she told Micah Winter.

"Bruised?" Anger resonated in his voice. "You were supposed to protect her, Taylor."

"I screwed up."

"He didn't," Rachelle protested. "Knock it off, Micah. Cal did everything possible to safeguard me. He was outnumbered."

"Sit rep, Taylor."

She scowled at the harsh tone and clipped speech.

Cal summarized the events since they'd returned from Mexico.

"What's your next move or do you even have a plan?"

Rachelle's breath caught. "Micah!" What was his problem?

Cal kissed her temple before answering. "If I'm not convinced Rachelle is out of danger, we'll be going on vacation until the rats are caged."

"Plan to do that anyway. Leave tomorrow before the sun comes up. I'll authorize the use of the jet. Take one of your teammates for backup. If Rachelle comes back to work with so much as a scratch on her, I'll ensure that you take on the worst missions known to man until you're old and gray. Am I clear?"

"Yes, sir."

"Micah, that's not fair," Rachelle protested.

"He's right." Cal threaded his fingers into her hair. "I should have suspected the attack on the other safe house was a decoy. Because I didn't, you were kidnapped. I won't let you down again."

She growled. Why wouldn't either of these infuriating men pay attention to her? No matter what Micah and Cal said, she knew the man she loved hadn't screwed up. After the events of the past week, she knew as well as anyone that sometimes things happened that were out of your control despite your best efforts. Her abduction was one of those things. "What about my job, sir?"

"Your job will be waiting for you when you return. Enjoy yourself, Rachelle. Rest and relax. Heal. Taylor?"

"Yes, sir?"

"If you don't treat her like a princess, you'll be unemployed."

"Copy that, sir."

Micah ended the call.

Rachelle rounded on Cal. "Don't do that again."

"Don't do what?"

"Take on the blame for something that isn't your fault."

"Baby, I miscalculated, and you almost died."

"I'm the one who chose to leave the safe room to protect Mrs. Grady. That's on me, not you."

"You shouldn't have had to make the choice in the first place."

She sighed. There was no winning this argument with Cal at the moment. Later, though, she would prevail. Time to change the subject. "So, we're going on a vacation, huh?"

A slow smile curved his mouth. "Looks like it." He cupped her chin and tilted her face up to meet his gaze. "Who do you want to accompany us?"

"Jackson."

"Why him?"

"He's lonely and needs a little fun in his life."

A blink. "How do you know?"

"Woman's intuition." And observation in moments when Jackson thought no one was looking.

"I'll ask. If he has other obligations, are you okay with Rafe coming along?"

"Of course. I enjoy being with your teammates."

"Good. You'll be with them often. Teams like ours spend time together on missions and off. It's how we keep our bond strong."

Cal captured her mouth with his. Long minutes later, he eased away, his breathing elevated and his eyes glittering with heat. "You're potent and addictive, beautiful lady. I need to talk to Zane about the accommodations for our beach vacation."

By the time Cal finished the phone call, Rachelle was stunned speechless. She couldn't believe Brent and Micah had made arrangements for Rachelle's and Cal's families to join them at the beach for the next two weeks.

Cal slid his phone into his pocket.

"We talked about meeting each other's families soon. I never expected it to happen this fast."

"I can rent a condo for us and Jackson a short distance away if you're uncomfortable with the arrangement."

She shook her head. "It sounds like fun. I love you, Cal. I'm sure I'll love your family, too."

She was right. She adored Cal's parents and siblings, especially his nieces and nephews. They'd had so much fun cooking out and entertaining the kids.

For this last night of their two-week vacation, though, Cal had arranged a date for them, something special that he was keeping a secret from her. From the broad grins she received from both families, they knew the secret. Must be a good one since the women had gone together to purchase an outfit for Rachelle to wear tonight.

When the time came to change for her date with Cal, her mother brought the dress to Rachelle's room. Eyes wide, Rachelle stroked the soft fabric of the royal blue dress. "Mom, this is gorgeous."

"Special occasions deserve special attire." She held out a pair of flats of the same color blue.

"Give me a hint."

A light laugh. "I'm not spoiling Cal's surprise. Trust me, you'll be glad I kept my mouth shut. Change clothes, honey. This will be a night you won't forget."

CHAPTER THIRTY-ONE

"What if she turns me down?" Cal pivoted and paced the other direction, passing his amused teammate.

"If she does, you haven't been doing your job." Jackson smiled. "Stop worrying, will you? Rachelle loves you. Why would she turn you down?"

"I'm not a good bet. None of us are. Life with an operative isn't easy."

The medic leaned one shoulder against the wall, watching Cal pace to the other side of the room again. "Depends on the operative. If she decides you aren't worth risking her heart, I'll go after her myself."

Cal glared at his friend. "Try it and you die a slow, painful death."

Jackson laughed, raising a hand to hold Cal off when he stalked toward him. "Couldn't resist yanking your chain. In all seriousness, though, you're raising your blood pressure for nothing. When you walk into a room, your woman doesn't see anyone else. She's totally focused on you." He sobered, shadows evident in his eyes. "You're a lucky man, Cal."

He blew out a breath. "I know. That's why I don't want to blow this."

The medic clapped him on the shoulder. "You've got this."

His gut clenched when he glanced at his watch. Time to pick up his date for dinner. "Any last words of advice?"

"Show her your heart." With those enigmatic words, he opened the door. "Go get your girl."

Praying he'd find the right words to say and patting his jacket pocket one more time, Cal walked upstairs.

He knocked on her door. When she opened it, he had to fight to keep his jaw from hitting the floor. "You look incredible."

"You look ready to be on the front cover of GQ."

Cal captured her hand and kissed her knuckles. "Ready?"

"Where are we going?"

"Not far." He led her downstairs and out the back door to the deck.

As soon as she saw the cloth-covered table, covered dishes along with the battery-lit candles, strands of white lights illuminating the deck railing, and the small vase filled with baby roses, Rachelle gasped. "Oh, Cal. You did all this?"

"Most of it. I had a couple of fairy godmothers who set the table. I've never been able to figure out why anyone needs more than one fork, spoon, and knife to eat a meal." His mother and Rachelle's had set the table with formal place settings.

He seated her, removed the covers from the salads on the serving cart, and placed one in front of her. The next hour passed with a lot of laughter. He could see them sharing meals like this for the rest of their lives, love and laughter a daily part of who they were together.

After they finished chocolate mousse for dessert, Cal stood and held out his hand. "Walk with me?"

"I'd love to, but we should probably take the plates inside first."

"Our fairy godmothers have that covered tonight."

"Oh, that's so nice."

He carried her across the loose sand until they reached firmer ground. He set her on her feet, then slid his arm around her waist. They strolled for a short distance before he stopped and turned to face her.

Cal drew her into his arms and kissed her, his touch soft and gentle. He eased away from her. This was it. Either Rachelle made him the happiest man on the planet or shattered his heart into a million pieces. "When I first saw you, I was stunned by your beauty. The more time I spent with you, the deeper I fell. I love you, Rachelle. Being with you brings me endless joy and contentment. You own my heart. I want a lifetime with you. A home and a family."

He dropped to one knee and pulled out a velvet-covered box. Opening the lid, Cal removed the ring. "Will you marry me, Rachelle Carter?"

"I love you so much, Cal Taylor. I'd be honored to marry you."

Thank God. He heaved a sigh of relief as he slid the one-carat diamond ring on her finger. Rising, he took her into his arms and kissed her, holding her close. "I adore you," he whispered. "Thank you for making me the happiest man on the planet."

She smiled. "We'll have to plan a wedding around your deployments."

"Got that figured out."

"Is that right?"

He shrugged. "I'm a SEAL. We're mission driven. Unless you want something different, I'd like to return to this beach in six months and marry you here. What do you say?"

Rachelle threw her arms around him. "It's perfect. I've always wanted a beach wedding. Now, I'll be able to marry the man of my dreams on the beach where he proposed."

"You won't regret saying yes. I'll make it my mission in life to make you happy."

She smiled, cupping his cheek. "You already have."

SEAL'S PROMISE

REBECCA DEEL

ABOUT THE AUTHOR

Rebecca Deel is a preacher's kid with a black belt in karate. She teaches business classes at a private four-year college outside Nashville, Tennessee. She plays the piano at church, writes freelance articles, and runs interference for the family dogs. She's been married to her amazing husband for more than 25 years and is the proud mom of two grown sons. She delivers occasional devotions to the women's group at her church and conducts seminars on personal safety, money management, and writing. Her articles have been published in *ONE Magazine*, *Contact*, and *Co-Laborer*, and she was profiled in the June 2010 Williamson edition of *Nashville Christian Family* magazine. Rebecca completed her Doctor of Arts degree in Economics and wears her favorite Dallas Cowboys sweatshirt when life turns ugly.

For more information on Rebecca...

Signup for Rebecca's newsletter: http://eepurl.com/_B6w9

Visit Rebecca's website: www.rebeccadeelbooks.com

Made in the USA
Monee, IL
11 September 2020